THE GRIEF OF GOODBYE

BOOK ONE OF THE CAMINO FAMILY TRILOGY

K.D. FIELD

K.D. Field loves to meet and chat with fans! Reach out to her at kdfieldauthor@gmail.com

Book Cover by Tatiana Vila

First edition 2023

For Jeff
With you, nothing is impossible.

Camino de Santiago

Camino Francés

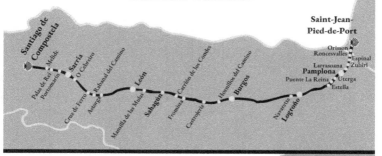

Author's Note

In 2017, I walked the Camino de Santiago with my 15-year-old daughter. The adventure changed our lives, and I left Spain with a sense of peace and purpose. Returning to the US, my husband, Jeff, noticed a profound change in me. Unsurprisingly, I said, 'We should move to Spain.' Jeff saw that my smile was wider than before, my mind quieter, and my heart more open. He was all-in. In Spring 2018, we moved to Spain with four suitcases and no clue what we were doing. It was then I started writing this story in earnest, and the stories have never stopped. The tale of Tess and Pen captivated me as I had begun it in my head while on my first Camino. While the characters are pure fiction, I knew each of them as if we had walked together for 800 km in the hot Spanish sun. Theirs is the story I needed to tell, and I am grateful to you, dear reader, for listening to it with your whole heart. I also invite you to follow my blog—www.vivaespanamovingtospain.com, where you'll get a view into my brain on any given day—the good, the bad, and, well, we'll leave it at that. But this invitation is just for readers of my books. Shh... don't tell anyone.

P.S. Don't miss the book club questions at the end of the book!

PART I

THE DECISION

ONE

I DON'T HAVE TIME FOR THIS

Tess stood in front of the mirror in the sterile grey bathroom, leaning against the white marble counter, willing herself not to sway. Keep it together, she thought. Her calendar was cleared, and John waited for her in the lobby. She looked into her blue eyes and studied her tired face, which seemed to age a hundred years overnight.

She couldn't remember the last time she'd stopped and taken stock of her life. There was always too much to do. But if ever there was a time, it was now. She ran her hands under the water and patted her pale cheeks. Water dripped down the front of her blouse, but she barely noticed, not bothering to wipe it away. On the outside, she was the same woman in the business suit she had been the week before. But on the inside, her thoughts were beach balls bouncing into every corner of her mind.

Tess was not a patient person. Always anxious to get on with it. But she was confused more than people knew, and sometimes it felt as though life was just a series of encounters where she wasn't in on the joke.

She didn't consider herself a great mother, though she tried her best. But as a wife? Well, that was for John to judge.

She could be self-indulgent. She knew that. Drinking strange concoctions of vitamins and herbs, convinced it was the cure for almost anything. It seemed, now, none of that had worked.

Tess could be rough around the edges, and sometimes, she cut people in the process. But she hoped and prayed for forgiveness.

And she had breast cancer.

Two

When Love is Not Enough

'Penelope Elizabeth!' Tess called down the hall for the third time, shaking her head, walking back into the gourmet kitchen where her husband waited. Her daughter never made things easy. Tess was sure Pen could be nice. But only when she wanted to be, and this would not be one of those times. Pen was 15. Eye-rolling was compulsory.

After meeting with her doctor, the day before, Tess asked to take a few days before deciding what course her treatment would take. There were drug therapies and surgery options, and she wanted to take a breath to weigh them. The one thing not up for negotiation was leaving her job. The first thought that popped into her head when her doctor uttered the word *cancer* was, 'I'm done.' She and John decided to delay telling Pen about her cancer until they had a plan. Their daughter didn't do well with ambiguity.

The calm Star Trek-like voice of the alarm sounded. 'Door Open' announcing that a back door out to the pool was breached. John had installed it for safety, but Pen was an excellent swimmer. She'd slipped out the back. Tess watched her husband make for the front door to head their daughter off at the gate. He wasn't going to allow a delay in this conversation.

Tess closed her eyes and sighed. Pen tried her patience at the best of times, but usually, she got along with her dad. John always called her 'Lucky Penny' and kept a shiny copper coin minted in the year of her birth in his wallet. For Good Luck. Ever since she was little, they'd left pennies on her bedside table when they would travel for work. So, she'd know they were thinking of her. Tess had recently seen the large jar filled with them; her daughter kept on the desk in her room. Tess closed her eyes. This conversation was just the first of many, and it would require all the luck they could get.

She heard John open the front door for their angry teenager, who marched in ahead of him carrying a backpack. Tess waited in the kitchen, still dressed in her work clothes. Louboutin's, a black sleeveless dress. Her big Celine tote perched precariously on the stool by the kitchen island. Her battle uniform, she called it—an appropriate sentiment for the occasion.

John took a deep breath and started them off.

'We want to tell you some news. Your Mom has decided to quit her job and spend more time at home—' Skip a beat. '—with us.'

Tess could almost hear the voice in Pen's head. Tess didn't *do home*. They had a cleaning service, a gardening service, and a pool service. They used *Fresh!* and *Home Chef* to cook dinner, or they ate out. Amazon delivered their groceries. Most nights, Tess wasn't even home in time for dinner. When they were little, and people complimented her kids on their manners in restaurants, Tess always bragged.

'My children know how to behave in restaurants, and they know how to order.'

Over the years, she traveled a great deal for work, sometimes at the last minute, and she knew her kids would find out she was in a city across the country when their dad got home from work. He was an email contact on her corporate travel account. They often laughed that he knew Tess would get on a plane before she did. And now she was suddenly staying home. Pen's reaction wouldn't be pretty.

'Why?' Pen's question hung in the air, sounding more like an accusation.

Again, John stepped forward. 'She wants to spend more time with us. You know she's away a lot. She wants to make sure she doesn't miss out.'

Pen's face was an unreadable mask. She was clearly wondering why her dad was playing the role of her Mom's publicist.

'Time with us?' Pen questioned sarcastically. 'Now?'

At last, Tess chimed in, hoping to smooth things over.

'I have dreams, too. There are a lot of things on my list that I've never been able to do because I was working all the time. Now I'll have a chance to do those.' She said, smiling, not sounding quite as confident as she'd hoped.

Tess could feel the ice-blue eyes boring into her.

'Like what? What things have you wanted to do that you've never done? You do whatever you want.'

Pen wasn't wrong.

'That's not true,' John stepped in again. 'Your Mom has been the main breadwinner for the lifestyle we've all enjoyed. She's tired. It's her turn to rest, and let us pick up the slack.'

Tess had never rested in her life.

'Now, I can take you to school in the mornings and pick you up from soccer practice. I'll be able to go to your games, too.' Tess cringed at the sound of her overly cheerful voice. Like she was selling a used car, and she was the car.

Teenage eye roll. She saw it was just what Pen had been dreaming of—more parental involvement in the business of her life.

'Yeah, well, you've made me walk home from soccer practice for years. And I don't remember the last time you went to one of my games, 'Mom,' using air quotes. 'I don't need you to do any of it. I got it. You always said your job was to raise independent kids. Well, you did. Now you can go back to work.' Pen said flatly, crossing her arms.

A look passed between John and Tess.

'I'm staying home from now on.' Said Tess, with as much patience as she could muster. 'End of story.'

The discussion was over.

'Great!' Pen said with mock cheerfulness, 'I need cupcakes for my team fundraiser tomorrow. You can get right on that, right?' Pen grabbed her backpack and headed for her room. They both flinched at the sound of the door slamming.

'Wine.' Said Tess, letting out the breath she'd been holding. 'Time for wine.'

'I'll pour' John grabbed the glasses and a bottle, then headed outside to sit in the warm Arizona evening sun. Tess followed, still a little stung, although not that surprised. Pen was Pen.

John handed her a glass filled, unapologetically, to the top. He clicked his glass against her own, offering 'Sláinte.' The toast from their Irish honeymoon. A usual toast for an unusual day.

'How do you feel?' he asked, grasping her hand. It was a loaded question.

'I don't know.' She whispered. 'A little adrift, I guess.'

'To be expected. I don't imagine they're happy at work.'

'No.' she exhaled loudly. 'Ken wasn't happy at all this morning. When I said I'd give him a 2-week transition period, he said he felt like I'd sucker-punched him.' She took a long pull on her wine.

'I get it,' said John, squeezing her hand. 'But he'll have to deal with it. You've made him a lot of money for a long time. He can take over for a while until he finds a replacement.'

'I know. I'm not going to a competitor. Then he would have tried to throw money at me or walked me out. But when I told him I was *staying home,* he laughed. Ken says he gives me a month before I climb the walls. He's hoping I have a change of heart.'

John took a sip of wine. 'Well, we both know that's not going to happen.'

They sat contemplating the sunset over the pink desert and the unspoken truth behind her sudden departure from her job.

'I couldn't sleep last night. What's coming? I feel like I'm trapped. There are so many things I want to do, and I always thought I would have plenty of time. *We* would have plenty of time. But I'm sick. And based on what they told me yesterday, I will only get sicker. Even if this doesn't kill me, I'll be too ill from the treatment to contemplate going to Bali or hiking the Camino de Santiago. For a very long time. You know that's always been at the top of my list.'

'I know.' He said quietly. Watching the sun dip below the horizon.

Later, Tess lay awake in the dark next to John's softly snoring form. She generally believed life was math — just a series of equations that, when unbalanced, caused worry and difficulty. Solving for x was what she'd always done. But with cancer, she could find no missing variable to plug in to instantly balance the equation. She knew this was why sleep eluded her.

Her cell phone lit up and repeatedly buzzed on the nightstand. Tess looked at the screen, surprised at the unfamiliar number.

'Hello?' she said softly, trying not to wake John.

'Hello, is this Pen Sullivan's mom?' said a frantic voice on the other end of the line.

Tess's heartbeat went from groggy to marathon runner in an instant.

'Yes.' She said, confused. 'What's going on?' Pen was in her room asleep. What could this be about at midnight on a Thursday night?

'Um.' Tess heard rustling and then a moan.

'Who is this?' Tess asked.

Silence. And then. 'I'm a friend of Pen's.' Said the male voice Tess didn't recognize. More rustling with muted voices in the background. He was covering the phone.

Tess shot out of bed, running barefoot down the hall, opening Pen's bedroom door, and switching on the light. The lump in the white canopied princess bed made Tess settle momentarily. When she shook her daughter, it was just a pile of pillows under the duvet.

'Oh, my God.' She said to no one in the room.

'Ma'am?' The voice on the phone shook her back to reality.

'What's going on?' Tess asked with a dry mouth, still struggling to put this new reality together. 'Who are you, and where's my daughter?'

'Pen's here at my house. Um. My parents are out of town, and I had a party. She smoked some stuff, and she's really sick. I think you need to come.' He said he was texting her the address.

'Is Pen OK?' she asked him, worried out of her mind.

He sounded angry and scared. But Tess was undeterred.

'Would you give up your life to save her?' she asked him, 'Right now, if someone walked in with a gun, you'd put yourself between them and her. I know you would.'

She was right, but he didn't react. All they'd been doing over the last three days was reacting. She could tell he would pick another time to try to talk her out of it. Today, they needed to focus on their daughter. Getting Pen on a plane was going to take some maneuvering. But, in her heart, Tess knew it was the right thing to do.

Tess was 50 years old. She could count the years and knew the time had passed, but it had slipped away. She'd missed so much precious time with her children. There and not there for them. John was around when they needed him. But she had traveled so much and been preoccupied. Always a crisis at work.

She remembered taking her son, Charlie, to the office when he had a fever because she couldn't miss a meeting and stay home. Back before, *working from home* became an actual thing. He'd slept on the couch in her office. Tess's assistant made sure he ate chicken soup while she was in meetings. When the smartphone arrived, she was connected to work 24/7 — home, but not at home.

Was she a bad mother? She didn't honestly know. Everything she had done was to give her children more than she ever had. Pen would be out and off to college in three years: the most challenging child. Maybe Tess had made the wrong choices.

She closed her eyes, filling with tears. Look forward, she told herself. You've got a lot to do. Don't get bogged down in self-pity.

Pen was back in school the following week, and Tess and John had returned to work. One evening, John glanced over at his wife sitting on a chaise lounge by the pool, with the warm light of the desert sun shining on the face he'd looked at for more than 25 years. It had some wrinkles now, and Tess had stopped coloring her hair, so her dark brown bob was laced with some grey too. It was a face he knew well, but it was a mask today. Tess was holding back. That was clear.

John had broached the topic of the trip she proposed. Again, insisting she reconsider in the light of day and making every logical argument against it. He looked up cancer statistics and peppered her with them. But Tess was more determined than ever, calling her doctor to discuss options while in Spain. She was barely listening to the reasons this wasn't a good idea.

'I'm going to see Charlie in Seattle before we leave.' Tess said suddenly. 'I need to tell him myself about all this. In-person,'

It caught John off-guard. 'Is that necessary?' He whispered.

Tess looked over at him but said nothing. John closed his eyes and took a deep breath, feeling the wind blow the collar of his pink golf shirt. It was her show now, and he needed to back off and give her space. It was his role since the very beginning. And he knew how to do it.

The following weekend, John dropped Tess off at the airport for her trip to visit their son. It made her smile his asking if she had everything she needed. Tess could pack in her sleep.

Before she knew it, she landed in Seattle, driving through the familiar city they'd lived in for over 20 years. Charlie was Tess and John's firstborn, and from the moment he entered the world, it was clear he was an old soul. Tess knew you weren't supposed to be friends with your child—you were the parent. But Charlie was unique, and his birth added a rudder to her life that she didn't know had been missing. She needed to spend time with him now. It would do her heart good.

Walking across the grass, she smiled as she laid out the blanket so they could sit and have a long-overdue chat. No longer a Seattleite, her tan gave her away as someone from out of town. But today, the Northwest sun was shining, and she closed her eyes, turning her face to the sky to take in the warmth before starting them off.

Charlie with his glasses. Remembering back to when he was in kindergarten and got his first pair. They made him seem more intelligent than all the other kids. And then, as the years went by, it turned out he was—getting a full scholarship to college for her genius son. She and John were so proud.

Sitting on the hill overlooking Lake Washington, Tess looked around at the tall Douglas fir trees she remembered from living there. So different from the desert where they live now.

'I'm so glad I got to see you.' she told him. 'It's been too long. But I came to talk to you about something important.' Tess took a deep breath. 'There's no other way to say this. I have cancer.'

'It's gone beyond my breast, and it's serious. But I need to do some things before I have surgery, and I wanted to come here and tell you in person.'

Tears fell down her cheeks as she searched her jacket pockets for tissues.

'It's going to be OK, though.' Tess assured him, trying to smile. 'I was upset, too, when I heard it. But your dad and I, we've talked a lot about it. And we've decided that I will go for a walk in Spain. It's a pilgrimage of sorts. Before I have surgery and start all that chemo and radiation stuff. They say people get miracles when they reach Santiago. So, who knows? Maybe there is a miracle waiting for me there.'

As the sun went behind the clouds, the wind picked up. Tess smiled to reassure her clever son.

'The doctors support my decision to wait until I return from my walk. They believe in a mind and body approach, and since this is so important to me, they think I'll be in a good position to focus on getting better after I've done it. Dad supports it, too. And,' She took a deep breath. 'I'm taking Pen with me.'

'I know, I know. It seems crazy, but I'll tell Pen about my cancer on the walk when the time is right. You know we have a tough relationship. And this trip is my chance to spend time with her and tell her in my own way. And there's something else.' She went on to describe the night of the party, leaving nothing out.

'I bet you're wondering how this could happen. It's a question for which I have no answer. And frankly, neither does Pen, if you ask her. She's not the Pen you knew. We're still trying to understand it—your dad and me. But we can't ignore it. And we can't ignore that I have cancer.'

Tess closed her eyes. She longed to see her son's smile.

'I'll be fine. Don't you worry. If you look at me now, you'd never know I'm ill. It's only eight weeks, and then I'll be back and getting better. And listen to me.' Tess said calmly. 'I'm getting Pen out of Arizona to try to reach her, however futile that sounds. And at the same time, I get to do something I always wanted to do.'

Getting up on her knees, Tess gathered the bag from the shop where she'd stopped from the airport—pulling out all of Charlie's favorites—beef jerky, Snickers bars, Smarties, and Red Vines. And then the flowers Tess put in the vase at the base of the stone. She kissed her fingers and outlined the deep engraving of her son's name etched in the granite marker.

'I Love you, my wonderful boy. I'm so glad I got to see you today. I'll be back right after I get home from Spain. And don't worry about me—I'll be just fine.' choking up. 'Because I know you'll be watching over me. I'll keep you posted along the way.'

It was all Tess could do not to hug the cold stone that anchored her son to the ground. She gathered the blanket and slowly returned to the car after stopping at her grandmother's grave a few yards away and placing a single yellow rose on the brass marker.

Tess was staying overnight in the city but had one other stop on her itinerary. Driving north, she craned out the window, examining the houses on the street just off Roosevelt Way. Circling the block, parking in front of a small bungalow with dormer windows on the roof. It looked just like the house from the book *The Little House;* she used to read it to her kids when they were small.

Tess wasn't entirely sure she had the right place with all the new construction in the area as she opened the car door to get out, stepping onto the sidewalk. Suddenly, the memory of this house from when she was a child became clearer. Back then, the house was a red brick color with white trim. She and her siblings used to sleep up in the attic. There were stairs they climbed through a secret door in her grandmother's closet, up under the eaves. They slept on metal beds made up with old, soft linens and quilts. Tess loved how they felt. Large wood and leather steamer trunks were full of old stuff—newspapers and random things. Once, they discovered a mangey black fox stole. They used to terrorize each other with it. Well, mostly, they tormented her since she was the youngest—Tess chuckled at the memory.

Tentatively walking up the cement steps to the front porch, she looked down, smiling. On the walkway, five handprints, from very small to large, were still visible in the pavement.

Tess's Dad put in this walkway for their grandmother on a grey summer day. Tess was probably five years old, and when the cement had set up a bit, he had them press their hands into it.

Tess bent down and put her freckled adult hand over the imprint of her younger self. It seemed like a million years ago, yet here she was again, at this house, she hadn't thought about in more than 40 years.

She smiled, remembering that cloudy day so long ago. Time slipped through her fingers, but she vowed to use the remainder more wisely.

Driving to the hotel in downtown Seattle, she handed the keys to the valet and ran a bath when she got to her room. It hurt. Her heart was breaking for so many reasons. Tess was sick, but that didn't matter. She missed her son, an ache that would never go away—and worried about Pen and John and how they might fare without her — especially Pen. She called John from the bubbles, and they talked until midnight.

The following day, Tess turned in her car, passed through security, and waited for her flight home. Ready to enter the next phase—The Walk. The books she read all said your Camino didn't begin in Saint-Jean Pied-de-Port in France. It started at varying points before you left home. Now Tess understood what they meant. For her, it had already begun.

PART II

THE WALK

THREE
PHOENIX TO ST. JEAN PIED-DE-PORT

Driving to pick Tess up at Sky Harbour airport in Phoenix, it hit John all at once. The weight of her diagnosis; what had happened with Pen. All of it. It was heavy, and it sat in his chest like a boulder.

Tess always had a plan. But sometimes, he wasn't included in whatever strategy session she had in her head when she hatched it. Now it turned out his superhero wife was a human like the rest of them. John found he was somehow angry about it, and that surprised him. In the last 25 years, he wondered if she needed him. But he knew she needed him now.

On the one hand, John agreed that this trip was important for her and their daughter. Tess believed this was the only way to save Pen from herself.

On the other hand, he wanted to yell at her, 'You're gambling with your life, and if I lose you, it will destroy me too!' But he wasn't the one with cancer. He couldn't imagine how that felt. And seeing Pen at the party had scared the hell out of them both.

Tess was right. Pen could have died. The potential of losing his wife and daughter in one fell swoop was a wake-up call. He knew Tess was trying to keep both things from happening, and he couldn't fault her for that.

John contemplated taking a leave of absence to walk with them. Tess could get sick or hurt, and she might need him. But he also knew that she needed this time with Pen and that his daughter was at a critical moment, just like her mother. They had things to work out. He would save his leave for when she was back. When treatment started, he could help her through it.

John didn't have a crystal ball. This trek might be the last adventure of her life. He'd written her a letter and would put it in Tess' backpack before she left, so she could read it when she got there. She was entitled to go and to be free in doing it. But that didn't mean it wasn't the most challenging thing he had ever done.

John recalled the evening they sat Pen down to tell her about their plan.

'Your Mother is going to walk the Camino de Santiago in Spain when school gets out next week,' John told their daughter matter-of-factly. 'you're going with her.'

'What?! I'm NOT going to Spain.' Pen protested like they were crazy. 'I have soccer camp all summer. If I don't go to the camp, I can kiss playing on the first-team varsity next year goodbye.'

Tess had remained silent.

'I canceled your soccer camp after the drug thing.' He took a deep breath, 'We're taking you away for the summer, and you and your Mom are going to do something together.'

Pen looked from her dad to her mom. They weren't messing around.

'I have friends here. We have plans.' She'd pleaded.

'Plans around drugs and the booze in our liquor cabinet?' asked Tess. 'Or is it just the pills from the medicine chest? We know you've been stealing that stuff from the house.' The arrow hit the mark. They were going for a little shock and awe. Pen looked very surprised they knew about the rest of it.

'No.' she whispered. 'I'm never doing drugs again.'

'Well, I'm sure you mean that now.' Said John. 'But we're not taking any chances.'

'You'll be coming with me on this walk.' Tess told her. 'You'll still have some time with your friends when you return, but we'll spend a large chunk of this summer in Spain.'

John could tell Pen wanted to protest. She wanted to yell at them for not trusting her. But the words melted in her mouth. Since the incident, they weren't lording it over her. Yet they no longer trusted her.

Tess wrapped her arms tightly around her daughter before Pen pulled away and returned to the other room.

Tess shoved the photo and the letter into the envelope and stuffed it in her pack. Grabbing her toiletries, she headed for the bathroom, catching a glimpse of herself in the mirror. The woman staring back looked tired and unsure. Something she often felt but usually kept hidden.

That night, Tess had a nightmare. She couldn't remember what it was about, but it woke her before the sun was up, as summer lightning flashed outside the window. She lay in the dark listening to Pen's breathing, much like she used to when her daughter was little and she couldn't sleep. Her thoughts were all over the place. Of home. Of her trip to see Charlie. Of John. She wondered how Ken was getting on at work. Did he pull the deal together? He'd only called her a few times to ask questions, but mostly he'd been on radio silence.

At that moment, Tess missed the familiarity of her work. She knew how to do that. No matter what was happening in any other area of her life, Tess could bury herself there. But she didn't know how to do what she was about to do—choosing to take Pen on this trek to find a way to save her daughter. And she was even less sure how she would save herself.

As dawn broke, Tess gently woke Pen to get packed up and into the taxi she had ordered to take them to Barcelona-Sants station and the train to Pamplona.

Pen groaned, rolling over.

'Why can't we shop in Barcelona for a few days? I'll need school clothes, and we'll be getting back right before school starts.'

Tess just smiled.

'We need to get started on our walk. But even if we did buy some stuff, you'd have to carry it for 800km from France across Spain.'

Pen rolled her eyes as she padded to the bathroom to brush her teeth and put her long hair in a ponytail. To Tess's surprise, she hadn't packed any makeup and was ready in record time.

They caught the train to Pamplona, then waited for the bus to Saint-Jean Pied-de-Port, where they would begin the following day. Sitting in the Pamplona bus station, Pen studied the route they would take over the next month. Tess smiled. Her daughter was taking an interest.

'It says here the trail goes right through Pamplona.' Pen pointed to the map. 'Why are we taking a bus to St. Jean if we could just start from here? It seems like a waste of time.'

'Because the walk starts in Saint Jean.' Tess reminded her, 'I want to walk the whole thing. And I read the Pyrenees section is an important part of the experience. I don't want us to miss it.'

'You get that the Pyrenees are mountains, right?' She looked down at Tess skeptically. 'Are you going to be able to climb that?'

'I guess I'll find out.' Tess smiled. 'But I have you to help me if I need it, right?'

Pen had gone back to studying the map, ignoring her.

An older woman sitting beside them at the bus station watched with interest. The woman spoke up when Pen left to get a Coke at the bodega.

'Are you waiting for the bus to Saint Jean?' she asked Tess in heavily accented English.

'Yes, we will start the Camino de Santiago tomorrow.'

The woman studied her for a long moment. 'You're American.' She declared.

'Yes.' Tess confirmed.

'And you are taking your daughter the entire Way to Santiago de Compostela?'

'Yes. I am.' Said Tess.

The old woman pursed her lips, carefully examining her from beneath a sea of wrinkles.

'This is good.'

'Have you ever walked the Camino?' Tess asked her.

The woman smiled.

'Portions of it. I had always intended to do it entirely. But time got away from me, and now I am too old.'

A quote from the writer George Eliot flashed through Tess's mind. *You're never too old to become what you might have been.* But that wasn't strictly true, as this old woman knew well.

Heading through the mountains, passing many of the towns they would walk back through in the following days, like Pen, Tess thought about how much easier it would be to get out and start from there. But she kept it to herself. Walking the Camino wasn't about taking the easy way.

An hour later, the bus dropped them off in Saint-Jean Pied-de-Port, a town whose origin dates back nearly a thousand years. The buildings are crafted of stone and stucco, half-timbered, with low doors and small windows as though Hobbits had constructed them centuries ago.

Tess and Pen searched in vain for the albergue, where they would stay the night before starting their Camino early the following day. Albergues dot the route from SaintJean Pied-de-Port in France to Santiago de Compostela on the west coast of Spain, where believers will collect the Compostela, recording their completion of the pilgrimage. Albergues are places for pilgrims on the road to sleep, shower, and wash their clothes. The local municipality or a church sometimes runs them. Sometimes by the local convent or monastery. Still, others are run by ex-peregrinos, as pilgrims of the Camino are called. To provide shelter and keep giving back to others walking the Way.

They found their albergue across an ancient stone bridge and gratefully set their packs down in the small reception area. Their host was an elderly Frenchman who had given his little speech thousands of times. He held out his hand.

'First of all, I need your American and pilgrim credentials.' Tess handed over both for her and Pen. All pilgrims need a credential or pilgrim passport to stay in the Albergues. Each accommodation along the route imprints the document with a bespoke stamp. Included for the price of a few euros per night is a bed fit for a monk. A pilgrim meal is often available for an extra charge. These are hearty, three-course meals to be eaten communally with the other peregrinos.

'I get to give you your first stamp!' Said the French *hospitaliero*, grasping the worn wooden handle, faithfully ensuring the rubber was smothered in ink, before loudly pressing it to each of their pilgrim passports with a flourish. Satisfied, he handed them back to Tess.

'So, you might find a few things helpful as you start your journey. First of all,' Pointing to Pen, 'this is not a race. You are not trying to compete with the other people on the Way. There are no medals at the end for finishing before everyone else because, well, that would be foolish. Walking the Way isn't about speed or keeping up with others in front of you. You will walk your own Way. As each person must in this life.'

Tess watched Pen's face as the albergue host was speaking. She could tell her daughter wasn't remotely bought into the ideas this guy was selling. *Competition* was Pen's middle name. But the host smiled knowingly.

'You will see.' He chuckled.

'And to you.' addressing Tess. 'You are walking the whole Way?'

'Yes.' Said Tess.

'With your daughter.' A statement, not a question.

'Yes.'

'Low or high boots?'

'High.' She held up her foot.

'Okay. If you do not want your legs to hurt.' Pointing at the front of his calves. 'How do you say? Hmm.'

'Shin splints?' offered Pen.

He tapped his nose and nodded, smiling.

'Exactly this. If you don't want *shin splints*,' said the Frenchman, mimicking Pen's sharp American accent, 'then you will not lace your boots to the top. And not too tight. You need to be able to move your ankle front and back. You will save yourself a lot of pain if you do this. And do not forget to tuck in your laces. Very important.'

Tess took note and decided she would follow his directions.

'It's something I've always wanted to do. What about you?'

'I just graduated from university and am now a fully qualified computer engineer. I'm celebrating with this walk before I start my career.' He explained.

'Very smart.' Tess smiled. 'I wish I had done something similar. But hey! It's never too late, right?'

Herman laughed. 'Of course not.'

Just then, they saw the sign on the pilgrim office change to 'Open.' Herman wished her 'Buen Camino.' She did the same as they sat before the administrators to get their stamps and shells to commence their respective walks.

Pen appeared unmoved by the experience as the French woman explained each day's stages and elevation maps. Tess listened closely and took notes.

'If you lose your way, look for the yellow arrows or shells. Sometimes, you must return to the last one you saw on a building, fence post, pavement, or stone. Anywhere. But you will always find your way.'

With their pilgrim passports officially stamped and their intention to walk to Santiago de Compostela registered in the official logs, they were peregrinos now.

'Buen Camino,' the administrator said, waving them off to select a shell from the box. It means 'Have a good way' and is the official blessing for pilgrims on the Way.

Stepping out onto the street, there was no place to go but back the way they had come. Tess was grateful it was downhill. She called Pen over, and they took a photo of their feet, taking the first step of their journey next to a brass marker embedded in the cobbles, indicating the start of the Way. Then she texted it to John.

Two possible routes mark the Camino Frances start from Saint-Jean Pied-de-Port to Roncesvalles, Spain. The Valcarlos route runs along a flat road but is a bit longer. The other is the Napoleon route over the Pyrenees mountains through the Roncevaux Pass, a few kilometers shorter. This route is the most popular, and the one Tess had chosen for their first two days until they reached the village of Roncesvalles in Spain.

Other pilgrims were up and starting to walk out of town. Instead of looking for the yellow arrows, Tess and Pen followed people who seemed to know the right direction. They walked past the Albergue where they'd stayed the night before, continuing up the road and out of the old town.

Initially, Tess was winded. She had reserved beds for them at a place called Orrison, so they only had to do 8km on the first day. No sense in risking injury and hurting themselves. They needed time to build up their endurance. And books said that the first day was the most difficult.

They walked on pavement up hills, similar in gradient to those she remembered from living in San Francisco in her 20s. The path led to a rolling road and beautiful views of the surrounding mountains and farmland.

This wasn't so bad, thought Tess. The guidebook made it sound difficult. Maybe she was in better shape than she thought.

Further ahead, they rounded a corner that went off to the right. From there, Tess could see the road up ahead would take a sharp left 200 yards further. At that point, it went straight up.

Tess stopped. She put down her trekking poles, removed her pack, and got out the guidebook. It looked like what they described. Well, in truth, it looked worse. How would she ever get up that hill, let alone walk the other 800 kilometers?! She knew her daughter was watching her.

'Come on.' Pen whined. 'Other people are passing us. I don't want to be the last one to get to the top.'

'Don't you remember what the man from the Albergue said last night?' Tess reminded her. 'It's not a race.'

'Yeah, right. Let's go.' Pen bent down and grabbed her poles. Tess struggled into her pack without help from her daughter, securing the buckles. In a way, Pen was right. The sooner they started, the faster they would finish for the day.

They walked the 200 yards to the base of the big uphill and stopped. Tess looked up to the top—then down at her feet, trying her best not to hyperventilate. She took one step and then another. After 50 yards, she was so winded she stepped to the side to catch her breath. Pen continued up the hill, walking backward with a withering look of pity for her mother. Tess could see she was on her phone texting someone. Tess turned around, looking over the valley filled with farms and villages. It was beautiful—an idyllic setting for a picnic and a glass of wine. Just standing there, her breathing came fast. Scores of other Peregrinos passed her. All were greeting her with 'Buen Camino.'

Seriously? She thought. Buen? So far, the *good* part had escaped her. She heard Pen's voice from above.

'Come on, Mom. Let's go!'

Tess had no choice. She had to start walking, climbing, to be exact. So, she did. And every 25 yards or so, she stopped, and others passed her. Pen stayed about 100 yards ahead, looking back in frustration, anxious to be done with it. At one point, Tess had to lie down on the side of the road. Was she this out of shape? When did that happen? She'd worked out consistently all her life. At home, in hotels, a gym near her office. She refused to believe the cancer was already getting the better of her.

Pen saw her Mom on the ground and texted her Dad.

Pen: *mom is gonna die.*

John: *What?!?*

John sprang out of bed, his heart leaping out of his chest. He was lying in the dark, wondering how it was going on their first day out. The photo of their feet had woken him. Pen's text was the last thing he wanted to hear. Frankly, John was surprised that Tess started by telling Pen so soon.

Pen: *she's lying on the side of a road that isn't even steep. never gonna make it to Santiago*

John: *Where r u?*

Pen: *like one minute out of Saint Jean. I'm like a mile ahead of her, but I can see her down there.*

John: *Why aren't you with her?*

Pen: *she's too slow, and it's hot—I want to get to the hotel and stop walking.*

John: *Does she have water?*

Pen: *I have her water. It was too heavy for her to carry.*

John: *Go back down and give her some water. Honestly, Pen—Help her when she needs you.*

Pen rolled her eyes. *fine.*

Sullenly, Pen walked back down the hill and handed the water to her Mom.

'Thank you!' Tess drank deeply from the plastic bottle. 'It's so hot. I was dying.'

She said the words before their irony hit her. Giving the bottle back to Pen, she got up. All she had to do was make it up to Honto. Orrison couldn't be that far beyond it. Using her poles and putting one foot in front of the other, she finally made it to the top.

There was a spot on the stone wall circling the lone cafe, and she sat down and drank more water. It was humid, and the sun was blazing down. Tess took deep breaths. She could do this. After 15 minutes of rest and watching Pen pace back and forth, she got up, put on her pack, and started again.

This stretch of road was less steep. But then, the Camino veered off the pavement and onto a dirt track, where it started gaining elevation. From this perspective, Tess could see the path zig-zagged up the mountainside, back and forth, skirting pastures where cows and sheep grazed. As they made their way up the mountain, others began to stop and rest, so she felt less conspicuous.

A regular cadence set in. Hike 50 yards and rest for 3 minutes. Hike another 50 yards and rest for another 3 minutes. After an hour of gaining elevation, she reached what she thought was the top of the mountain when looking up from below. But, when she got there, Orrison wasn't there.

Tess stopped and turned around. Looking out, she could see Saint Jean off in the distance at the bottom of the valley. Others were coming up the track she'd just walked. Older people and those pushing bicycles loaded with all the gear they would need for the ride to Santiago. A man who looked like he had just left work and decided to walk the Camino in his khakis, dress shirt, and office shoes. He appeared so out of place; he caught Tess's attention. This man didn't seem winded. He passed her by on his way up the mountainside as though it was his daily commute.

As a kid, Tess had played Gretel in a local school production of *The Sound of Music*. She wondered if this was what Maria von Trapp had felt climbing the Alps, one step ahead of the Nazis. Only Tess wasn't fleeing from Nazis. Just cancer, and she already knew she couldn't outrun it. If she could keep it at arm's length for the duration of this adventure, that was the best she could do.

In just one day, who Tess had always been, began to peel away. The masks she had worn to protect herself wouldn't work here. And they were too heavy to carry anyway. She couldn't get anything more up this mountainside than herself, and her body betrayed her to everyone who passed by.

She saw Herman, the German guy from the pilgrim's office, when she was lying by the side of the road down below. He smiled and waved as Tess burned with embarrassment. Herman wasn't having any trouble getting up the hill.

Tess turned and started up again, knowing Pen was somewhere up ahead. After more steep hills, she finally spotted stone buildings around a bend. A group of people were sitting outside around tables with cold drinks in their hands, laughing and enjoying the sunny day. As if they had driven there in a car and not walked up from Saint Jean. Her daughter, Pen, was among them.

After lunch, they received bunk assignments, and Pen made a friend, spending the afternoon kicking around a soccer ball. While she had a moment, Tess lay on her bed listening to the hum of voices outside.

Various perigrinos spoke a multitude of languages on the terrace below. The sound was like a hive full of bees punctuated by laughter. Tess closed her eyes, marveling at how so many people from around the world found themselves at the top of this mountain. She had no idea who they were, and they didn't know her, but Pen was already making friends with another teenager she met an hour before. It was going to be OK. They could do this.

Later that evening, those staying in the Refugio in Orrison gathered for the three-course meal of soup, meat, and a traditional Basque cake for dessert. The wine flowed, and a guitar strummed with a harmonica as voices sang the same U2 song. Prompted by the host, each person introduced themselves and their country of origin. In the room was a couple from Brazil celebrating their 20th wedding anniversary with this walk. And others from Korea and Slovenia. Many were Germans or French. And there were even a few Americans, just like them. Pen smiled when she won the distinction of being the youngest peregrino in the room at fifteen. People wanted to know why she was walking, and Tess held her breath.

'Because my Mom wanted to, so I came with her.' She said, blushing as the room broke into applause.

Her daughter seemed to be in a better mood with all the camaraderie. The glimmer of hope Tess had for Pen flickered and burned a bit brighter. Tomorrow they would cross over to Spain and climb down the other side of the Pyrenees.

At last, Tess crossed the border between France and Spain through a livestock gate. Then she moved through the forest alone, running at times after becoming spooked by every snap of a twig or rustle of leaves under her feet.

All at once, she felt her bootlaces catch, barely catching herself from falling with her poles. It was in that moment she remembered the Frenchman's advice in Saint Jean and realized she'd already forgotten to tuck in her laces. No one was around to help her if she fell or became injured. She would have to wait for the others to catch up. Bending down, Tess tucked them in, vowing not to forget again. She stood up and looked forward, then back. Still no one and no sign of Pen. Where could she be? Tess had to keep going if she was going to find her daughter.

In the afternoon, she reached the other side of the mountains, where the big downhill climb began. The dark threatening clouds that loomed over them all day dumped rain mixed with hail as the path in front of her split in two. The pilgrim office in Saint Jean recommended taking the way to the right. The route to the left was shorter and direct to Roncesvalles in the valley below, but it was steep and treacherous. To the right was more gradual but more exposed to the elements.

Tess wondered which way Pen would have chosen. Her daughter had heard the speech from the woman, but Pen was a teenager and had a well-documented independent streak. Tess decided to take the woman's advice. Walking right, she could see the lights from the village in the valley far below, just through the fog, like a beacon calling her.

After emerging from the trees, a strong gust came at her from the left, knocking her to the ground. Large blond horses ran past like the devil was chasing them as rain and hail hit her face, blinding her. It was all Tess could do to regain her feet with the heavy pack weighing her down. Struggling, she looked back, but no one was there.

Turning around, she looked down, hoping someone might be within calling distance if she encountered more problems on the steep muddy trail. She saw a red dot far below—someone who had gotten there a half-hour before her but was too far away to hear her call. She had no choice but to start down alone.

'Slowly.' Tess said to herself out loud. 'You got this. It's not a race, and we can take as much time as we need.'

The sound of her voice was oddly comforting. The path was slick and slow going, using her feet to brace her descent and her poles to help keep her upright. The wind whipped around her, and the melting hail ran down her neck, soaking her shirt. Rain seeped through her jacket and pants. Shivering, she took another step while singing a made-up song she used to sing to her kids when they were babies. 'The Sham Sham song' they'd called it. She would sing it for hours until she was hoarse. Pen and Charlie had demanded it and would fall asleep to it most nights before they outgrew the ritual. Now she used it to calm herself, trying to quiet the rising fear. Without warning, Tess slipped and fell, scraping her hands on the loose gravel as her knees sank into the deep mud. She began singing louder so she could hear the familiar tune over the wind as she got up and examined the damage. Moving forward was her only choice.

Eventually, she reached some trees, and while the path was steep and slippery as chocolate pudding, she was better able to stay upright protected from the wind. Finally, after winding her way through a field of cows with enormous horns blocking the gate to the village, Tess went in search of Pen. She found her daughter sitting in one of the two cafes in town, drinking a Coke the owner had given her more than an hour before. When she saw her Mom, she laughed.

'You look like a drowned rat.'

Tess took deep breaths.

'You left me and ran ahead. I had no idea where you were!' Tears flowed at the relief of seeing Pen. 'If you were hurt or fell off a cliff. I spent the whole day rushing to find you.'

'I'm fine. You were walking too slowly, and those people were boring, so I kept going. I got here like two hours ago. You're a slowpoke.'

Pen looked down at Tess's pants covered in mud. 'Did you fall?' She asked her Mom with a flicker of concern that almost surprised Tess.

Tess nodded. She was cold and tired, barely able to gather a coherent thought.

'Well, we need to check into the monastery.' said Pen, 'But you have our documents. So, I couldn't get us beds yet.'

Pen gave the owner her empty bottle and said, 'Thanks for the Coke.' Tess paid and thanked him in Spanish, and he responded in kind.

Pen put her arm around her Mom. 'Come on. Let's get you cleaned up.'

They made their way to the registration desk at the monastery to reserve a couple of beds and have a shower. The host led them to their bunks and explained that the showers were at the end of the hall. Being the first to get their bed assignments, Pen offered to stay with their things while Tess took a warm shower. She was cold to the bone.

Tess stood under the blessedly hot water until she warmed up. Drying off, she exited the stall, looking forward to her clean, dry clothes. Looking up, she found a line snaking from the showers out the door she had come in. But there was something curious about that line.

'Why are there only men in this line?' She inquired to no one in particular, blood rising to her cheeks.

One grinning person enlightened her, 'You are in the Men's shower.'

The entire assembly chuckled.

Her eyes widened, cheeks turning crimson. Each man was in various stages of undress, but they all had smiles.

'Oh, my God! I swear I didn't see anything. I swear.' Realizing she wasn't wearing anything either, clutching her clothes, Tess ran back to the stall, closing the door. Struggling, she pulled her clothes over her wet skin and wrapped her hair in her towel. Leaving the shower room, the sign that confirmed it was indeed reserved for Men. Red-faced, she rushed back to the bunks.

'What's wrong with you?' asked Pen, seeing her flustered mom.

'Nothing.' Said Tess, busying herself with organizing her bunk. 'By the way, the showers are at the end of the hall, then to the left. It's a bit tricky.'

'I'm sure I can find the women's showers.' Pen assured her, marching off to get cleaned up. 'I'll just look for the picture of the international symbol for 'girl in a dress.'

Tess lay down on her bottom bunk, wrapped in her sleeping bag, wishing for John and his steady hand as exhaustion overtook her. She didn't awaken when Pen left to eat the pilgrim meal with the others. Nor hear the church bells tolling, signaling the pilgrim's mass to receive the blessing. She'd planned to light a candle and pray for their journey and her daughter. But she slept until morning and was only awakened by the Spanish cyclists on the opposite bunks preparing to head out.

SIX

THE ROMAN ROAD TO PAMPLONA

T ess and Pen stood outside the monastery, donning oversized rain gear to cover themselves and their packs. The mist had started to come down, and a rain shower was imminent. Tess helped Pen with hers first.

'Please don't run ahead today. I don't know what this next stretch to Zubiri is like, and I would be grateful if you could stay with me. I would like us to spend time together.'

Pen didn't respond, and after Tess struggled with getting her own rain poncho over her head, she turned around, and Pen was gone. Closing her eyes, she took a couple of deep breaths. It would be another day alone. She would have to walk with the other pilgrims; they were all going in the same direction.

Tess trudged the crowded, muddy path. It began to thin out in the woods until she was, again, all by herself. She started walking quicker, hoping to catch up to other pilgrims who might be ahead, but there were long stretches where she was alone. Alone and scared. She shook her head. Insecurity was not like her. She knew she could take care of anything, but she wanted Pen with her. The illness was, no doubt, making her feel more vulnerable.

Tess had a list of things she wanted to discuss with Pen in her pack. Of course, there was the moment she would tell her about her cancer. But there was more. She needed to talk to her daughter, with whom communication was so hard and so painful, about many things.

Tess compiled it because this might be her last opportunity to spend a large block of time with Pen without being focused on her illness. Things that they might have talked about later, when Pen was in college or out in the world. But Tess knew that might not be in the cards for her, so she wanted to have them in the next few weeks before she told Pen about her diagnosis. So, these conversations would be untainted by what was to come.

After several hours of walking, Tess entered the village of Viscarret-Guerendiain, stopping to rest at a cafe. She put her pack against the fence in the courtyard with the others and went inside. With a sea of occupied tables, she asked a man sitting alone if she could share his. He was enjoying a coffee, as well.

'Of course.' He offered her the chair opposite as she settled her coffee on the table. 'Where are you from?'

'I'm from the US.,' she said in response. She took a sip of her coffee to avoid saying more.

'Ah.' He said.

Something in his tone made Tess turn from looking out at the courtyard back to the man.

'And where are you from?' She asked him.

'I am from Madrid.' he said, drinking from his cup.

'So, like most Europeans, you started your Camino at your front door?' asked Tess. She had heard of others who started in The Netherlands or France. They had already walked 1000km or more before arriving in Saint Jean and hadn't found the climb to Orrison that first day quite as exhausting as she had.

'Originally, yes. We walked from Madrid to León. This year we came to Saint Jean and are walking to Santiago.'

'You said 'we.' Are you walking with your wife?'

A shadow passed across the man's tanned face.

'No. With my son. But he found someone with whom he would prefer to walk today. We met her yesterday on the trek from Saint Jean to

Roncesvalles. At the meal last night, they arranged to meet up today to walk to Zubiri. So, I am left on my own.'

'Coincidentally, I'm walking with my daughter, and she has gone ahead for the second day in a row.' Tess told him.

'Is your daughter in high school?' he asked.

'Yes, why?'

'I think she may be walking with my son.'

Tess pulled up a recent photo of Pen on her phone and showed it to the man.

'Yes.' He confirmed. 'Her name is Pen?'

'That's her.' Said Tess.

'An unusual name.' he observed.

'It's short for Penelope. She prefers her nickname.' she explained.

'Ah.' and the man took another drink of his coffee.

There was an awkward silence. Tess didn't know what to think of this man and his son, who knew Pen. Why hadn't Pen mentioned this boy and his father at the monastery? Or told her she wanted to walk with him today?

'What is your son's name?' Tess asked him.

'I'm sorry. I should introduce myself.' He held out his hand for Tess to shake. 'I am Javier Silva. My son is called Mateo. He is nearly seventeen and will complete the final year of high school next year before attending University.'

Tess gulped. Pen was only fifteen, and she said so. Javier chuckled, and a smile broke out when he saw her surprise.

'Pen seems like a very self-possessed girl, and my son is a gentleman. I do not think anything untoward will happen while they walk to Zubiri. We have nothing to worry about.'

This man seemed so sure of what he was saying. The memory of Pen hunched over a bucket at the party just a few weeks before was still fresh.

'And your name is?' Javier asked.

Tess realized she was being rude.

'I'm sorry. I'm Tess, Tess Sullivan. It's nice to meet you.'

Javier smiled and finished his coffee. 'Well, since our children are walking to Zubiri, would you like to walk there with me? It seems I could also use a friend today.'

Tess breathed a sigh of relief. 'I would love to have the company. I've been feeling a little lonely the last couple of days.' she admitted.

Javier took their empty cups to the bar and met Tess by the fence as pilgrims filed in to rest at the café. He helped her with her backpack and then shrugged into his own. Making their way through the village following the yellow arrows, they walked in silence. Tess didn't know how to strike up a conversation with this man who, somehow, she had fallen into walking with because of Pen. Javier solved the problem for her.

'So, what made you come to Spain to walk the Camino to Santiago de Compostela from Phoenix, Arizona?'

Tess was surprised he knew where she was from but remembered they had walked with Pen the day before.

'I've dreamt of walking the Camino since reading Paulo Coelho's book *The Pilgrimage*. It's been over 25 years since I first read it, but it has always been in the background. I recently quit my job, and my husband supported my need to come to Spain. I decided to bring Pen with me, hoping to find a way to bridge the divide that has opened between us since she became a teenager.'

Javier nodded.

'You said you started in Madrid before. Why are you and your son walking the Camino?' she asked.

Javier stopped, staring at his boots before facing her. 'We are walking in honor of my wife and Mateo's mother. Alejandra passed away five years ago. It has been a difficult time for us. Very difficult for Mateo to lose his mother at such a young and crucial age. We decided last year that we would walk this Camino for her. For ourselves too, but in her honor.'

His thoughtful response moved Tess. It was clear he had loved his wife very much, and this was something he was carrying with him. Mateo must have been through a great deal over the past few years.

'So, you both walked with Pen yesterday.' She said.

'Yes. We came upon her as she was returning from taking photos of the statue of the Virgin Mary. She had crawled up the rocks, and when she appeared from the fog, we were surprised to see her. She was pleased to have gotten the photos, entertaining us the whole way to Roncesvalles.' Javier smiled. 'We were taken with her enthusiasm.'

Tess cringed. She didn't want to know that Pen had taken chances in the Pyrenees the day before. But hearing that her daughter was taking photos was encouraging, considering Pen's often sullen silences around her mother. The Pen he described was not the Pen she knew. Tess decided to change the subject.

'So, Mateo will finish high school soon. Does he know what he would like to study at university?' she asked.

'Yes. He will study medicine, like me.'

Tess hadn't considered that Javier was a doctor. He hadn't introduced himself as one. In the US, the doctor's title would have dropped into the conversation back at the café.

'You're a doctor?' She asked, surprised.

'Yes. Family Practice. Most of my patients are geriatric. I like treating that generation. They have a lot of wisdom. While helping them, I learn a great deal in the process.'

It sounded kind and compassionate, and accurate.

'Will he follow you into your practice?' Tess asked.

'I don't think so. Mateo would like to be an oncologist. His mother died of cancer, and he hopes to treat patients and conduct research. He wants to be the person who discovers a cure. A noble endeavor.'

Tess gulped and continued walking before finding her voice again.

'Yes, a very noble endeavor.' She agreed. 'Is he a good student?'

'Excellent. Mateo can accomplish anything he sets out to.' Javier said with certainty.

Tess smiled. 'You're a proud father.'

He smiled. 'I have much to be proud of in my son.'

They reached the base of a steep incline. Tess got out her water bottle and realized she had forgotten to fill it at the café as planned. She'd been distracted by the conversation with Javier. He saw that she was drinking the last few drops.

'Here. Have some of mine and put these salts into it. You look a little red in the face, and I think you're not drinking enough water."

He filled her water bottle and put the salts in. Within five minutes, she felt ready to climb.

'Shall we?' he offered.

'Thank you. I feel much better.'

'Good'

It was only another 7km to Zubiri, but the old Roman road was steep, uneven, and rocky. Javier helped her through the worst, handing her down so she wouldn't slip on the smooth wet stones. And walking slower than she was sure he was capable of going.

Soon they were at Puente de la Rabia, the old stone bridge crossing the Rio Argainto the village of Zubiri, then went in search of their kids. They found them sitting outside at a cafe on the corner of the two main roads in the town. Pen was drinking a Coke and laughing at a shared joke.

'When did you arrive?' Javier asked his son while removing his pack.

'About 2 hours ago. Pen likes to run. We've had lunch and staked out the best albergues. I wasn't sure if we were staying here tonight or going on to Larrasoana. But Pen said they were staying here.'

Javier smiled. He looked at Tess, who shrugged.

'Sure. We can stay here tonight. Which albergue do you think is the best one?'

Mateo and Pen pointed it out. They had been listening to other peregrinos, and Mateo's guidebook confirmed it.

'Watch our packs. Tess and I can go and reserve beds.'

They paid for four beds and returned to the kids, joined by people they knew. Pilgrims, who were coming and going, regaled them with their stories when suddenly, fatigue washed over Tess. She needed a shower and to take her meds.

'I'm going to the albergue and get cleaned up. I'll meet you there for dinner.' Staring intently at Pen, expecting a response.

Mateo kicked her chair with his foot.

'Fine.' Pen said without looking at her Mom.

After a shower and a change of clothes, Tess felt human again. Taking her pills, she laid down to rest before the pilgrim meal. Tess was getting her feet under her. In the books, they said, 'The Camino provides,' but she had no idea how well until now. They would probably walk with Doctor Javier and his son for a day or two more. Once they reached Pamplona, it would get busy, and chances were good they wouldn't see them again. Tess was sure Javier was going slower for her. But everyone needed to go at their own pace. Everyone's Camino was their own to walk.

The following day, they took their time getting up and having breakfast, not walking to Pamplona until after 7, which is late on Camino time. Most pilgrims talked about getting up at 4:30 or five so they could walk when cool. Summer heat in Spain can be brutal, and pilgrims embraced anything that alleviated the hardships on the trail.

As they walked back across the old bridge to take up the path, it was clear to Tess that Pen would be walking with Mateo again. It meant she would be walking with Javier. He was a pleasant, undemanding companion, not expecting her to talk, but when he spoke, it was usually to ask a question or expound on something they saw. A student of history, Javier seemed to know a lot about the Navarra region.

The dappled path wound through forests, punctuated by small villages along the Arga River, and looked so much like Washington State Tess felt awash in homesickness. Their children had gone on ahead towards Zabaldika, where she was hoping they might meet up.

Crossing the narrow stone bridge into the village, they spotted a café on the riverbank. Tess recognized familiar faces who greeted them with shouts and raised arms beckoning her to join the group. Even the Austrian, Peter was there with his jagged stick and scarves.

'You made it!' said one of the Germans.

'Yes. Did you doubt it?' Tess asked him, smiling.

'Well, we were taking wagers after seeing you lying on the road up to Honto. But I won! I figured you'd push through.'

Javier looked at Tess questioningly.

'I had a rough time that first day. It was so hot, and frankly, Phoenix doesn't provide a lot of elevation to train.' She stopped herself and laughed. 'Okay. I was unprepared for that climb.'

'Ah,' he said.

Tess was quickly learning this word had multiple meanings.

'Listen.' She said to him. 'If I'm slowing you down, you can walk faster. I know I'm slower than most, but it's my pace. Yours is probably much closer to Pen and Mateo's.'

Javier frowned.

'I'm walking as quickly as I like. I'm enjoying your company and the scenery. I have no desire to go faster today.' The intensity of his gaze made Tess uncomfortable.

'I'll get us some coffee.' She offered in reconciliation. 'Would you like tortilla?'

'Sí. I'll find us a table.'

Coming outside with the food, she found Javier sitting with the group.

'Hey, Tess.' said one of the guys from California. 'We saw your daughter this morning while resting by the river. She was with a boy we hadn't seen before.'

'How long ago was that?' She asked him.

'Maybe an hour or so. They were walking pretty fast. Might already be in Pamplona by now.'

'The boy is my son.' Said Javier proudly.

'Very handsome kid.' The Californian laughed, 'You'll have to watch out, Tess. If you hope to pry Pen out of Spain by the end of the Camino.'

Free-range chickens pecked at the food dropped at their feet. Tess closed her eyes momentarily and listened to Javier talking to her friends. Once you cross the Pyrenees with people, you consider them friends. Soon, with the coffee and tortillas consumed, it was time to go. Saying their goodbyes, they picked up their packs.

The next stretch was hot. The map showed Pamplona was 8km away, but the river route added more distance to their walk. They were sweaty and tired when they arrived in the city, and the four of them checked into the Albergue Jesus y Maria. When Tess came out of the showers dressed in clean clothes, she found Javier had done the same.

'Where are the kids?' Tess asked.

'They pleaded for a few euros 10 minutes ago. To get some pizza.' He explained. 'How about some wine?'

The warrens of the old town of Pamplona were packed with restaurants and shops. The famous Spanish jamón proudly displayed in shop windows, with plastic renderings of the pinchos, in which each café specialized, front and center. It was the first-time Tess had confronted a sizeable Spanish city since Barcelona, having to navigate the menu and the language barrier. Javier was an expert guide.

'I've spent a lot of time up here. San Sebastian is further north and is known for its food and spectacular coastline. But Pamplona also has good food and a lively nightlife.'

Tess followed, watching as Javier spoke to each proprietor, examining the food on display in the cases. Finally, he chose a small place after discussing it with the man behind the bar. The man escorted them to a table, and the wine arrived almost immediately.

Javier tasted it and nodded. The waiter poured Tess a glass and topped up Javier's before departing to the kitchen.

He raised his glass. 'To new friends and new adventures. Salud.'

Tess inclined her head and then took a sip. The wine he had chosen was crisp and sweeter than she anticipated. She closed her eyes and tasted every bit of it as it slid across her tongue and down her throat.

'You like the wine.'

She opened her eyes to a smiling Javier while he studied her face.

'Yes, very much.' She said.

'I ordered food for us. I hope you don't mind. Ordering in Spain can be difficult for people not from here, and ordering in Navarra can be even more of a challenge because they often prefer to speak in their language. I am lucky that I know some Basque, so it makes things easier.'

Tess had watched him converse with multiple people until they found this restaurant. It was clear he knew a great deal of the Basque language.

'We will start with *pintxos* and see how we feel after. If we are still hungry, we can get something more.' He held up his glass. 'And, of course, there is always the wine.'

The food arrived, and Tess relaxed, enjoying the atmosphere immensely. The flavors were so different, mixing fish or meat with peppers; and sauces and spices she was sure she had never encountered before. The hard bread was just a delivery mechanism. Already, she decided on favorites and took pictures with her phone.

"I see Americans do this all the time in Madrid.' Javier observed.

'What?' asked Tess, confused.

'Take pictures of their food.'

Tess laughed. 'Oh. I'm not a foodie, posting my meals on Instagram. I want to show the picture to someone in another restaurant. Because I'll never remember the names.'

'Ah.' He smiled.

Tess took this for approval. She wondered how Mateo was faring, trying to find something Pen would eat. Her daughter was not a culinary pioneer, and this food was definitely outside her comfort zone. Javier brought her back to the present.

'So, you said you quit your job to walk the Camino.'

Relaxed due to the wine, she'd almost forgotten about everything else. Suddenly she tensed. Another glass or two, and she might have told Javier everything, but she had known him less than 36 hours even though they had already slept in a room 3 feet apart and would do so again tonight.

Javier was watching her intently, patiently waiting for her to answer.

'Yes.' She took a swallow of the last of her wine. 'I decided I wanted to take time off. Reassess.'

His gaze was intense as though he was waiting for something more.

'I'll figure out the next steps when I get back home. Right now, I'm just enjoying the adventure. I have a list of things I want to talk to Pen about as we go along. But I think Mateo might not want to hear that stuff.'

He smiled a crooked smile.

'You're a very organized person.' Drinking more of the wine he had chosen. 'If you need time alone with Pen, I'll ensure Mateo is otherwise occupied. I know they enjoy each other. Perhaps, even a summer romance. But there are more important things, and I don't want us to get in the way.'

'Thank you.' she smiled, 'I appreciate that. But we have a long way to go, so I'm sure there is plenty of time to check things off my list.' she hedged before adding, 'Although, I must get through all of it before we reach Santiago.'

Javier asked if she wanted another glass or to explore a bit. She opted for walking. The evening was warm, and the narrow stone streets were heating up with crowds out for the night. The shops displayed nods to San Fermin, the patron saint for which the fiesta celebrates the world-famous running of the bulls. And the scallop shell, the symbol of the pilgrim, was prominently displayed in various forms to entice the peregrinos, who were so crucial to the local economy. Tess saw a bracelet in one shop and opted to buy it.

'You know this tourist stuff is all along the Camino?' he teased.

'Yes. But if I buy it here, I'll remember this evening whenever I look at it. I like to do stuff like that when I travel. Like taking a picture, only better.'

She chose a ribbon with all the towns from Saint Jean to Santiago embroidered on it for 2 Euros and insisted upon wearing it with the help of Javier. Afterward, she held up her wrist.

'Look!' She said with the enthusiasm of a child. 'I'm traveling with my map on my arm now. And I'll be able to chart my progress. All the places I've been and all the places I'm going.'

Javier chuckled, a bit surprised. 'You're a romantic. An organized romantic. Interesting combination.'

'That's me!' Somehow, Tess liked the sound of that.

They strolled down the cobbled streets, enjoying another glass of wine before returning to the albergue. At the door, Javier stopped her.

'You're a lovely person.'

Tess smiled. 'Thank you. You are too. I appreciate you shepherding me through the world of *pintxos*. The next dinner is on me.'

He smiled. 'It was my pleasure.'

They got ready for bed and heard the kids come in a little later. That night Tess slept deeply. In the morning, she woke, hearing Pen's breathing on the top bunk. Rolling over, she saw the bed next to her was empty. Javier and Mateo were gone.

SEVEN

THE ROAD TO LOGRONO

Tess woke Pen. Her daughter slowly climbed down from her bunk, still bleary-eyed, and immediately asked where Mateo and Javier were.

'I think they already headed out.' Tess told her.

'That's not possible.' She looked confused. 'We made plans to take pictures in front of the sculptures at *Alto de Perdon*. Mateo said it's famous. He wouldn't have gone without me.'

She looked around and then at her Mom. Her eyes narrowed. 'Did you say something to his Dad? Did you do something that made him take Mateo and leave?'

Tess thought back to their conversation from the night before. She had told Javier about the list. He said he would see to it she had the time she needed with her daughter. But not so soon. Pen was angry. Of course, she blamed her Mom.

'No. I didn't tell Javier to take him away. I know you like him. Javier probably wanted an early start to stay out of the heat. He talked about it last night, but I didn't think he was leaving this early. Maybe we'll catch up to them.'

'Are you kidding? You're the slowest person on the Camino. We'll never catch up to them.'

Pen grabbed her things and began angrily stuffing her pack. By the time Tess was ready, Pen was sitting outside the albergue on a bench by the door, arms folded, pouting. She got up, sullen, and walked beside her Mom. After a brief search, they found the first yellow arrow of the day. Tess endured another mile of silence. Finally, she decided to break the sound barrier.

'So, you really like Mateo, huh?' Tess asked with false cheerfulness.

'Yeah, so?' Pen challenged, as only a teenager can.

'What do you like about him?' Tess asked her.

'What do you mean?' Pen scowled.

'Well, I know he is cute so we can check that off the list. And you could be brother and sister with his height, blond hair, and blue eyes.'

'Yeah, so?' Pen looked over at her. Her daughter was curious about where her mom was going with this.

'But what else?' Asked Tess.

'I don't know.'

'Sure, you do.' Tess prodded. 'Is he smart?'

'Yeah. Mateo's smart. He wants to be a doctor like his Dad.' Pen offered enthusiastically.

'So, you like that he's smart?' Tess nudged her again.

'I guess.' said Pen, guarded.

"Does he play sports?'

'He plays soccer. But here, they don't have sports in school, so if you want to play, you gotta join a club.' explained her daughter.

'Ah,' It just slipped out. Tess sounded just like Javier.

'He's almost 17.' She put her hands up to fend off her Mom's reaction. 'Don't freak out. His birthday is while they're walking the Camino. I thought we might find a way to have a party or something. But since they're gone, and I have no way to contact him, I don't know how that would happen.'

'You didn't friend him on Facebook?' Tess asked—hoping that was a possibility.

'Facebook? Seriously?' Pen mocked her.

Tess smiled. 'Ok, Snapchat or Tik Tok, then.'

'I didn't think about it at the time. I didn't know they were leaving.'

'Where did you guys go last night?' Tess asked, trying not to sound concerned. 'You came in kind of late.'

'We met some other kids, listened to music at this place, and ate pizza.'

'Did you have a beer or anything?' Tess tip-toed around the topic.

Pen hesitated. 'Well, someone ordered a beer, and I had a taste. I don't like beer, so I ordered a Coke.'

'Ah.' There it was again. Tess didn't want to start a fight, but her stomach did somersaults thinking of Pen and alcohol. She knew Pen was expecting more of a reaction, but she held her tongue. For now.

'So, you really like him.' She restated, hoping to change the topic.

'Yes. I 'really like him.' Pen said, mimicking Tess. 'Why?'

'Just wondering.' Tess told her cheerfully.

More silence.

'Have you kissed him yet?' She asked.

'MOM!!' Pen looked horrified. 'Why are you asking me that?!'

'You've spent hours walking with this boy. You were out late last night. I just figured he probably tried to kiss you by now.'

'Well, he didn't.' Pen waited a couple of steps. 'We did hold hands.'

'Ah.'

'You keep saying that.' Pen was almost yelling at her now. 'It's no big deal.'

'I didn't say it was a big deal.' Said Tess calmly. 'I don't care if you hold hands or kiss a boy, Pen. You're getting older. I'm not stupid. You'll be doing a lot more than that in the next few years.'

Pen looked uncomfortable.

'How do you know I'll 'do a lot more than that'?' mimicking Tess again. 'Did you do a lot more than that?'

'Yes, I did.' Tess said matter-of-factly.

'In high school?' Pen's eyes widened.

'Yes.' Said Tess, but she didn't elaborate. Yet. It was like fishing—don't set the hook too soon.

'What did you do?'

After four days of walking without her daughter, she had Pen's attention now.

'My boyfriend and I got caught by the cops making out on a secluded road near the Rose Gardens in Portland.' She admitted. 'I was in a state of significant undress.'

Her daughter's jaw dropped. Tess knew she was admitting to something Pen didn't want to think about her Mother doing on her worst day. Not their usual dinner conversation.

'You can lift your chin off the ground.' Tess laughed. 'I was once your age, you know. I remember what it felt like, and it wasn't that long ago. Being a teenager and figuring all that out isn't easy.'

'Duh.' laughed Pen. And then, 'Did you love the boy you were dating?'

'Love?' Tess smirked. 'Oh, I probably convinced myself I did to justify my actions. Back then, if you really loved each other, it wasn't as bad as if you just wanted to have sex. We were still teenage Puritans in the '80s.'

Looking over at her daughter, she could tell Pen's mind was reeling from these revelations. This was not the Mom she thought she knew. Tess savored the moment.

'I've made a lot of mistakes, and confusing love and sex were just some of them. But I finally sorted that out. You can have love without sex and great sex without love. The best is when you have both. But you need to be clear about what you want.'

'So, were you a total slut?' Pen asked, incredulous.

Tess frowned, then laughed.

'First of all, I hate that word. There is no such thing as a slut. Girls who control their sexual experience however they want are strong, not weak. No one would call the guy in that circumstance anything but 'lucky.' Anyway, I liked having sex. I had it on my terms, using protection. But you'll notice I didn't tell you to avoid having sex.'

Pen appeared to mull over these new revelations.

'My friend, Jenny, is kinda religious.' Pen said. 'She said her mom told her that if she has sex with her boyfriend before she gets married that she's definitely going to Hell.'

Tess laughed. 'I'm sorry, but I think God has bigger things to worry about, like wars, poverty, disease, and climate change. A young woman having sex before she gets married so far down that list.'

Pen thought about it.

'So, if I had sex with Mateo, you wouldn't care?' She asked her Mom—intensely studying her for a reaction.

'Oh, I'd care very much. I hope that before you do it, you and I will discuss it. I'd want to ensure you had birth control and used a condom. But sex is a natural part of life. Let's face it, it's fun, and if it is between two people of legal age who agree why they're having it—love or just fun—then it can be great! And eventually, when you're older, you can do all kinds of things to enhance it. But we won't go into that now.'

Tess knew, back home, Pen would have avoided this conversation like the plague with *the Ice Queen*.

'Does Dad know all this?' Pen asked, glancing over at her as they walked up a steep hill.

Tess laughed.

'Uh, yeah. That's generally one of the things you do early on in a relationship. You tell each other your crazy relationship stories. Your first love and your first time. So, he knows my *everything*, and I know his.'

Pen's eyes widened again. 'Dad did stuff like that?'

'Yes. Dad did stuff like that, too.' Tess smiled. 'He was in a fraternity, you know. Well, it was for engineering students, but still.'

Pen was surprised.

'Dad? Really?'

'Dad. Really.' Tess repeated. 'We were people, just like everyone else. Even before we became the high and mighty, perfect parents you see before you today.'

Pen laughed.

'Anyway, I want you to be safe in whatever you decide to do, and it's not just about not getting pregnant. You don't want to catch something you can't get rid of. And you want to make sure that the person you're having sex with cares about you as a person. Respects you.'

Tess was shocked when Pen readily agreed.

'OK. I'll talk to you about it before I have sex with someone.'

'Great. You can even talk to your Dad if I'm not around.' She offered. 'He and I are on the same page about all this stuff.'

She didn't think Pen would go to her Dad about sex, but at least she had a backup, just in case.

The conversation seemed to spark something else in her daughter.

'Did you or Dad ever smoke pot—' Skip a beat. '—or other stuff, like I did?' Pen whispered.

Tess gulped and looped her arm through her daughter's. 'That's a conversation for a different day.'

By this time, they had climbed a steep hill overlooking the valley, passing *Alto de Perdon*. They stopped and took some goofy pictures with the rusty pilgrim sculptures and the windmills off in the distance. The wind whipped around them, and she heard Pen's laughter carried away with it. Tess couldn't remember the last time she had seen her daughter this light-hearted.

Walking into Obanos, they were tired, and instead of going on to Puente la Reina, as planned, they decided to stay at the only albergue in a town named *Primo*. Somehow, the name appealed to Tess.

Their night went much like the others. In bed before the sun went down. Tess lay in her bunk. Secretly, she had hoped they would see Javier and Mateo here, but she figured they had gone on to Puente la Reina since that was the official stage in all the books. They wouldn't catch up with them again and had no way to contact them. Tess wasn't sure why she was so sad about that.

'We're leaving early in the morning,' she told Pen, 'So we can beat the heat. And I saw an albergue called *La Casa de Misterio* in Villatuerta in the app. I think we should stay there tomorrow night. Any place called 'The House of Mystery' should be experienced.'

Tess decided that she would ship her pack the next day. There were services all along the way who would take a pilgrim's pack to their next albergue if they felt tired or injured. Tess needed a day without the weight.

Pen was up early the following day, ready to go, when Tess walked out the door. The sun wasn't up yet, and they made it to Puente la Reina as it was coming over the horizon.

'Turn around, Mom. To see the sunrise!'

The view gifted the pilgrims a painting of the ancient town with a backdrop of reds, blues, and purples as they passed over the medieval Puente la Reina (Queen's Bridge) in the morning light, reflecting on the water below it. Tess couldn't remember seeing anything more beautiful.

Continuing through small villages, Pen played shield for her Mom when she had to pee by the side of a barn.

Most pilgrims were going on to Estella as the next official stage, but because Tess had decided to ship her pack to *La Casa de Misterio* in Villatuerta, they would be one town short.

Arriving early, before the albergue was officially open, the cleaner directed them to leave their things in the reception area. Tess's pack was already delivered. The woman led them to an open courtyard where she said they could wait until the opening time. It was like paradise, complete with a pool.

Tess gathered their dirty laundry to pop into the washing machine before other pilgrims arrived. The owner checked them in and gave them the pick of beds in the large room on the floor above. Single beds, not bunks. Pen was so excited she declared the place 'Heaven.'

They each chose a bed in a separate nook, complete with a rare exclusive charging outlet. With unlimited Wi-Fi access and an outlet, Pen plopped herself down and plugged in. Tess smiled. After only a week, simple things now meant so much to her complicated teenager.

Tess took a shower, then ventured out for a walk in the village alone. There wasn't much to it, but she did find a store with some supplies and snacks to keep them happy.

Back at the albergue, she stashed the purchases in her nook, then went down to retrieve the wet laundry and to hang it out to dry on the clotheslines by the pool. It was oddly satisfying to wash and line-dry her clothes daily. She found it grounding to perform such simple tasks. Making her way back through to reception, she climbed the ancient tile staircase.

'Tess?'

Turning, she found Javier and Mateo standing below her, just inside the door by the check-in desk. Both looked hot and tired. Tess held her breath.

In English, Javier turned to his son and said, 'I told you they would stay at a place with *Misterio* in the name.'

Mateo's smile widened.

'How did you know?' she asked Javier.

His very tanned face made his teeth glow with their own light. 'You're an organized romantic, remember? I thought the mystery would appeal to you.'

She laughed, admitting. 'That's just what I told Pen last night.'

They smiled at each other until Tess looked away.

'Well. I'll let you get checked in and cleaned up.' Then she took the stairs two at a time to tell Pen they were there.

'What?!?' Pen sat up when she heard the news.

'They're in the lobby. I just spoke to them.'

Pen scrambled off the bed. 'But I haven't had a shower yet!'

'Well, I suggest you hurry; they'll be coming up the stairs any minute.'

Pen grabbed her pack and dug out clean clothes. Tess handed her the shower bag and the new bottles of shampoo and conditioner she'd just bought at the store. Her daughter looked at them like she had never seen anything so precious and hugged her Mom. So far on the Camino, they'd been washing their hair with bar soap or body wash to save weight in their packs. Neither of them was happy with the results.

'There's a blow dryer on the wall in there.' Tess told her, smiling.

Pen let out a cry of joy and ran from the room—the sound of water from the shower next door could be heard through the wall.

Other pilgrims filled the beds in their room now, so she assumed that Javier and Mateo would sleep on another floor.

Tess was feeling stronger, with more energy and none of the side effects of the medications she was for which she was on the lookout.

The other three joined her later at a table in the courtyard. Javier's salt and pepper hair was still wet and wavy. He wore a white linen shirt, shorts, and flip-flops and was tanner than before Pamplona, which seemed impossible. Mateo regaled Pen on their last two days. Smiling, Javier enjoyed listening to his son's enthusiasm.

'We stayed last night in Uterga. I thought maybe you would catch up to us, but we didn't see you.' Mateo explained.

Pen beamed, happy to hear he missed her.

'We stayed in Obanos.' She told him. 'We planned to go to Puente la Reina, but we were too hot and tired. We thought you were probably already there. We got up super early this morning and left by five am. I hoped we might catch up as you walked out in the morning.'

'We didn't leave until six, and we were behind you the whole way.' He countered.

They laughed in unison, and Javier smiled at their miscalculations. He turned to Tess.

'I was thinking of getting a glass of wine before the pilgrim meal. Would you like to join me at the café up the road?'

Relaxed, Tess was all for continuing that feeling.

'I'd love a glass of wine.' They left the kids to work out how to avoid losing each other again.

This time, Tess paid for Javier's selected wine, and they took it outside. It was a hot, sunny day, and the shade at the table was welcome.

'So, did you get to check off some things from your list?' He asked as he poured the wine.

'I knew that's why you left so suddenly. Without a word.' After she said it, she realized it sounded like an accusation.

Javier blanched at her reaction but concentrated on the ruby liquid inside his glass.

'First, I thought you might need the time with Pen. It seems she has not walked with you so far, and your chances of having the talks on your list were not high if she continued walking ahead or with other people. Secondly, it never occurred to me that our children had not exchanged phone numbers or connected on one of the apps they spend so much time on. When I found that they had not, and we had no way to contact either of you, I worried we wouldn't see you again. I asked several people yesterday at our albergue and today on the trail, but while they knew of you, they had not seen you. It's why we stayed in Uterga. We sat in the café out front, and I thought, surely, we would catch you walking by, but we didn't. You should have heard Mateo insisting we sit there for hours. I like coffee, but yesterday I had more than usual. It was a sleepless night. I thought he would kill me for getting him up early and not waking you when we left the albergue in Pamplona. I have never seen him like this.'

It was the longest set of words this man had strung together since she had met him four days before.

'Well, we did have one of our talks, and I was able to check 'Sex and Love' off my list.'

Javier looked surprised.

'That's quite a talk.'

'It was. I was honest, and after some awkward moments, Pen asked good questions, and we had a nice discussion. I think she found out I'm human and not *the Ice Queen from another planet* that she and her friends call me when they think I can't hear them. Once she picked her jaw off the trail, she seemed to take it all in.' Javier chuckled at that. 'However, this was after an hour of total silence, following serious recriminations when we left town. I suffered the accusation of saying something horrible to you that night in Pamplona. Driving you to take Mateo away from her forever.' She dramatically flung her arm across her eyes, pretending to faint.

'Ouch.' Javier grimaced.

'Oh, yes. That was fun.'

'Well, for that, I apologize.' He raised his glass. 'I was trying to help. But I see the lack of communication on my plan—perhaps leaving a note or getting your mobile number in WhatsApp—would have been a better approach.'

Tess smiled.

'Maybe. But you're here now, and we are having wine and enjoying the afternoon, so no permanent damage has been done.' She took a larger sip and let herself taste it completely. Javier knew wine without a doubt, and he knew the people who made it. It was the best five euros she had spent so far.

'Can I get your mobile number?' he asked. 'Just in case there is a next time.'

Tess read it out, and he put it into his phone. Then he messaged her so she would have his. She was creating a new contact for him when John texted her.

John: *'Good Morning, Sunshine!'*

Tess gulped but wasn't sure why.

Tess: *'Buenos días. Or Buenas tardes here.'*

John: *'Everything, Ok?'*

Tess: *'Yup. Just enjoying a glass of wine with a new friend on the Camino. Pen has met a boy, and I'm chatting with his Dad.'*

John: *'How was the walk yesterday and today? I didn't hear from you.'*

Tess: *'It was good. Do you remember I made the list of talks I wanted to have with Pen? Had the 'Love and Sex' one with her yesterday.'*

John: *'Wow! Jumping right in, I see!'*

Tess: *'you know me.'*

Javier cleared his throat and made to get up. 'I'll go back and leave you to talk to your husband.'

It was then Tess realized she was being rude.

'No. Stay.' She reached over and grabbed his hand. Just let me tell John I'll talk to him later.'

Tess: *'Hey, I don't want to be rude to Javier since we are sitting here. Can I text you when I get back to the albergue?'*

John: *'Javier? Sure.'*

Tess: *:)*

Tess put her phone down and turned it over. Javier studied her but said nothing.

'It feels strange sometimes, being here, on the other side of the world, having this experience. My husband isn't here with us. I know, at times, he feels disconnected from what we're doing. It's hard for him, and I don't think I'm communicating very well.'

'I think you are very hard on yourself.' Javier observed.

'What do you mean?'

'Your expectations for your part in other people's happiness seem very lofty. I'm not sure it is achievable.' He said, watching her frown.

'Please. Don't hold back.' She said a bit sarcastically. 'Tell me what you really think.'

'I'm sorry. It's none of my business.' He said, taking another drink.

Tess stopped herself. 'No. You may be right.' She grudgingly admitted. 'I think sometimes I have to try to make everyone happy. And when I can't, I feel guilty for being happy myself.'

'Are you happy sitting here enjoying this wine with me?' He asked.

Tess didn't hesitate. 'Yes. I feel light. Like I'm nowhere but right here. John's text threw me a bit. It reminded me that this other place wasn't right here. Home. I can't adequately explain it.'

'I understand. But being happy here doesn't mean that the *other place*, as you call it, isn't important. But you are here. It's OK.'

He was right. Even John would agree because they'd had similar discussions before. She would call him later.

'Sometimes, I cry on this walk when I'm alone. Today, when Pen walked a bit ahead of me, I found myself crying. Thinking about things. I'm not an overly emotional person.'

'An organized romantic. I know.' He smiled.

Deep down, Tess knew why tears came so easily. She needed to talk to someone about her illness, but she was afraid to do that until she'd told Pen. The previous two days had been pleasant with her daughter—an unexpected detente. She didn't want to rock that boat.

'I worked a lot. Back home. *A Lot.* Raising our kids daily mostly fell to John. I traveled and was gone two or three weeks out of every four for nearly 20 years. I missed so much of their daily life. My children had everything I could provide for them materially. I just wasn't physically there much of the time.'

Javier shrugged. 'I'm sure they were not neglected.'

'But I always felt guilty. I think about it while I'm walking. Regrets, I guess.'

'How old is your son?' He asked.

'Charlie?' Tess gulped, then whispered. 'Eighteen.' But then he would always be eighteen, wouldn't he? She wasn't sure why it was so hard to talk about his death. It just was. 'And then there's Pen.' she said, redirecting the conversation.

'Yes. Then there is Pen. She is strong-willed. And she's smart and beautiful. In a few years, she will be a force of nature.' He raised his eyebrows and smiled. 'Sort of like her Mom.'

Tess pulled a face.

'What? Are you not strong-willed? Are you not smart? You are beautiful—but you already know that.'

This man didn't mince words.

'What's your point?' She asked, uncomfortable with the compliment.

'You have raised capable children. They're independent, and they will do well in their lives. The choices you made and the example you set ensured that. And while you think you were not there, you were. They could count on the fact that you would come home from a business trip. If they needed you, they could reach you.'

'They could.' she conceded.

'I can honestly say that Mateo would have given anything if his mother just became an executive and traveled all the time. Rather than dying.'

This statement felt like a punch to the gut. She couldn't breathe, so she took a big gulp of the wine he had just refreshed.

'I always see it in my practice when people bring their children to me for treatment. Children are much tougher than their parents ever imagine. More than the parents, even. They can endure pain and smile through things that would break you or me. We often project our feelings and insecurities onto our children. I know I have done this with Mateo after his mother's death. I was in the darkest place of grief for a very long time. He recovered before I did, yet I still treated him like he would break. I did things I would have told you were for his benefit, but they were for mine because I couldn't face it. I wasn't ready to have a life without her.'

Tess watched him talk. Saw the shadows of his pain wash across Javier's face. The torture of talking about his wife and what he went through was still close to the surface. His eyes glistened. She wondered if this was how John would be after five years if the monster inside her won. She realized she was getting a front-row seat to the aftermath. But Javier didn't apologize for his feelings or try to minimize them. He just sat with them like old friends, as if he'd grown accustomed to their presence over the years. He picked up his glass.

'Your husband is a lucky man.' He told her before taking a drink.

'I'm the lucky one.' She whispered, wondering if she should say more. Then finally, deciding. 'He wrote me a letter and left it in my pack. I didn't find it until we were at the hotel in Barcelona.' She hesitated. 'I'd like you to read it.'

Javier nodded thoughtfully. 'Does it have anything to do with the medication you've been taking?'

Tess held her breath, and her eyes narrowed.

'Partly, yes. Did you go through my pack?' she whispered.

'No.' he told her. 'You dropped one of the prescriptions in the bathroom at the albergue in Zubiri. I picked it up and saw that it was yours. I also saw what it was. Before dinner, I put it with the rest of your meds. I didn't want to pry.'

Tess sat there, stunned. Terrified cancer had invaded this little bubble she had created for herself, but she was also relieved to be talking about it with someone. Her following words came out sharper than she had intended.

'So, Doctor Silva. Any advice as I walk the Camino with this thing inside me? When you asked me in Pamplona why I quit my job, you already knew I had cancer.'

'Yes.' He said quietly. 'Based on the medication. But it wasn't my story to tell, and you would have told me if you wanted me to know. Since you want me to read your husband's letter, I think now you want me to know.'

She took a couple of deep breaths.

'Can we walk back to get it and then go down by the bridge before you read it? I need to make sure Pen isn't around, and I know I will cry.'

'Of course.' He whispered.

Javier grabbed the half-full bottle and waited for her to lead the way. They walked down the hill in silence, and he remained in reception as she went up to her room. Neither of them saw Mateo or Pen, which was a blessing.

When they got to the river, they crossed to the middle of the bridge, and Tess stopped. She needed to know she could go either way if she had to. Planning an escape route against an enemy from which she could not run. When she handed Javier the letter, she had forgotten the photo was still inside. He caught it before it fell to the stones. Studying the image, he looked up and smiled.

'Smart man. I would have fallen in love with you, too.'

Then he unfolded the single sheet of paper and read it. Tess studied his face. He was breathing heavily, and she watched as he read it, again.

'John is a good man. He loves you very much; this is clear. He is afraid.' Javier studied the paper. 'And he should be. Why are you here? Why did you not start treatment right away? If I was your husband, I could have never let you do this.'

Tess had already started to cry, and with Javier's words, she began to sob. He wrapped his arms around her and felt her body vibrate. It was a moment before Tess realized he was crying himself. She pulled back, wiping her cheeks.

'It may seem ridiculous to everyone else, but I need to do this walk with Pen. There is so much you don't know about everything; we need to work through difficult things. I'm taking my meds, and at every church, I light a candle and pray for my family.' She stopped herself before whispering. 'And selfishly, for a miracle for myself. But I needed to come here because I may never get the chance again. To live like I don't have cancer and to try to reach my daughter.'

Javier was silent for a moment before responding.

'Your husband clearly understands this. And so do I. I promise I won't play doctor to you. And I won't play cancer's widower. I will be here with you if you'll let me.' Squeezing her hand. 'I am lucky I get to be around someone who is truly living. Fully.'

Tess nodded gratefully and wiped her eyes.

'I haven't told Pen yet. I need to find the right time in the right way. She's been so happy for the first time since as far back as I can remember. I want to wait until we're further along before I rain on her parade.'

Javier seemed surprised she had not told her daughter, but he hugged her again. They stood on the bridge for a while, then slowly returned to the albergue. They could hear the kids in the pool when they reached the front door. Tess remembered her clothes were drying on lines next to the water and rushed out to get them before they got soaked as Javier stood watching the kids. It looked so normal, but nothing was further from the truth.

At dinner, Tess reminded herself that she'd come here to walk the Camino, to get closer to Pen, and to talk to her about what was coming.

Now she had told Javier, a relative stranger, before she had told her daughter. Tess needed to look for the right moment. But seeing Pen's face smiling at Mateo, she knew she would wait a little longer.

Their next few days took on the same cadence, including an afternoon punctuated by a torrential thunderstorm, hiding in a shepherd's stone hut to avoid lightning. Tess was able to get in some stints walking with Pen, but she didn't work in any of the talks on her list.

Finally, it was on to Logroño for an overnight in the largest urban area since Pamplona. Entering the city, it felt strange to have to worry about traffic on the crowded pedestrian mall. But Tess restocked their supplies that were harder to find in the small village stores along the way.

The next day, they could breathe again, crossing through the region of La Rioja, known for its wine and endless fields of grapevines. Tess had lived briefly in Northern California wine country right out of college, bringing back fond memories.

The vineyards of La Rioja are very different than those in California. Here, the vines are lower to the ground, with old men out in force along the rows pinching offshoots with their bare fingers. Few machines or industrial equipment were in view: just weathered hands, faces, and strong backs.

Javier called out to one of the men, who looked up with surprise, ambling down the row to embrace him. Mateo smiled as the short-stooped man said something to him, encircling him in a monster hug, then fiercely grabbed his face.

'This is my *Tío*, Uncle Diego.' Said Javier, solving the mystery. Tess said, '*Buenos Días.*' Then introduced, Pen. Javier translated. Diego tipped his cap.

The man's weathered face told the story of a life spent outdoors, and his well-worn plaid shirt was torn and stained in several places. The men spoke for a bit, then Uncle Diego invited them to the house. Tess assured Javier that he didn't need to bring them along. She had planned to stay in Ventosa and explained that they could meet up with them later if he wanted to spend time with his family.

Javier pulled a face.

'Don't be ridiculous. Come.' He and Mateo loaded their packs into the bed of his uncle's battered truck. Pen and Mateo climbed into the back, and Javier opened the door to the cab.

'Your chariot, my lady.'

Laughing, Tess slid to the middle of the threadbare bench seat. Javier sat beside her as his Uncle Diego hopped behind the wheel. He navigated the dirt roads like an Indy car driver before pulling up to a large, old stone house surrounded by palm trees. Looking at Diego in the fields, she would never have thought he would live in such a grand place.

'These are my family's vineyards.' Javier explained. 'My father grew up in this house before he moved to Madrid for university and became a surgeon. I spent every summer and most holidays here as a child, pampered by my grandmother. And my grandfather and my uncles taught me about grapes and sheep.'

Tess smiled. Just another side to this complicated, quiet man.

Javier's aunt came to greet them and usher them inside. In no time, they were sitting at a table in the center courtyard of the house, coffee and plates of warm pastries placed in front of them. His uncle spoke no English, but Javier translated when needed. Mateo excused himself to show Pen around, and his *Tia* shooed them away, laughing as they ran off.

'*Amor Joven*,' she said, smiling at Tess.

'Young Lovers' translated Javier. He saw the startled look on her face. 'I mean *young love*. Completely innocent. My aunt wasn't implying anything.'

Tess laughed as he turned crimson, then using the time while they were talking to look around. The house was an oasis. A beautiful place to grow up, and Javier must have loved coming here as a boy.

Tess excused herself, stepping outside. It was 3 o'clock. She could try to catch John before he left for the office.

'Where are you?' he asked when he answered her call.

'We're almost to Ventosa. We crossed into the La Rioja region yesterday. Right now, we are at the home of Javier's uncle. We were walking through the vines, and he spotted the man. His uncle drove us up to the house for coffee and pastries. They don't speak English and, by the looks of it, are having a serious discussion. Mateo is giving Pen the grand tour, so I thought I would catch you before you left for the office.'

'Sounds like it's getting serious.' Said John.

'I think Pen might be having a summer romance with this boy. Nothing more.' She assured him.

'I wasn't talking about Pen.' John said quietly. 'Javier has brought you back to meet the family.'

'Ha. Ha. We happened to come upon his uncle. We would have passed right through without stopping if we didn't see him.'

But John was not laughing on the other end. She supposed jealousy was natural, even though she hadn't done anything wrong.

'How are you feeling?' he asked, changing the subject. 'Are you taking your meds? Any side effects?'

'Actually, I'm feeling much stronger. I haven't had fatigue since the first few days. No nose bleeds. My thigh has a nasty bruise from the second day in the Pyrenees, but it's not getting bigger. I'm keeping an eye on it.'

'Good. If it does, you promise me you'll go to a doctor.' He asked, needing to hear she would.

'Javier is a doctor. So yes, I'll ask for his advice if I'm concerned.' She said.

John was silent.

'Does he know about the cancer?' He asked quietly.

Tess wanted to talk to John about what she was seeing and doing. She didn't want to talk to him about her illness.

'Yes, he knows.' She said impatiently.

'So, you haven't told Pen, but you told Javier.' He said, almost accusingly.

Tess sighed.

'I didn't tell Javier. He found a medicine bottle I dropped in the bathroom at an albergue more than a week ago. He knew what the meds were for.'

'Oh.' Whispered John.

'Listen, John. I know this is hard. I want to tell Pen, but you should see her. I've never seen her so happy. It's as if the drug thing never happened. I want to wait until we're closer to the end. Maybe in León or Sarria before I drop this on her.'

John sighed. 'Are you sure you're not just hiding from this?'

Her silence hung between them. John broke it.

'Anyway, Tess, I meant what I said in the letter I wrote to you. I understand that I'm not there seeing this miraculous new version of Pen. But I think I'm entitled to be a little jealous of this Doctor Javier, who is spending so much time with my wife. Don't lie. He looks like a Spanish movie star, right?'

Tess wondered if she should tell him the truth and decided she would.

'Actually, he does. Right from central casting.'

'I knew it! I can hear him now, *'Welcome to Fantasy Island.'*

Tess broke out laughing at his Ricardo Montalban impression from the 1970s.

'It's not quite like that.' She told him. 'He's not wearing the white suit.'

'Well, I said you were free to do what you needed. I meant it.

She knew John was trying to deflect from what he was going through. He was struggling, and she took no pleasure in it.

'But, this Javier.' He said quietly. 'You guys are spending a lot of time together.'

'Pen and Mateo are glued at the hip. I think he started walking with me by default. I know I walk much slower than he does.' Tess told him honestly.

'Yet he could have gone ahead or walked with other people.' John told her.

'He could have. Listen, John. I do like him. He's a quiet guy. A lot like you, in that way. He's a good listener, and he's very comfortable with silence when I don't feel like talking. Javier lost his wife to cancer five years ago. He and Mateo started their Camino from their front door last year. That's how they do it here. They walked from Madrid to León. Then took it up again this year, starting in St. Jean, dedicated to her. They met Pen on the trail in the Pyrenees on the second day. I'm glad she didn't walk alone through that. So far, I've just walked with the guy and slept on bunk beds beside him.'

John quietly absorbed her words. 'I didn't know he'd lost his wife to cancer.' He had written a letter telling her she should do what made her happy. He had given her a pocket full of free passes. But jealousy was to be expected.

'Are your conversations helpful?' He asked.

'Very. We don't talk about cancer, but Javier does talk about the grief of losing Alejandra. It's still with him every day. He talks about Mateo, being alone, and dealing with his loss. I know I'm still new to all this, but it's helped me understand what you're going through. What you will go through if I lose this battle.' She had never spoken the words out loud before.

'Listen to me.' John told her. 'We aren't going to lose. You'll be home in 6 weeks, and we will win. I'll accept no other outcome.'

It was Tess's turn to be silent.

'Don't mind me.' He said. 'I woke up in a funk today. Please re-read my letter. I meant every word. Go and do what you need to. Whatever that means—but I need total honesty, Tess. We've always had that between us. That can't stop now. No matter what. Agreed?'

'Of course.' She whispered.

'Finish this, then come home. I will be in New York next week, so I'll be closer to your time zone. Awake earlier. We can talk at lunchtime your time.'

'That will be good. I'll let you know when we get to Burgos. I think I'll treat us to hotel rooms. Pen and I have been sleeping in bunk beds for ten days now. Sometimes the only girls in a room full of 50 smelly, stinky men. I could use a private bath with a tub and a bed without side rails.'

'Sounds great. Go all out. Five stars, with room service and good sheets.'

John was a bed linen snob. Good sheets in a hotel meant a lot to him.

'Yes, sir.' She laughed, sniffing.

'I need to get up.' She heard John pull back the covers and could tell getting out of their bed felt heavy for him. 'I love you.'

'I love you too.'

Tess hung up and stood looking out over the valley with vines as far as the eye could see. While their conversation had taken an awkward turn, John had reiterated his commitment to what he had written. Tess was glad he had got there in the end, but she couldn't fool herself about what this whole thing was doing to him. She liked being with Javier. All the things she had told John about him were true. His companionship was something Tess relied upon every day. She wiped her eyes with the tail of her shirt and went back inside.

Pen's laugh greeted her when she found them all in the courtyard. Javier's aunt had been busy. The large table groaned under piles of food. It was as if she had known they were coming and had been cooking for days. Javier saw her wide eyes and laughed.

'This is just a typical lunch here.' He explained. 'It will last for hours.'

Pen leaned over and whispered in her ear. 'Can you believe the amount of food?'

Mateo popped something mysterious into Pen's mouth. Food, Tess was sure, she would never have agreed to taste in Arizona.

'Mmm. That's so good.' Pen smiled dreamily at Mateo.

How different than anything they had back home, Tess thought. But it was relaxed and easy to sink into, so Tess decided to sink. Javier's aunt filled a plate and put it in front of her. She was sure she couldn't eat all of it, but she dug in. The wine was from the vineyard they were sitting in. The Farm-to-Table movements in the US would be audibly moaning.

Throughout the meal, an intense discussion ensued before Javier turned to her and said, 'My family would like us all to stay here tonight instead of Ventosa.'

Tess shook her head. 'Oh, I don't want to put them out.'

'There is not a thing in Spain for putting out family. They insist.' He told her.

Looking at Pen's eager face, she was outnumbered.

'OK. Please thank them for us.' But then turned to his Aunt and Uncle and smiled, '*Muchas Gracias.*'

'*Denada.*' they both replied, the decision made.

'Anyway,' said Javier. 'I'll be working for my room and board. My other uncle is having an issue with some of his sheep, who are lambing. He's coming down to pick me up and take me back to the sheep farm so that I can take a look. He's having trouble getting a vet out; they're all busy. I said I would help.'

Tess wondered how she might use Google Translate to communicate with his family while he was gone.

'Do you want to come along? It might be boring, or it might be exciting. Have you ever seen a lamb being born?' He asked her.

'No, I haven't, and I would love to come. But I don't think I'll be much help.' She laughed.

'I'll take our packs up to our rooms. You get the one meant for grownups. Mine still looks like it did when I was ten. Do you want to freshen up before we go?'

'I don't want to delay if it is urgent.' She said.

'It will be some messy business, and these clothes are fine until I return.'

'Then I'm fine too.'

Javier grabbed the bags and took the stairs two at a time. He came down just as his second uncle arrived. The man looked like an older, shorter version of his doctor nephew, and she was even more surprised by his introduction as *Tio Javier*. Tess raised her eyebrows.

'I know.' Javier smiled. 'He was my father's favorite brother, and we do look alike. But then, I look like my father too.'

The three of them piled into another equally battered truck and drove under an hour to a sheep farm north of Logroño. They left the paved road and continued up a track for a few kilometers, past a large house near some small cottages to a large barn.

'Is all this your uncle's farm?' Tess inquired, surprised at the size.

'Yes. We are now in the Basque Country region. The farm is quite large and has been in our family for a very long time. Long before the vineyard. My uncle has no children, so I will probably be a sheep farmer someday. I have always liked it here.'

The truck stopped in front of the barn. The cries of ewes could be heard like a chorus through the walls. Javier explained the situation.

'Ewes usually give birth in the corrals. The birth leaves them vulnerable to predators who will smell the blood and are attracted by the afterbirth. It's a dangerous time for them and their babies. During this time, my uncle and those working on the farm were out all day and night. They try to check if any of the ewes are in trouble and take care to let predators know, like the neighbor's dogs, that the sheep are not alone. We have dogs of our own as well. They consider that the sheep belong to them, so they're very protective.'

'Why are these sheep here in the barn?' She asked him.

'These are the ones my uncle and his people have found in distress. For some reason, there are many of them this year, and it's late in the lambing season. They brought them to the barn, and I will see if I can help. Come, I'll show you.'

Inside there were more than 40 ewes. All of them struggled to deliver their lambs on their own.

'They can't go on like this for long. If they do, they get too stressed. And then, even if they deliver, they could die of shock or never recover from the birth, leaving the lamb as an orphan. Failure to deliver is a big concern, then both mother and lamb will die. This is the worst possible outcome.'

Javier washed his hands in the old sink and dried them on a clean flannel he had taken from a pile for just this purpose. He said something to his uncle, who pointed at one of the ewes. Javier went over to her and listened to her belly with a stethoscope.

'This one is young. It is her first birth, and she's been showing signs of labor since this morning, but she is not progressing. We need to get the baby out. I brought a tub and a bucket from the vineyard. They're in the back of the truck. Can you get them for me, please?' He asked Tess.

Tess ran to the truck and got the items he'd indicated.

'Fill the bucket with hot water and soap and rinse it out. Then fill it up halfway with boiling water and add a cup of the solution in that blue bag under the sink.' Javier told her.

Tess did as he directed.

'Put several flannels into the bucket to soak and bring it to me.'

Tess did this and brought him the bucket. He had been petting and soothing the ewe through it all. Then, Javier gloved up, took the diluted antiseptic flannels, and cleaned the area thoroughly. Next, he put on a plastic sleeve from a box his uncle had brought him and asked Tess to squeeze the lube from the tube from his bag into his hand. Again, she did what he asked and then watched as he waited for the contraction to subside before inserting his hand into the opening.

'The lamb is in distress. But the good news is she is almost in the right position.' He said it in both Spanish and English. Uncle Javier followed his nephew's directions, then Javier turned to Tess.

'Wash out the tub with the hottest water and bring me more flannels.' He told her.

He was very calm through it all, speaking with deliberation. Tess went to do what he asked, and when she returned, he had the straps his uncle brought him inside the ewe and explained he was attaching them to the legs of the lamb. It happened relatively fast after that. He didn't yank but waited for a contraction and pulled, checked, and pulled. Suddenly, the lamb was born. He rubbed the baby until it was showing signs it was vital enough and bleated. He let the mother clean her baby and bond with it.

Javier got to his feet, stripping off the plastic sleeve and the latex gloves. He asked his uncle which ewe was next and began to repeat the process. First, evaluating and then deciding the plan. The process for each ewe took time. But Tess was a quick study, and swiftly she cleaned the bucket with soap and water. She filled it with the hot water, antiseptic, and flannels and took it to Javier. Tess was ready with the lube and didn't have to be asked to fill the hot water basin. She also brought him soap to scrub up in between. Javier watched her do her assignments unbidden and smiled when she returned with the next bucket.

'You'd make a great scrub nurse.' He smiled.

'Yes. doctor.,' she said in a flirty way that surprised them both.

Hours went by. It was late in the night when they got to the last one. The good news was they saved all the ewes. They had delivered two stillborn lambs where the mother had just labored too long. These were hard for Tess, but she tried to focus on the meaning of their work and all those that thrived.

Uncle Javier clapped his nephew on the back and shook Tess's hand. He said something in Spanish and to Tess, 'Thank You' in his heavy accent.

'We will stay here tonight.' Said Javier. 'Or this morning since the sun is coming up in a few hours. I will tell my Uncle Diego to tell the kids we will not be walking today. Tess was so tired she readily agreed. Uncle Javier took them to the farmhouse in his truck and gave Tess a pair of well-worn pajamas, showing her where to sleep. She handed the bottoms to Javier.

'I'll share.' She smiled, exhausted.

'Muchas Gracias. For that, you can have the first shower.' He laughed.

Covered in a mixture of fluids, looking at herself in the bathroom mirror, she laughed. Her hair was barely in her ponytail, and dirt covered her face. If her old colleagues could see her now. No one would ever believe she'd had her arm up a sheep all night, learning to deliver lambs. A month ago, she wouldn't have believed it herself. But here she was, in this house on a farm in northern Spain. Staying with people she didn't know 24 hours ago. Trusting this man, she didn't know ten days before. None of this was like her. Indeed, not the Tess she had been for the last 25 years.

After a shower, Tess donned the ancient soft flannel top and slid under the covers. She was so tired she forgot the clothes she was wearing on the floor in the bathroom and was asleep before her head hit the pillow.

Sometime around noon, she woke up, taking a moment to remember where she was as the springs of the old bed groaned beneath her. Looking around the stone room, she remembered her dirty clothes in the bathroom. But when she went in to retrieve them, they were gone. The talking from below reached her, and she had no choice but to go down the narrow stairs in just the oversized pajama top. The landing creaked, announcing her arrival into the kitchen with a low, timbered ceiling.

'There she is.' said Javier standing by a coffee machine. 'Would you like a coffee?'

'I would love a coffee.'

Uncle Javier said something to him in Spanish, and Javier rebuffed it but didn't translate.

'Loco,' said his Uncle, and he patted Tess's shoulder before heading out the kitchen door. She watched him start his truck and drive away through the small window.

'What did he say?'

'He's going to check on the new mothers and their babies.' He told her, handing her the coffee and sitting again at the ancient kitchen table.

Tess stood at the window, sipping her coffee. When she turned around, she saw Javier watching her, a bowl in front of him filled with bright green apples. Her stomach growled as she hadn't eaten anything since the enormous lunch the day before.

'Want an apple?' she asked, grabbing one for herself and taking a bite.

When she looked up, the raw desire in Javier's eyes took her breath away. The electricity in the small kitchen was a lightning storm striking them both. She set the apple on the table as he wrapped his arms around her waist and buried his head in her stomach, rubbing it back and forth. The thick stubble tickled through the fabric as she wrapped her arms around his head, running her fingers through his hair.

'I cannot go on like this.' He said into her belly.

Standing up, cupping her face with his hands, he kissed her. Lightly at first, then deeper. Tess kissed him back hungrily, surprising herself. Javier pulled away and picked her up, carrying her up the uneven staircase to the room where he had slept. Instead of laying Tess on the bed, he deposited her on her feet. He kissed her again as he undid the pajama buttons, then slid the top over her head. She stood before him, completely naked.

'You are perfect. Just like I imagined.' He whispered.

'You imagined?'

Javier pulled a face. 'You know I've imagined since Pamplona. No harm in imagining.'

'Hmm.'

'You didn't imagine?' he asked.

'Maybe a little.' She admitted breathlessly.

'You have looked hungry for the last week.' He told her boldly.

'Hungry?'

'Yes, very hungry.'

He knelt and put one of Tess's tanned legs over his shoulder. It exposed her to him completely, and she had to hold on to his head for support as he held her upright with his left hand and stroked her with his right. She was sure she would pass out from the sensations flooding her body, and he began exploring her with his tongue. Tess moaned so loud she was afraid the neighboring farm could hear her cries. Javier tilted his head back so he could see her face.

'I think you're enjoying this.'

Tess looked down at him. 'Don't stop.'

'Si, *señora*.' And he didn't until she came loudly and almost fell over, taking him with her. But he held her up and slid her leg off his shoulder so she stood on two feet again, swaying.

'Oh, my God.' She said drunkenly.

He stood, smiling, and kissed her again. She could taste herself on his lips and tongue. Then he picked her up and laid her on the bed before he took off the big pajama bottoms, and she got her first look at him.

She wasn't disappointed with what she saw, and he stood there looking down at her. He clearly wanted her, and she scooted to the edge of the bed and reached out. She stroked him with her right hand as he closed his eyes and swayed a little. When she slid him in her mouth, he moaned loudly and said something in a language she didn't understand. She licked and teased him and smiled as she pulled her head back to look up at him.

'I guess you're enjoying this.' She smiled, using his own words, and she took him deep in her mouth before he could answer. Again and again. He held her head and pressed into her. She could tell he was close as his breathing quickened, and he whispered something in Spanish that she thought might have been 'Oh God.' Suddenly, he pulled back and pushed her on her back.

'I think we both want this.' And he plunged himself inside her. No longer concerned about how much noise they made or who might hear them. It wasn't until they were lying together afterward that it occurred to Tess his Uncle Javier might be back from the barn and listening to the old iron bed getting a workout.

'My uncle isn't here.' He said when she brought it up. 'He will be in the barn for several hours.'

'How do you know? Did he tell you when he left? I thought he called you 'loco.' Doesn't that mean 'crazy'?

But Javier chuckled.

'Yes, it does. My uncle told me he would be in the barn for a while. He also told me that while he was gone, if I didn't make love to this beautiful

American, he would turn his out-of-date charms on you himself when he returned.'

Tess's eyes went wide. 'What did you say?'

'I told him he is too old for the job and to go out and check on his sheep. He told me I was crazy.'

'Ah.' She said — more than a little embarrassed.

'I didn't plan on taking his advice, but you were so beautiful standing there biting into the apple, and when the shirt slipped off your shoulder as you turned around to ask me a question, I don't remember what it was. I couldn't stop myself. Are you OK?' He asked, concerned.

Tess got up on one elbow. She traced the salt and pepper hair from one brown nipple to another.

'I'm OK.' She whispered, snuggling into him.

He knew they shouldn't be doing this, but he couldn't help himself. Tess was the first woman he had made love to since his wife had died, and he needed to be with her for as long as he could. They fell asleep until later; a noise woke them up.

'I think your Uncle is back.' She told him.

'Yes. We must head back to the vineyard and figure out what we're doing.' Javier said sadly.

'Can we take a shower together?' Tess asked shyly.

He playfully swatted her behind. 'Of course, we can.'

Javier reached for her hand, leading her across the creaking hall to the bathroom.

'I washed our clothes early this morning and hung them on the line. I'll get them and bring them up.' He left with the towel wrapped around his waist. Tess looked out the small window and saw him talking to his uncle, who was smoking a pipe on a chair in his well-tended rose garden. He said something to his nephew as Javier unpinned their clothes. Javier's response got him a chuckle in return.

'What did you say to your Uncle?' she asked when he returned to the room with the clean clothes.

'I told him he should back off. That you didn't need an old sheep farmer.' He said with a big grin that made Tess laugh.

'Is it going to be an awkward drive back to the vineyard?'

'Not at all.' And it wasn't. Uncle Javier serenaded them with song. He had the voice of an opera singer and seemed in good spirits on the drive back.

'Is he always this happy?' She whispered in Javier's ear.

'Oh, no. But all his ewes have all delivered. He'll sing for us the rest of the way.'

Eventually, Uncle Javier turned onto the dirt track that led to the big house in the vines. Pen and Mateo were out front to greet them.

'I heard you guys delivered baby lambs!' said Pen excitedly, hopping up and down as Tess exited the truck. 'I wish we went with you.'

Tess looked over at Javier. A little guilty.

'Well, your mother is a champion lamber. I couldn't have done it without her help, and now she can work on a sheep farm as her next career.'

Pen looked at her mom with surprise.

'*You* delivered baby lambs?!' She asked, surprised.

'Yes, I did.' said Tess proudly.

'Like she was born to it.' Said Javier, laughing at the expression on Pen's face.

Uncle Javier reached into the back of the truck and pulled out a perfect rose from his garden. It was a deep lavender color and smelled like fresh raspberries. He bowed and presented her with it, turning scarlet when she kissed him on the cheek.

The two uncles began speaking simultaneously and went inside to have coffee. Tess was hoping there would be another epic feast. She'd had just one coffee and two bites of an apple since lunch yesterday.

'Let's see what *Tia* has for us.' Javier ushered them towards the front door and out to the courtyard. A table had been laid in anticipation of their arrival. The surface groaned under the weight, and others from the estate joined the meal. Included in the group was Javier's cousin Isabela, who greeted them warmly.

'Isabela is helping at her parent's winery just over the hill. They have not been well, and she's taking time off from her job this summer as a professor at an American university.' He explained.

Tess looked over at the new arrival chatting with Pen and Mateo. Isabela was a fierce beauty, with her thick black braid, in her dusty clothes and cowboy boots. It seemed strong women were a valued part of the Silva family.

The heavy meal and little sleep from the night before made Tess's eyelids droop. It wasn't long before she had to excuse herself and head upstairs. She took the meds she had skipped and climbed into the bed. Javier's *Tia* knocked, then entered the room with a pitcher of water and a glass. She leaned down, kissed Tess's forehead, patted her arm, and smiled.

'Duerma bien,' she said, before turning out the light on the bedside table.

Wrapped in the warmth and love of this family, Tess couldn't remember the last time she felt this content. If there was a heaven, it must be exactly like this, and she would be a happy occupant. Her final thought as she drifted off to sleep.

Sometime in the middle of the night, Javier came in, wrapping his arms around her. She snuggled into him and went back to sleep. But when she awoke in the morning, he was gone.

The group were getting a late start by Camino standards. Tess found the others around the table when she came down the stairs with her pack, ready to leave. Javier put meats and cheeses on a plate for her.

'Protein is a good thing.' He reminded her.

Uncle Javier had returned to the sheep farm the night before but not before asking Javier to thank her again for her help.

'More precisely, he said, 'Tell the beautiful American lady I will need her to help next year in lambing season.'

Pen laughed. Tess wondered if it had ever occurred to her daughter that other people might think her mother was something other than ridiculous.

Soon they were at the front door hugging and thanking Javier's *Tia*, then loading packs in Uncle Diego's truck to be delivered back to the Camino. Once they got down to where he had picked them up, they said goodbye.

'Please thank him for caring for Pen while we were helping with the sheep.'

'You can thank him yourself. Just say 'Muchas gracias, por cuidar a mi hija.' So, she did.

He rewarded her with a tip of his cap and waved them off with a 'Buen Camino' before disappearing into the vines.

EIGHT

TO BURGOS

'We never talked about where we were going to stay tonight. Azorfa or Ciruena? 'asked Pen as they set off on the trail towards Ventosa.

'I think we should stay in Azorfa.' offered Javier, 'We should not try to push too much.' The kids would run ahead anyway, so they just needed to know where to stop and wait for their parents.

'Sure, that seems fine.' Said Tess. 'We will see you there.' Mateo and Pen were off like a shot. Tess waited for them to crest the small hill up the road before she stopped and turned to Javier.

'So. How do you feel in the light of day?' she asked him.

He smiled. 'It was the light of day yesterday, and I felt fine then. I still feel fine. And you?'

'I feel strange. Guilty, perhaps. I've done something I can never take back.' She saw his concern. 'I'm just being honest. John gave me a free pass, but I've never been with anyone except him for over 25 years. It's like my body is wondering what I'm doing.' She admitted, tearing up. 'And maybe my heart as well.'

Javier wrapped his arms around her and whispered into her hair. 'I understand. It's not a normal situation. For any of us.' He said quietly. 'Including John.'

'No. Especially for John.' She conceded.

Tess wiped her tears. They moved up the trail silently. It wasn't until Ventosa and another coffee that Tess found her voice.

'I'm splurging when we get to Burgos.' She told him.

'What is *splurging*?' He asked with a frown.

Tess smiled.

'It's like getting a treat or doing something extra special. John arranged for Pen and me to have rooms in Burgos. It would be nice to soak in a bathtub and sleep in an air-conditioned room with real bedding. I talked to John about it a couple of days ago. He booked two rooms at the Parador Hotel. He texted me this morning.'

A heavy silence fell over them.

'What's wrong?' She asked him.

Javier didn't answer.

'Listen. Let's discuss this right now. John and I have talked a lot. And I've told him about you.' She said.

'You told your husband about me making love to you yesterday?' His expression was pained and filled with shame.

'Not yet, but I will. I didn't go into detail before, but John knows we've spent weeks walking together. He also knows you're my friend, and our friendship has come to mean a lot to me. John gave me his blessing to find myself again on the Camino. He told me to drink the wine. Dance in the rain. He explicitly said to 'embrace romance,' So I won't wear a scarlet letter.' She said—unsure her words matched how she felt.

'The other day, while you were talking to your aunt and uncle before we went to the farm, I stepped outside and called him.' She reiterated the details of the conversation. 'He admitted to being jealous of you and our time together. But by the end of the conversation, he said it didn't change what he had written in the letter. He wants me to do what makes me happy. And he knows you're a part of that for me right now.'

Javier searched her eyes for something while she was speaking. She wasn't sure what. He took off his hat and ran his hands through his hair.

'I don't know if I could be so selfless in his place. I have never been *the other man*. I never cheated on Alejandra; if she did, I never knew about it.'

'John is a good person.' She said, reaching for his hand. 'And so are you. But we're not cheating. I would never do that to John. I don't want to spoil things, but I also don't want to pretend John isn't my husband or that he's not back home, waiting. I don't know what we're doing, exactly.' She said with tears in her eyes. 'Somehow, I need to be with you. And I think you need to be with me. But we can't pretend. Please tell me we won't do that.'

Javier examined his cup. When he looked up, it was with tears of his own. He reached out and stroked her cheek.

'If I have learned anything in this life, we only have today—this moment. I will not spoil it. But like John, I'll admit to being a little jealous myself.'

Tess smiled, but inside, she was hurting for them both. Because she knew she was the reason for their pain.

They walked to Azorfa to meet the kids and then did a few long days to make up for the extra night they had spent with Javier's family, so that they could reach Burgos for their hotel reservations. When they arrived, both Pen and Mateo were confused.

'Aren't we going to the municipal?' Mateo asked his father, referring to the albergue run by the city.

'We decided to splurge.' Javier used the word he'd added to his vocabulary a few days before.

Mateo didn't understand.

Pen explained, laughing. 'Finally, I get to translate something for you!' She looked at her mom, then hugged her.

'They have a pool, too.' Said Tess.

'Woo hoo!!'

Their group entered the cool, spacious lobby and checked into their four rooms. Tess was getting unpacked when she heard a knock at her door—surprised to find her daughter on the threshold.

'Is everything OK?' Tess frowned.

'Yeah.' Pen didn't say more.

'What's wrong?'

'It's just that the room is so big, and I'm used to sleeping with you now. It was OK at Mateo's family's house cause the rooms were normal-sized, and we shared a bathroom. But the rooms here are huge.'

Tess smiled. 'You mean, kind of like your room at home?'

'Yeah. But that seems like a year ago, and I feel we live in Spain now. In rooms with other people.'

Tess laughed. Her privileged daughter had discovered she didn't need so much after all.

'Are you going swimming with us?' Pen asked her.

Tess was surprised Pen was inviting her.

'I hadn't thought about it, but that sounds like fun for a little while. I want to go to the Cathedral and light some candles. We've also had a few long days, so I would like to have a nap.'

Pen smiled, bounding out of the room. Tess shut the door, wondering if she could bottle whatever was elevating Pen's mood. As she finished unpacking, there was another knock at the door. This time it was Javier. He had showered and was ready to go out in the city.

'Hi. You look like you're ready for a swim. Not exploring a city.'

'I promised Pen I would go to the pool with them. She came to my room to ask me. She's finding sleeping in such a big room unnerving after the albergues.'

Javier chuckled.

'But I want to go to the Cathedral and light some candles. And then I think I should lie down for a while. I'm admitting defeat today. I'm tired. Maybe I'll take a bath later.'

'OK.' He kissed her nose. 'Come and get me when you want to go to the Cathedral.'

Tess horsed around with the kids. After a while, Pen and Mateo were having enough fun that they wouldn't notice if she slipped out. Tess showered and got dressed in the last of her clean clothes. When she knocked on Javier's door, he was waiting for her.

At the Cathedral, they paid the fee for the self-guided tour. Javier had been there before and punctuated some of what they saw with the history of Northern Spain. Tess loved that he took such pride in the area where his family originated.

'I know your father left to become a doctor in Madrid, but you never talked about your mother's people.'

'My mother is from Madrid. It was a big problem when my father didn't come back to practice medicine in La Rioja or any one of the larger cities in the North. And he didn't marry a local girl. But my mother was too much of a pull for him, and she wanted to stay near her family in Madrid. My mother's family is Castilian. The Basques and the Castilians have a long bitter history. When he told his parents, there was a lot of shouting and recriminations. I have heard the wedding was very tense. My father's grandmother might have uttered a curse or two.'

'I can just imagine. An old lady, sitting in the church dressed in black lace, muttering under her breath.'

He tapped the side of his nose and smiled.

'Exactly this. My birth helped break the ice. When I would come North in the summer, my grandparents and aunts, and uncles taught me to speak Basque. I learned how to tend vines and the chemistry of winemaking. Helping on the sheep farm, but you know all about that—milking, making cheese, lambing, shearing the sheep. My mother never let my father hear the end of it. She didn't like her only child becoming a farmer. She considers me Castilian. My father's family is Basque. But he was never concerned with labels.'

'And what do you consider yourself?' She asked.

'I am me. I like both cultures and understand why the Basque people yearn for autonomy. It's in our independent nature.'

'And Mateo? How does he see himself?'

Javier thought for a moment.

'The superstitions or the old feuds do not burden this generation so much. Although I'm not naïve about what has happened in Catalonia, we can all take pride in our heritage without fighting about it. The younger generations seem more likely to fight over futbol. Besides, Mateo speaks Basque, and Gallego, the language of Alejandra's mother's people from Galicia. He is a melting pot of Northern Spain.' He smiled. 'His mother gave him her light hair and blue eyes.'

'You didn't marry a girl from the people on either side of your family?' She asked him.

'No. I married for love, like my father. Alejandra was the daughter of a very famous heart surgeon who was one of my professors at the Universidad de Barcelona. I instantly fell in love with her at a party he was hosting for his most promising protégés. He wanted his daughter to marry a doctor. She was rebellious, and I liked her spirit. And she was lovely.' Smiling, remembering his wife.

'When I returned to Madrid to do my specialty training at Universidad Complutense de Madrid, I grew mad about missing her. Her father would not allow her to move with me to Madrid. Sebastian saw that I lacked the same ambition he had, and I wasn't going to follow him as a heart surgeon. I enjoyed medicine because I could help people and make a real difference in their daily lives. In his disdain for my approach, he aligned with my mother, who had hoped I would be more ambitious.' Javier chuckled, 'If they saw me the other day delivering lambs? Uf! Tut Tut. A waste of talent.'

'What happened to change their minds?' Tess asked.

'Oh, nothing happened. There was no *mind-changing*. Except we ran away to Paris, and we came back married. Her parents were furious. It was a good thing I already had my place at the university in Madrid, or I think her father would have had me kicked out of school. As it was, he withdrew his support for his daughter. My mother was beside herself. She didn't get to plan a big wedding in Madrid and invite all her friends. My father was silent but would come and have coffee with me at a café near the university every week. He liked Alejandra very much.'

'My father's mother was very supportive. My grandmother told me that I had the passionate nature of her people. I think she took great pleasure in seeing my mother so upset. They threw us a big party in the vineyard—a lot of food and wine. My mother refused to come, but my father was there. And Alejandra's mother and her aunties and cousins made the trip. Hundreds of people came from miles around. We got married in the church in Navarette for our religious ceremony. It made my grandparents very happy.'

'How did you live during your medical training if everyone disowned you?' Tess asked him.

'Being disowned is different here. My mother was angry but wouldn't allow her only child to live in poverty. That would have looked very bad to her friends and family. So, they continued to support me financially. I came into the inheritance that was left to me by her parents when they died. So, we had a home in Madrid, and I set up my practice. Mateo was born in that house.

'What did your wife do?'

Javier smiled. 'She was a painter,' he told her proudly. 'She painted every day, and she was very talented. It was appropriate that we were married in Paris. Our house in Madrid has a room in the attic with large windows where she could paint all day, in perfect light, she said.'

Javier seemed lost in the memory as they silently walked through the chapels. But his sadness at remembering all that had come before faded quickly.

'Shall we go back so you can have your rest before dinner?' he asked.

'That sounds perfect.' Said Tess, taking his arm.

Javier left her at the door to her room.

'Get some sleep, and please don't forget to take your meds. Let me know when you wake up.'

She was asleep before her head hit the pillow. Later she woke to the sound of knocking. Tess sat up and looked around before she remembered they were staying in a hotel in Burgos and that she was in her own room. She got up and went to the door, where Pen stood vibrating with Mateo.

'I know we were all going to have dinner together, but there is a street party outside the municipal albergue, and we really want to go.' She pleaded, 'We can grab dinner at a café somewhere.' She pointed to herself and Mateo.

Tess was having trouble keeping up. She was still half asleep. It was Mateo who caught on.

'Did we wake you?' He asked, concerned.

'Yes. No. It's Ok. I'm still processing what you're saying. You want to go to this street party instead of having dinner in a nice restaurant with us old people. Did I get that right?'

Mateo smiled, and Pen laughed. The sound brought Tess fully awake.

'I guess that's what we're saying.' She told her mom.

'Except for the part about the old people.' Qualified Mateo, sheepishly.

Tess thought about it for a moment.

'Mateo, you know she's only fifteen. Will you ensure she stays out of trouble and is back in her room before midnight? I know that's early by Spanish standards, but we are leaving tomorrow for Hornillos, and you guys will be in no shape to walk if you're out all night.'

With a serious look. 'Of course.' He assured her.

Tess liked this boy and his influence on Pen.

'Did you ask your father?'

'Yes, but he said we needed to ask your permission before we could go.' She smiled at that.

'OK. Have fun. Midnight. No later.' She held up a finger to emphasize how serious she was.

'Got it.' They ran off towards the elevator.

Tess shook her head. Oh, to be young and in Spain. They would never have seen her again. She closed the door and called down to the front desk to see if her laundry was ready. She had the *Do Not Disturb* sign on the door all day—something that had not deterred Pen and Mateo. It was available, and they sent it up. She changed into the one dress she had brought and a pair of leather sandals. Brushing out her hair and looking in the mirror, she appeared tan and healthy, belying what lay beneath the surface. Discovering a lipstick in her toiletry bag, Tess put some on, then promptly removed it. After weeks of not caring what she looked like, it felt unnatural to mask her face.

Javier's room was on another floor. He answered the door, looking even more handsome if possible.

'Did you sleep well?'

'I did. The kids woke me up. They said you sent them to get my permission for their evening plans.'

Javier said something in Spanish under his breath.

'I told them they would need to get your permission. I didn't tell them they should wake you up, now, to get it. I will speak with Mateo.'

'No. I don't want to sleep the entire evening away. I'm starving. Do you have anywhere you'd like to go for dinner, or should we walk around town and see what we might discover?'

'I do have plans.' He said.

'Oh,' she was surprised. 'OK. Well, I'll find something to eat and see you later.' Turning to leave.

Javier frowned.

'After the kids asked to go off on their own, I made plans for us to have dinner in this room. I spoke to the manager at the restaurant and arranged to have our meal brought up here. I thought it would be nice to take our time. We have nowhere to be, and I've selected the wines, so we don't have to think about anything else.'

He seemed determined, and there appeared to be no room for debate. Tess liked that he had been so thoughtful.

Javier shut the door behind her. After calling down to let the kitchen know they were ready, he turned his attention to the bottle of wine chilling in an ice bucket, occupying himself with opening it.

'This wine is not from La Rioja. It's a white wine called Txakoli. I hope you like it.'

Tess took the glass he offered, tasting the fruit of pears, apples, and herbs. It was delicious.

'It's good, no?' Javier studied her face looking for her reaction.

'Yes, it's excellent. I don't think of Spain and white wine.'

'Many people don't, but I like them.'

He patted the couch at the foot of the bed. 'Come and sit with me.'

Tess did as he asked. Unsure of what was next.

'How was your nap?' He asked.

'I slept very hard until the kids knocked.' Javier frowned before she countered. 'But I'm glad I got up. I get to spend more time with you.'

He smiled and took a sip of his wine. Spanish guitar played very softly in the background, and he reached across the sofa and rubbed her neck. She closed her eyes, enjoying the light massage.

Tess felt him take the glass from her hand and heard him set it on the table beside him. He kept the pressure on her neck, then replaced it with his lips, planting soft kisses behind her ear.

'You're lovely.' He whispered. 'I missed you while you were sleeping. Thinking of you at the farm. I have ached for you in the days since then.'

Tess was desperate to have him touch her and feel him with her hands. He kept it up; eventually, it was too much for her. She turned her head and kissed him very deeply.

'Mmm. You taste good.' She said breathlessly.

Javier smiled.

'But we must wait. Dinner will begin soon. Besides, we have all night.'

He handed her back her glass and drank deeply from his own.

'I find myself energized these days.' He said, smiling. 'You've turned me into a teenager again.'

Tess laughed.

'There were no teenagers with your particular skills when I was in high school.' She assured him.

'Well, you didn't go to my high school in Madrid.'

'Mores the pity.'

The dinner arrived, and the staff set it upon the table in the room, complete with white linens. They would be back for the next course when he called down to say they were ready. Javier pulled out a chair for Tess to sit.

'I hope you don't mind. I took note of the types of food you seem to favor and went with something along those lines.'

They started with a seafood salad. Burgos is not exactly near the ocean, but seafood and Spain are synonymous. Tess took her first bite and groaned audibly.

'I'm glad you like it.' He said. 'It reminds me of holidays in Tarragona and San Sebastian. Both regions serve excellent fruits of the sea.'

'You know food.' She smiled.

'I like to eat. That's what I know. Frankly, I find I'm just showing off for you. Take me to the US, and I would be lost.' He said humbly.

Tess pulled a face. 'I doubt that very much.'

'Well, maybe not lost, but you would probably need to lead me through a meal in New York.' he said before taking another sip of the wine.

'That I could do. But I think your love for food is part of the passion you've talked about before. Tastes, smells, and feel on the tongue. All part of a passionate nature. No matter where you are in the world, you would bring that along.'

Javier considered this.

'Perhaps you are right.'

He looked down at her empty plate.

'Och. Americans eat so quickly.'

Tess frowned.

'Spaniards take so long to do everything.' She teased. 'Perhaps, I'm just looking to get past dessert to the main event.'

He wrinkled his brow.

'Tsk, Tsk. So very impatient. Digestion is essential. Anyway, I find that anticipation can be almost as good as 'the main event,' as you call it. Learn to enjoy the moment. What's to come will come. Relax.'

His eyes said *Big Bad Wolf*, yet his body language was the opposite. It was unnerving.

'How do you like this wine?'

'I like it.' She said.

'This wine is from my family's winery. My cousin, Isabela, gave me a bottle and told me to find the right time to drink it while walking. From *la Reserva*, that is just for the family.'

'You've carried a bottle of wine since Navarette?' said Tess, surprised. She'd done everything she could to limit any weight in her pack.

'I didn't mind. And now we are enjoying it. So, it was worth the extra weight for a few days.'

Tess smiled, closed her eyes, starting to relax. The wine made her think of their time with his family. It was hectic at the sheep farm but also dreamy. It sounded lovely when Javier had jokingly said she could have a career as a sheep farmer.

Since being on the Camino, they had awoken in the dark nearly every day, just in time to catch the sunrise out on the trail. Walking until noon, and after checking into an albergue for the night, they would eat, do laundry, and nap. It was a natural cadence, like the tides, a rhythm Tess found comforting and one she could get used to long-term. She was lost in this thought when she realized Javier was watching her closely.

'Where were you just now?' He smiled. 'You looked happy.'

'I was thinking about our life on the Camino. And how much I would like to live in Spain and become a sheep farmer.'

He laughed but quickly realized she was serious.

'I think you would make an excellent sheep farmer.' He told her. 'Would you let me come and live with you on your sheep farm? I promise to pull my weight.'

Since they were fantasizing, 'Of course, but you would be confined to the house, barefoot. I hope you will have meals like this on the table daily when I get in from the fields. As you know, being a sheep farmer gets the blood pumping.'

Javier liked this playful side of her.

'I would be ready to give you whatever you desired. Needing to keep you happy if I wanted you to stay down on the farm rather than going to seek your fortune in the big city.'

'No worries there.' Tess assured him, taking a drink from her glass. 'Big cities and I are finished with each other.'

'And why is that?' he asked. 'From how Pen talks, it sounds like you've spent your life working in big cities. She seems to admire your *epic shoe collection*.'

Tess was a little embarrassed by that.

'I have.' She said. 'But now, after walking through these small villages and towns, I like a quieter life. It will be hard to go back to traffic and craziness.'

'You never really told me what you did for work. You talk around it. Like it's some kind of poison, and you don't want to spread it around.'

'It wasn't poison.' She told him. 'I was good at what I did, but somehow, I'm not that person anymore.'

'What exactly *did* you do?' He asked.

'I found investment opportunities for my company—mostly small, early-stage start-ups or others who were further down the path and ripe for acquisition pre-IPO. I had a lot of relationships with incubators and accelerators globally. I would get calls and fly off to meet with them at a moment's notice. Sometimes I would introduce two struggling start-ups who could help each other.'

'One plus one equals four?' offered Javier.

'Something like that.' A little surprised, he understood so quickly. 'I'd watch to see if their collaboration showed promise, and then we'd acquire them both. They used to call me *The Unicorn*. I could see things others couldn't — market potential or IP to be monetized. I made a lot of money for a lot of people. Including myself.'

Tess took a large mouthful of her wine. She hadn't thought about her work since that first day climbing to Orrison. But the elevator speech had spilled out of her, like a rehearsed pitch at some incubator's demo day. Where it had come from, she didn't know.

Javier watched her as she spoke. A moment went by and then another before he said. 'You appear different when discussing your work. Very in charge.'

'I don't seem *in charge* usually? I'm not sure if I should be insulted by that.' She told him, only half-joking.

'No. It's just that as you were speaking, I could see the person you were. Dressed in a suit, in a boardroom meeting with important people. Making deals.'

Tess sighed deeply.

'And then I left it and came here. Dressed in clothes, I wouldn't have been caught dead in a month ago. It's all melted away like a wax doll in the hot Spanish sun. Who I was before doesn't matter here, and I'm glad about that. I'm sorry if I was testy about the *in-charge* comment. On the Camino, I don't have to drive anything. I no longer have to push deadlines, maneuver financing, or tap dance. My life is simple. Most days, I wash my underwear in a bathroom sink with hand soap, and I like it much better than before.'

Suddenly, it hit her.

'It's like I had to die to learn to live.' Whispered Tess. The statement took even her by surprise. Tears flowed down her cheeks, and Javier got up from his chair and made his way to her, holding her as she sobbed. Talking about her old life was like touching the third rail. Tapping into emotions that she could usually keep at bay, being so far away. Tess couldn't have done any of it without John by her side. At that moment, she missed him fiercely — his steady approach. His love for her reached out and touched her. At that moment, she hoped hers found him.

Javier pulled back, and Tess dried her tears with her napkin. She looked up at his face filled with love and understanding; she began crying, yet again. How had she found this man who had become so important to her in such a short time? How did she deserve this?

'Come.' He said. 'Let's have something more to eat. It will make us both feel better.'

He called down. Soon the servers were back with the main course, taking away the dishes from the starter and laying a fresh table. Tess regained her appetite when she saw the lamb chops looking prepared.

'Lamb chops for my organized, romantic sheep farmer.' Javier said with a smile while placing his napkin on his lap. Hoping he could prod her out of her funk.

Her mouth watered as she sliced into the perfectly seasoned grilled meat. Taking a small bite, then closing her eyes. When she opened them, she was back in the room with Javier.

As he suggested, they ate their lamb slowly and had more of the family wine. Tess felt lazy and sleepy after the meal.

'That was perfect. I don't think I could have eaten another bite.' She said, rubbing her stomach with her hand and looking across the table at Javier's thoughtful expression.

'What are you thinking?' she asked him.

'If I could,' he told her. 'I would stop time so that it replayed over and over, this night. Just us, in this room together, talking. Eating good food and drinking good wine. Nothing else would spoil it.'

'Mmm.' Closing her eyes. 'That is a nice thought.' No cancer, no regrets.

'Were you able to speak to John today?' He asked.

'Yes.' It still felt odd discussing her husband with him. 'He asked if you guys were staying here too.'

'What did you tell him?'

'I told him that both of you had rooms, and I had just returned from swimming with Pen and Mateo. He was a bit worried that I was feeling tired.'

'You are taking your meds, right?' Javier asked her, concerned.

'Yes, doctor. I'm taking my meds. I just needed to make sure I got some serious rest. Hence the nap.'

'But you didn't get a long nap—the kids.' He frowned.

'True.' she said.

He looked at his watch. 'Time to go.'

He got up and pulled her to her feet.

'Where are we going?'

'To your room. Don't you remember?'

'We're going to my room. I was only kidding about spending the night there. Here is fine too.'

'No. I promised to sleep in your room, and we'll do that. All your things are there, and it will make the morning easier for you.' They rode the elevator to her floor. Javier took her key and opened the door.

Stepping inside, she was amazed at the transformation. Soft music was playing, and some candles had been lit and flickered from the bathroom.

'How did you do all this?' She asked him, looking around.

'A simple phone call and an American-style tip. Come. You need to relax.'

He led her slowly into the bathroom. Bubbles filled the large tub, and Javier pulled her dress over her head, unfastened her bra, and tugged down her underwear. She watched him do all this as if from afar. He looked into her eyes, cupped her face, and kissed her lightly.

'Into the tub.' he said.

She did as she was told, slipping into the warm water whose scent smelled exactly like the rose from his uncle's garden at the farm.

He stood up and took off his shirt, and began to undo his belt.

'Are you coming to join me?' She asked—surprised.

'Suddenly, I think I am.' He smiled.

Tess made room, and he stepped into the hot water and lowered himself behind her, wrapping his arms around her waist. She leaned back and relaxed.

'You know,' said Javier, speaking into her hair. 'I just realized that you know a lot about me. But you haven't told me that much about you.'

Tess was confused.

'What do you mean? You know the most important things. You know about John and my kids. About my work.' she hesitated. 'About cancer. We've spent the last few weeks together for hours every day, walking in the heat. Talking. I think you know a lot.'

'Hmm.' He remained unconvinced. 'I think I know very little. You are good at talking about the surface things. You speak, but you don't tell me much. And you're very good at asking questions and redirecting the conversation. I think Americans are like peaches. It's easy to get to the fruit. But the heart?' placing his hand between her breasts. 'Not many people break through.'

'I don't think that's true. I'm an open book.' She told him. 'Your life is just more interesting.'

'Ha. If you are an open book, then the book is more of a pamphlet.'

Tess took a deep breath.

'OK, fire away. What do you want to know?' She asked, leaning against his chest, playing with the bubbles.

'Where were you born? Where did you grow up? What was your life like when you were a child? Where did you go to college? What's your favorite color?'

'Ah, you want the ancient history. Oh, my. Can I even remember back that far?' She asked.

'Try.' Javier whispered into her hair.

'Well, I was born in Oregon—that's the ironic state on the west coast of the U.S., filled with people who dress like lumberjacks but have never felled a tree. My father was a traveling salesman, and my mother was a homemaker. I am the youngest of all the kids in my family.'

This revelation surprised him. 'Really? I would have thought you were the eldest. Eldest children are very responsible, they say. Very driven.'

'Nope.' She said. 'The youngest and the clown of the family. I was the court jester who laughed in a house without laughter. Taking nothing seriously, it wasn't a trait that went down well in a blue-collar household. Hard work was the only thing of value, and humor wasn't on the agenda.

Where I grew up, a kid who liked to wear a ballet tutu and high-top tennis shoes to school wasn't considered interesting, just weird. Even in the 1980s. And embarrassing. Oof! In my house, *embarrassing* was the worst thing you could be. I mean, what would the neighbors think?' She asked in mock horror.

Javier chuckled. 'So, they cared about appearing as different.'

'Oh, yes. My mother wanted girls who would excel at Home Economics and marry well—marrying well meant a postman or a fireman—someone with a good government pension. No risk. She told me I'd never find a husband because boys don't like loud girls.'

Javier laughed at that.

'What is this *Home Economics*?' he asked, confused at the term.

'It's where they teach you to sew and cook in school—how to keep a house. I failed Home Ec. Seriously. I flunked it. I was *Destined for failure*. It was written in the comments on my report card by my Home Ec teacher in the 8th grade.' She told him.

Javier scowled.

'In Spain, they don't teach cooking and sewing in school. Most girls learn that from their mothers or grandmothers. But still, it seems very harsh. How old were you?' He asked.

'I was thirteen. And already *Destined for failure*.' Tess smiled. 'In many ways, it was a gift. My mother gave up on me. I didn't have to take Home Ec. after that. They had such low expectations of me in school and life that if I could live on my own and dress myself, they felt that was about all they could expect from me. They poured all their energy into my siblings. I heard my mother tell my father once, 'Why throw good money after bad?' when they were in the kitchen discussing my future.'

'That's not possible.' he frowned. 'How could they determine that from you failing cooking and sewing?'

'Well, that was what they had decided girls should do. And my mother was very successful in school in the subject, so she wanted me to do the same. I enjoyed other classes, like math and science. I played sports and was more of a Tomboy.'

'I don't know what this is. *Tomboy*.' He said, confused.

'It's like a girl who acts more like a boy is supposed to. I don't think you hear the term as much anymore, even in the US, because traditional gender roles for girls and boys are changing. But in the '70s and '80s, they were still very much alive and well. I was a constant source of frustration for my parents. I didn't fit into a box neatly like my sister. She was Homecoming Queen and looked like a beautiful princess. I cried when my mother made me wear makeup. Until the 9th grade, I looked more like I had grown up in a jungle, living in trees. My clothes were always ripped and covered in dirt. I was an expert at fort building in our neighborhood.'

'*Fort building*?' He struggled to understand.

'It's like taking scrap wood or fallen branches and building small huts or a clubhouse. I borrowed my Dad's tools a lot.'

She heard Javier chuckle behind her.

'You were a non-conformist.' He said happily.

'Exactly. And as you can see, I still am. My mother would die of a heart attack if she saw me here with you. It was hard enough for them when I told them I quit my job. When I said I was going to walk the Camino, they thought I had lost my mind—and taking their grandchild with me on this hair-brained journey? Well, that was the height of irresponsibility. I'm 50 years old, and my Mother asked me, 'Are you crazy? Who even knows about this thing you're doing?' They called John. As far as they're concerned, he's always been the adult in the room.

'How did they react when you told them about having cancer?' He asked her quietly.

Tess hesitated.

'I didn't. I knew they would freak out. And I didn't want to deal with that until after the trip, and I'd told Pen. My mother doesn't handle stress well. She was a serious alcoholic the entire time I was growing up. I don't need to stick a fork in the light socket to know I'll get a shock. It's the same with this.' She whispered.

Javier sat behind her, quiet.

'Why did your mother drink so much?' he asked quietly.

Tess waited before answering. She wanted to be honest.

'I don't know.' She said, thinking back. 'She won't talk about it. No one ever talks about it. I lived in that house for eighteen years and barely know my mother. But to be fair, she doesn't know me either.'

'So, you grew up feeling like the outcast.' He said sadly. 'What happened when you went to university?'

Tess smiled at the memory.

'I was free. I could do as I pleased and got positive feedback from my professors. Suddenly I wasn't constrained by the opinion of where I grew up. I had friends who were different too. For the first time in my life,' she told him. 'I wasn't alone.'

Javier hugged her tighter. He knew this trip down memory lane wasn't easy, but he didn't want it to end. He needed to know her, all of her.

'So how did you meet John?' He asked.

'You saw the photo in John's letter.' She reminded him. 'It was the exact moment we met at our friend's wedding. I knew right away that he was *The One*. John gets me. No one had ever gotten me like that before. It's weird, but since you read his letter, you know. Often, he knows what I need, sometimes even before I do. I'm lucky.'

'I would like to meet him someday. I know that's impossible, but he seems like a good man.' Javier said thoughtfully.

'He is.' Tess agreed, smiling. 'But he's not a saint, you know. He's human. His nickname for you is *TFG—That Fucking Guy*.' She felt Javier tense, but she continued. 'When John asked me to marry him, I hesitated. Not because I didn't love him, but because I loved him so much I didn't want to hurt him. I am a different sort of person, and I wasn't sure how it would go. 50% of marriages end in divorce. If ours hadn't worked out,

I would have been heartbroken because I knew it would cause him untold pain. I never wanted that for him.'

Javier rested his chin on the top of her head. 'I understand John's perspective about me. But I am lucky we had this time together, and I am sitting in this tub with you now. You are extraordinary, and I wouldn't have missed this for anything.'

Tess shut her eyes. Tears spilled out, and she leaned her head against his arm.

'I have been fortunate in my life. I've had real adventures. We've made a great family and a wonderful life. But above all, I've been truly loved and accepted. I think that is more than most people get.'

She turned over and got on her knees to see his face. 'I am so glad I met you. Right here. Right now. No strings. No promises.'

He reached up, brushed the stray hairs from her eyes, and held her face in his hands.

'I could be nowhere else.' He whispered, softly kissing her forehead.

The water had gone cold.

'I think it's time for our dessert.' He said, offering her his hand, she stood up, and he wrapped her in a terry cloth robe.

In the outer room, they grabbed a bowl of berries the staff had left for them and took them to bed.

'No funny business.' He warned her. 'If we make a mess, we will have to sleep in it.'

'Yes, sir.' Tess gave him a mock salute.

Later, they made love quietly. Afterward, lying side by side, holding hands.

'I am lost.' Javier whispered. 'You're all I seem to think about these days. I'm not too fond of the albergues, sleeping in those beds so far from each other. On the trail, I can't touch you.'

'Why can't you touch me? Mateo and Pen are usually a mile ahead.' Tess reminded him.

'We're outside. Other people could see us.'

'We could find a barn, maybe.' She laughed. 'We are very good with barns.'

Javier got up on his elbow.

'Are you telling me you would be willing to behave like a heathen? Not a real, chaste pilgrim?'

Tess smiled.

'Yes indeed, that's exactly what I'm telling you. I am willing to give up my *Real Pilgrim* status if I can touch you every day, even for a moment.' She looked up at him and smiled.

'I wish I had known that before now.' Javier chuckled mischievously, laying back down. 'The last few days might have proved very interesting in the poppy fields.'

Tess giggled. 'I want to make the most of our time together.'

'So do I.' He kissed her tenderly, then Tess snuggled into his arm with her head on his chest as they dozed off.

'My favorite color is yellow.' She whispered before they both fell asleep.

NINE
ON TO HORNILLOS

When Tess woke up in the morning, Javier was gone. She felt sad but also relieved. Tess had only woken up next to John for their entire marriage. The intimacy was something she would find hard to relinquish so quickly to another man—even Javier.

She showered and dressed. Then went next door to Pen's room and knocked. Mateo answered the door. He was shirtless.

'What's going on?' Tess hissed, her forehead creased by a deep frown. Looking beyond Mateo, she saw Pen in bed. She stepped into the room and closed the door.

'Mom, it's not what you think!!' pleaded her daughter.

'Not what I think?' Trying to remain calm. 'What do I think, Pen?'

'You think we were having sex.' Pen choked out the words.

'I do? That's what I think, huh? I come to the door, and you're in bed—looks like naked—and Mateo answers my 15-year-old daughter's door without a shirt on. It's obvious to me he slept here. And it's quote 'not what you think.' How stupid do you think I am?'

Mateo stepped in. He said something to himself in Spanish, then to Tess. 'I did not sleep in bed with your daughter.'

'I wasn't worried about the sleeping part.' Tess told him sarcastically.

'We did not have sex. Pen was ill.' He looked at his feet, ashamed. 'I slept on the couch.'

Tess saw the wad of blankets on the sofa at the foot of the bed. It was then she noticed Pen was a light shade of green.

'What's wrong with you?' She asked.

The kids exchanged a look. Mateo decided to represent the situation.

'Pen had more to drink at the street party than was probably a good idea.' He explained.

Speechless, Tess looked at Pen, shaking her head. Deep breaths.

'What!?' pleaded Pen. 'Someone gave me a sangria, and then I had another sangria, and then I think I had something else. We were on the street, and I got caught up with all the other kids there. It wasn't a big deal.'

Tess turned back to Mateo.

'I didn't see how much she had until it was obvious that it was too much. I brought her back here before midnight. I was worried she would become sick on the street.'

Tess's face was crimson now. She looked at her daughter.

'Pen?' She said, barely able to contain her emotions.

'It's not Mateo's fault. We were all singing, and there was dancing with people playing music. He didn't know. He took care of me all night. I've been really sick, and I'm never drinking again. Not because you'll tell me not to but because it's not worth it.' Pen started to cry. 'I know, after this, you'll never trust me.'

Tess could tell Mateo wanted to go to her, but he wouldn't with her mom in the room. Suddenly, an odd smell reached her.

'Has she been throwing up?' She asked him.

Mateo nodded, hanging his head.

Another deep breath.

'OK.' She said, gathering herself. 'I told you that we're walking today. And we are. Just maybe a little later and a little slower than we thought. But we are going to walk. First, you both need to rehydrate, and you need food. I'm not sure how your father will react to this, Mateo.'

His head whipped up to look at her.

'I haven't decided if I'm going to tell him yet. But both of you need to take a shower and get ready to go. I'll run interference for you for a half-hour, so you should get going. You and I will discuss this in detail later, but not right now. Move!'

She watched Pen jump out of bed, wobbling, bringing the sheet with her.

Tess retrieved her pack from her room and went to the lobby restaurant. She ordered the buffet and a café con leche and took her time eating. Javier came down, ready to go, surprised to see her lingering over her breakfast.

'Healthy appetite this morning, I see. Very good.' He smiled.

'Well, someone wore me out last night. I was ravenous when I woke up, so I thought I would find some extra breakfast time and relax.' She said, taking a drink of her coffee.

'Good. I stopped by Mateo's room, and he was just getting out of the shower. It seems he and Pen had a late night out at the party.'

'Yes.' Tess acknowledged.

Javier cocked his head. He was sure there was something she wasn't saying. Looking past Mateo, he noticed the bed was made up. He raised his son to be polite, but Mateo didn't make his bed in a hotel. Javier would ask him about it later.

The kids finally came down, and Pen looked unwell. Javier was going to point this out to Tess, but he saw her studying her daughter as she encouraged her to eat something and drink a lot of water.

'I have some Tylenol and some hydration salts in my bag. After you've eaten, you can take some.'

Pen looked miserable but said nothing, then wandered to the buffet with Mateo. While they were getting their food, Javier leaned over to Tess.

'Pen looks unwell.' He whispered.

'Hmm. Yes. She does. She'll be fine after she eats something and has some electrolytes. I'm sure she has a raging headache from dehydration.'

'Should we skip or shorten our walk today?' He offered.

'Absolutely not. I think she'll be Ok. But maybe a little slower than usual.'

She smiled at Javier over her coffee cup, but it didn't reach her eyes. He didn't press her.

They set out for Hornillos. As predicted, both the kids lagged behind their normal pace. Javier and Mateo walked ahead by 50 yards. Tess caught a word or two but couldn't understand what they were saying as they spoke in Spanish. She turned to Pen, who was staying close to her.

'So. How are you feeling?' She asked her daughter.

'Not good.'

Tess sighed. 'I can imagine.'

'Look, Mom. I didn't mean to get drunk. I was just having fun, and some people gave me different drinks, and I didn't know how much I had until it was too late.'

Suddenly, she lurched off the trail to the bushes and emptied her stomach of her recent breakfast. Tess followed her and held her hair back as she threw up, flashing back to when she'd done this before. Her heart constricted.

Pen stood up, wiping her mouth on her shirt. Tess retrieved crackers from her pack with Aquarius water and offered them to Pen.

'Do you want to sit down for a bit on that rock?' Pointing to the side of the trail.

Pen nodded, removing her pack. She sat down before she fell, holding her head in her hands.

Tess paced back and forth, trying to calm herself down.

'This is hard for me, Pen. Harder than I think you even realize.'

Struggling to gather her thoughts, Tess chose her words carefully.

'Grandma, my Mom, was an alcoholic the whole time I was growing up. As a kid, I cared for her in the mornings after a long night of drinking more times than I can even remember.'

Pen looked up, surprised. 'You never told me that. She never said anything about it.'

'Yeah, well, there's a long line of alcoholics on her side of the family, going way back. The trail of destruction they left behind has a long tail. I'm the only one in my whole family who hasn't had a serious problem with addiction. Sure, I've had my share of overindulging. But I can go weeks without having something to drink. It's just never been a thing with me.'

She tried to remain calm.

'But I've lived with people, your Grandma in particular, who drank every day. And I can't begin to tell you what that does to you as a kid. The unpredictability, the anger, and sometimes violence. Taking the blame for being the cause of their drinking and then learning to blame yourself. The unimaginable painful scars that never go away. It marks you. Even now, there are days it overtakes me. I won't have thought about it for a long time, then it's suddenly there. Sometimes, I struggle, especially when I'm alone traveling and have no distractions. Your Dad knows it's tough for me. So, you'll have to understand why seeing you at the party, and holding your hair back as you vomit, might bring up some difficult emotions. It scares the hell out of me.'

Tears flowed, but Tess fought to control her emotions.

'I can't handle watching you sink into that world. Since you smoked heroin, I wondered if you inherited that gene from me. And I don't know how I would ever forgive myself if that's the case.' Closing her eyes. 'I would never forgive myself.' she whispered.

Pen didn't look so much sick anymore, as scared.

'Thank goodness Mateo looked out for you. I don't like to think about what could have happened or where you would have ended up. This is just what we were talking about the other day. You're growing up. You'll drink, I know that, but after the heroin incident? I can barely process this.'

She squeezed her eyes tight, then looked up at the sky, shaking her fists. 'We had a deal, you and me! I told you; I won't let you have her!'

Tess looked back at her daughter as tears streamed down her face. Pen's face was awash with fear as Tess lost control. It took Tess a couple of deep breaths before finding her voice again.

'I never told you or Charlie about this stuff from when I was a kid because I wanted to keep all this darkness, the black cloud, away from you.

To keep it far away from the life I've made with your Dad. But it's been there, lurking. And Pen, I prayed to God so many times that it would never touch you, my beautiful girl.' She cried. 'But it's found us, and I want to fight like hell to make it stay the fuck away from you.'

Tess couldn't believe she was having this conversation with her daughter at fifteen. But this was one of the topics on her list—'Drugs and Alcohol.' And after the last few months, it was probably the most important one.

'I thought we dodged it with you both. Charlie was always into science and math and computers, ' she whispered. 'before the accident. Like your Dad. Not parties. And you've always been an athlete. So, I wasn't paying attention as closely as I should. I let my guard down, and it slithered in through the back door like a snake when I wasn't looking.'

Pen sobbed. She looked up at her Mom, seeing her intense pain and despair. But love, too.

Tess felt utterly lost as she wrapped her arms around this girl who seemed in such a big hurry to grow up. Neither of them wanted to let go. Brushing back the hair that had fallen out of her daughter's ponytail, Tess smiled weakly—gathering herself. 'You look like hell.'

'I know.' sniffed Pen. 'I feel like hell.'

'You earned it. Don't forget this feeling.' She cautioned her daughter. 'It's another warning. You don't get many of those until you have a serious problem.'

Pen couldn't argue with that.

'Mateo is talking to his dad about it right now.'

'I didn't tell Javier.' Tess assured her.

'You didn't have to. Mateo is an honest person. He will have told his father himself. He feels terrible not protecting me after he promised you.'

'He's not to blame. He brought you back to the hotel as soon as he understood the situation.' Tess chose her following words carefully. 'You can be a lot to handle sometimes, Pen, even for your parents. Mateo, bless him, tried his best last night. But he's only sixteen.' She reminded her. 'Besides, if he thinks he can control you, he's in for a rude awakening.'

Pen hung her head. 'Was this one of the talks you wanted to have with me out here?' She asked.

Tess was surprised.

'What do you mean?'

'Mateo told me they left Pamplona so early so that you and I could have some important mother/daughter talks. You had a list, and his dad thought we needed space to have them.'

'Ah.' This caught Tess off guard. She hadn't meant to reveal her plan to Pen. But, now that she had, it might be easier to carve out the time and space.

'I do have a list.' She admitted, wiping her nose, 'I didn't know Javier would take Mateo off so we could have the time to talk, especially since we had no way to get in touch with them again. But it all worked out.'

'What was this one?' Pen asked her Mom.

'Drugs and Alcohol.' Said Tess.

Pen smiled weakly.

'Well, we've covered the *Alcohol* part. And I guess I covered the *Drugs* part before we left home.'

She decided to be completely honest with her mom.

'People were smoking pot in the square last night.'

Tess closed her eyes. She knew her daughter would have to make these choices in the future without her looking over her shoulder. Pen put her mind to rest.

'I promise.' She whispered. 'I'm done with all that.'

Tess searched Pen's face and released the breath she was holding.

'Good girl. Because honestly, Pen, that just about broke me, seeing you at the party. When I came back into your bathroom that night, and you were lying on the floor for a second, I thought you were dead, and I was so afraid I was paralyzed. I should have protected you and realized then that I couldn't.' She stopped before whispering, 'Not even from yourself.'

Tess broke down again, as Pen wrapped her arms around her mom. Finally, Tess composed herself, wiping her eyes on her sleeve.

'We have to go. All we need to do today is get to Hornillos and see if we can't get you through a nasty hangover.'

Pen nodded and got up to put on her pack, but not before helping Tess with hers.

After several hours of walking in the hot sun, they reached the village and found an albergue with a lovely garden. Pen wanted to lay down in her bunk to rest, and since Mateo had spent the day walking with his father, he was eager to spend time with her.

When Javier asked Tess if she wanted to go for a walk, she laughed.

'You know. These days, I don't get the opportunity to walk enough outdoors.'

He pulled a face and playfully pushed her towards the door.

'Don't get cheeky.'

They walked across the bridge and along the small river until they found a shady spot.

'You and Mateo looked very serious today. I don't think either of you spoke to us after we left Burgos.'

'We had a lot to discuss.' He told her.

'Such as?'

'I believe you're aware of the events of last night.'

'I was there, remember?' She smiled.

He shook his head.

'Not those events. The events involving our children.'

'Yes, I'm aware. I went to Pen's room this morning, only to have the door opened by a shirtless Mateo. Pen looked like *10-miles-of-bad-road*, and the room smelled like vomit.'

Javier cringed, sucking air through his teeth.

'I didn't get all those details, but it's obvious that Mateo didn't look after Pen at the street party last night as he promised.' He told her.

Tess frowned.

'Wait a minute. I don't blame Mateo at all for Pen's condition. She can be headstrong and admitted he didn't see how much she drank.' said Tess.

'I think if he had, he would have stopped it and brought her back to the hotel sooner. He looked frightened this morning.'

'I told him he needed to keep a closer eye in the future.' Said Javier.

'Look,' Tess stopped him. 'I don't expect Mateo to babysit my daughter. No matter what, I had him promise. Part of the reason I made her walk today is because I wanted to teach her a lesson. But I also wanted to talk to her. I think she got the message loud and clear. You guys were walking ahead, so you didn't see her throw up her breakfast in the bushes. It was a tough day for her.'

Javier was visibly upset.

'Mateo is a wonderful kid, and I like him very much. And the influence he's having on Pen. Please, let's not spoil the day. He was awake all night taking care of her, and they both suffered the consequences today.'

Javier reached out and hugged her.

'I see you possess the ability to see this from multiple perspectives. Maybe I have been too hard on Mateo about this incident.' He admitted.

Tess didn't respond.

'They're still children, after all.' Said Javier.

He got there in the end.

'Pen was missing John today.' She told him. 'I think she needed to reach out and touch home, so we called him from the trail when we finally got service. It was good to hear his voice, and Pen surprised me when she teared up, telling him she missed him. When I got back on the phone, he sounded pleased. He said he thought this Camino might be magic for all of us.'

Javier smiled. 'It seems your relationship with your daughter benefited from her misstep last night. I can see that now.'

Tess thought about it.

'It's interesting. I had *Alcohol and Drugs* as a topic of one of our talks. Today we got to have that discussion, and the consequences of Pen's choices were top of mind. So, in a weird but terrible way, I think it couldn't have worked out better. I should buy Mateo a present.' She smiled, hoping to lighten the mood.

'I don't think you should go that far.' He said with raised eyebrows.

Javier opened his day pack and removed the blanket he had smuggled from the albergue. He shook it out and laid it down on the side of the small river under the trees. Sitting down, he patted the space next to him. Tess smiled and sat down, leaning over and kissing him lightly.

Javier liked this side of her. Cool-headed and less stressed. Maybe her husband was right. The Camino might be magic for all of them. Perhaps that magic would extend to a cure for her cancer. But he pushed the thought aside. He was a doctor He had seen miracles happen. But he had never experienced it himself when they were desperate for one for Alejandra.

'I need to tell you something important, but I don't want it to cloud how you feel about us—me and Pen.' Tess told him.

'That sounds serious.' He said, concerned.

'It is. And normally, I would have kept this to myself, but after today I think it's important that you know all the reasons Pen and I are here. Together.'

Tess told him the story of Pen using drugs. The pain of finding her daughter in that situation and choosing to walk the Camino with her, even though she was very ill herself. When she finished, he blew out a long breath. His son was spending a lot of time with Pen. And after last night, Tess felt he had a right to know the backstory.

'OK. Now some things about you being here make more sense. I don't know what to say. I've never encountered this type of thing with Mateo. He has never broken my trust in this way. If you had told me about this, and I didn't know Pen, I would probably judge her harshly. But I do know her now. She is a good person; maybe this experience taught her something she needed to learn. And, in retrospect, perhaps the events of last night helped reinforce the message.'

Tess closed her eyes, praying he was right.

'Do you worry about your son hanging out with someone who would do those things?' She asked.

Javier was thoughtful.

'No. I don't worry about Mateo spending time with Pen. She's a headstrong teenager, but I do not believe she's not a drug addict.' He waited before saying, 'Thank you for telling me. For trusting me enough.'

'I just wanted to be honest.' She said.

They napped on the riverbank, then walked back to the village. The kids sat on the bench outside the tiny store, eating bocadillos and playing a game on Pen's phone. They both looked up when Tess and Javier approached.

'So, you guys have eaten. I was going to ask you if you wanted pizza or paella, but if you're full already,' Tess left it hanging.

'No!' said Pen. 'I'm starving.' She held up the sandwich. 'This was to tide me over until I could get real food.'

Ah, the tail end of a hangover, thought Tess. It called for spicy food.

They found a cafe serving the pizza and paella she had promised. Not too difficult a feat since nearly every bar on the Camino served a combination of these. Larger towns might have restaurants where the menu varied with locally grown food and chefs catering to those other than Peregrinos.

They grabbed a table outside in the small walled courtyard festooned with umbrellas, decorated with the now familiar 'Estrella' beer served everywhere. Tess noticed Pen had ordered two bottles of water. Smart girl, she thought.

'Salud' Javier raised his glass, and they all did the same.

'So, how are you feeling, Pen?' Javier asked.

'Much better. I think I'll survive. But I'm not doing that again.'

Tess raised her glass.

'Here's to experiences—and surviving them.' She said to the group.

Javier inclined his head and took a sip of his wine.

Pen leaned over. 'Did you tell Dad?'

'No. I haven't spoken to him since the trail today.'

Pen chewed her lip.

'Are you planning to?' She asked her Mom.

'I haven't decided.' Tess told her daughter.

Pen took a big swig from her water bottle. They'd never spent this much time alone in one stretch. It was as if they were getting to know each other for the first time.

The food arrived, and they were all hungry. Tess and Mateo ordered the black paella made with ink from an octopus. Javier and Pen had pizza.

'I don't know how you eat that stuff.' Javier said to Tess. 'It's the worst version of paella I've ever seen. Just wait until we get back to Madrid.'

Tess was stunned at the statement.

'What?' he said. 'You're coming with us to Madrid when we finish, correct?'

Tess's head spun.

'I don't know.' She said, frowning. 'I hadn't thought that far.'

Pen and Mateo smiled at each other.

'Well, based on my calculations, we will finish the Camino in another three weeks. That will leave you some time before returning to the US. I thought you might like to visit Madrid and see how we live there. We can eat real food, not from the McDonalds of Spain.' Pulling a face.

Tess held her fork suspended in front of her mouth. It was one thing to do what she was doing on her walk. John had told her to get as much from it as she could. It was quite another to return with this man and his son to his real life, home, and stay.

Pen saw her hesitate.

'Please, Mom.' She pleaded. 'Let's go to Madrid with them and see the city.'

'But we're flying out of Barcelona.' She pointed out. 'Those cities aren't near each other.'

Javier could tell she was uncomfortable.

'But we haven't been to Madrid.' Pen continued, 'I'm taking Spanish and could spend time talking to locals.'

'You could do that in Barcelona.' Tess pointed out. 'Or if we stay in Santiago.'

Tess's heart was beating very fast. She needed some space to breathe, getting up to go to the ladies' room. The other three looked at each other in silence.

When she returned to the table, Javier held her chair.

'Listen, you don't have to come to Madrid. We are enjoying ourselves so much, and I thought having you as our guests in our home would be nice. If that won't work with your plans, then it's fine. I am not offended.'

Tess took a deep breath.

'No, it's OK. It's a generous invitation. Let's see how we feel when we get to Santiago.'

She forced a smile and took a drink of her warming rosé.

'I'll get you a fresh glass.' Javier headed to the bar.

Pen looked at her mom, furious.

'I'm done with my pizza. Can we go back to the albergue? I want to lay down.'

Tess shook herself.

'Yes, of course. Both of you go.'

They got up and passed Javier as he returned with the wine.

'Where are they going?'

'They asked to go back to the albergue.' She said absently.

'Listen. You caught me off guard. I hadn't even considered going to Madrid until now. At some point on this walk, I'm unsure when, I need to tell Pen about my illness. I don't know how that will go or if I should make definite plans after the Camino. I'm unclear what she'll need or what I'll need after I've told her.'

Javier listened to the flood of her words and nodded.

'Pen is upset because she doesn't know of your condition. She will understand when you tell her.'

Tess looked out beyond the sunset behind him.

'Right now. I just want to enjoy...' She was at a loss. 'I don't know. Right now. I don't want to plan beyond 24 hours at a time. Can you do that for me?'

He took her hand and kissed her palm.

'Of course, I can.' He smiled.

It was the first moment on the trip that she felt afraid of the future. Just breathe.

TEN

THE MASETA TO LEÓN

The following day, they woke up before dawn. Like most mornings, Pen shouted, 'Turn around!' from up ahead on the trail, rewarding them with a sunrise more beautiful than the day before. Tess looked forward to them as they each took her breath away.

The path to the hill town of Castrojeriz was rutted with hard-packed dirt and plagued by swarms of flying black bugs. Passing the ruins of St Anton, catching sight of their next destination on a hill with a ruined castle gazing down over the residents, was like something from a postcard.

Winding their way through the old streets, they found a wonderful albergue with individual beds and a reputation for an excellent pilgrim's meal. The one drawback was that the *hospitaliero* who ran it tried to separate men and women, so they were placed in rooms by gender. As Tess and Pen were unpacking, one of their fellow pilgrims invited them to a birthday party in the square for a Peregrino who was staying nearby.

'You gotta come!' The woman told them. 'It's gonna be fun.'

Pen looked at her Mom with pleading eyes.

'Ok.' Conceded Tess.

Pen pumped the air.

Tess saw Javier outside the showers and told him about the invite.

'I'll try to come later. I have a couple of phone calls to return regarding my patients.'

Tess and the kids walked up the hill to the village square. Someone had a Bluetooth speaker, and music and drinks were flowing. Pen ordered a Coke, and Tess accepted a glass of red wine from a short, portly man sitting beside her.

'This is so fun. Whose birthday is it?' She asked the man.

He pointed to the large older gentleman, who was long past counting the beers he had consumed.

'Ah.'

She turned to the birthday boy and wished him a 'Happy Birthday.' He responded by raising his glass to her.

The man who had given her the wine asked where Tess was from. She told him, then enquired about his background, a little surprised when he said he was a priest from Scotland.

'Oh, Scotland holds a special place in my heart.' She told him.

'Really? Do you know where Fife is?'

'Yes, I've been there. I love that area. Edinburgh is magical.'

He seemed pleased.

'It is indeed.' He said, with a mischievous twinkle in his eye. And his next question, delivered in a thick Scottish accent, confirmed it.

'So, Tess, the American pilgrim. Care to share what you've learned so far on your Camino?'

She thought about it. What did she have to lose by being honest with a total stranger? The man was a priest, and her daughter and Mateo were dancing with other people out of earshot.

'I've learned a lot...' she told him some details.

His face turned red. 'Good God, girl! It would be best if you slowed down on the transformation. You're only a few weeks in.'

Tess laughed at his sputtering.

'At this rate, who will you be when you walk into Santiago in three weeks?' He asked her.

Tess thought for a moment.

'I'll be a butterfly and fly away.' She said, smiling.

The priest took a long pull on his mug of beer.

'I don't doubt it for a moment.' He said with a thoughtful grin.

After more wine from the various revelers, Tess started to feel the effects. She waved to Mateo and Pen, leaving them to their fun, walking back to the Albergue to lay down before the legendary pilgrim's dinner.

It wasn't long before she was fully asleep and dreaming; she was in Madrid with John and Javier. They enjoyed dinner at a beautiful restaurant, sitting outdoors at a table under the stars, with twinkling white lights overhead, drinking wine and laughing.

When it came time to depart, they stood outside on the pavement. Both men reached for her hand to go with them in opposite directions. 'Tess.' John pleaded as Javier waited for her to choose before saying quietly, 'Tess, we're waiting.'

She wasn't sure what to do—when a voice broke through her dream. It was Javier gently shaking her and calling her name. She sat up, not sure where she was. He sat down on the bed, wrapping his arms around her.

'Where am I?' she said.

'We're at the albergue, mi amor. You look like you had a bad dream.'

She wiped the sleep from her eyes.

'No, I was just dreaming. You said, 'We're waiting,' and then I woke up.

'I did say that. The dinner is about to start, and Pen and Mateo are already seated. They're saving our places.'

Tess got up and smoothed her hair and skirt. 'I'm sorry. I slept after the birthday party. Let's go to dinner.'

Javier took her hand and led her to the patio, where long trestle tables rested. The paella was cooking on an outdoor fire. The smell of the freshly baked bread made her mouth water.

Tess took her place at the table beside Pen.

'Wow. I'm glad Javier woke me up. I don't think I would have been able to find my way out here.' She said, still groggy from her nap.

Pen broke out into a smile.

'I think maybe it was the wine in the hot sun at the birthday party.'

Tess chuckled. She deserved that after the lectures she delivered in the other direction over the last two days.

Pen studied her mother's face and realized her mom looked tired. Not a little tired but exhausted. She would stop teasing her today. Perhaps the walk was taking a toll, and she hadn't noticed before. They would take a rest day in León, and she thought maybe her mom needed it. Javier and Mateo would be visiting some people on his mother's side of the family.

After his mom died, Mateo's dad made sure he remained close to her family. Javier was a good guy. Pen wished she and her mom were like that, but they had too many issues. She could almost admit that some of it might be her fault. Her mom was right. There were moments she knew she was difficult. Sometimes, she couldn't help herself. But while they were walking, her mom was trying. Maybe she should work a little harder at it, too.

Javier suggested an early night. Tess was grateful, and Pen didn't argue. They were getting up very early now because the afternoons were much hotter in the *Meseta*. Pen had heard that this stretch between Burgos and León was considered boring, but she thought it was beautiful so far. A difficult few days were in front of them, they said. Hot and flat. But it didn't appear that way to her.

They woke up in the dark the following day and climbed *Alto de Mostelares*. Turning around to catch the spectacular sunrise from the top, Pen watched her mother for signs of fatigue, but Tess appeared to be holding her own. Pen shook her head. Not sure why she was so concerned, she picked up her pace with Mateo, and they were off to the village where they would stop and wait for their parents.

The walk that day was hot and dusty. The last stretch was brutal, without a tree in sight and no way to fill water bottles. Javier shared his water with Tess and ensured she rested when they saw shade—even if they had to walk far off the trail to enjoy it. Tess and Javier arrived at the albergue where they were staying, where Pen and Mateo had been for hours.

Tess laid down immediately and slept. Later, the others were surprised when she put on her bathing suit, opting to swim in the pool at sunset. The water felt only a few degrees cooler than the air, and she enjoyed the feeling of it on her skin. Javier sat on the pool's edge, dangling his legs over the edge, watching her swim back and forth.

'You like water.' He observed.

'I do. I was on the swim team in high school. I used to swim every day. Then life got in the way, and I was too busy. Everyone thinks if you have a pool in Arizona, you always swim. But it's not true. In summer, it's too hot to swim. And too cold in the winter because you got used to it being so hot all summer.' She turned and swam the length of the pool. 'This is nice, though. I could live in Spain.'

He smiled. 'I could enjoy you living in Spain.'

Tess kept up her laps, eventually pulling herself out of the pool and wrapping herself in her sarong. She sat in a chair facing Javier, enjoying the twilight. Acutely aware of her fatigue, Tess was afraid of what it meant. She'd promised John she would tell him if side effects or symptoms sprang up. But she wasn't ready to pull the ripcord yet.

'Time for bed?' He asked.

'Yes, I'd like to make it an early night.'

Neither noticed Mateo, who watched from the window as they returned inside.

The morning walk through Fromista was stunning along the canal. The sunrise reflected on the water, turning it blue, then a fire orange before breaking the horizon. The foursome pushed through to Carrion de los Condes without stopping. They checked into an albergue run by singing nuns, who performed with pilgrims before the dinner. Those staying in the albergue were requested to contribute food or drinks and to help cook a communal meal.

It was a fun change of pace, and Javier shined in the role of head chef. He seasoned and flavored the meat dish and the vegetables and helped open the wines pilgrims contributed before the meal began. Tess enjoyed watching him feeding the others.

A few days later, they reached Mansilla de las Mulas, just one village before the large city of León. The *Rio Esla* runs through the west end of town, and Tess informed them of her intention to swim again.

'I need to be in the water. I don't know why—maybe because it's so hot. But I need to get into the cold river.'

Javier suggested they all go. And while Pen and Mateo ran up the stairs to dig into their packs for their suits, he decided to intervene. Something he had promised he would not do.

'Are you feeling alright?' He asked tentatively.

'Yes, why?' asked Tess, a bit irritated.

'I don't know.' He frowned. 'You seem more tired. This desire for swimming over the last few days is new. We've stayed at places with pools before Burgos, and you never looked to swim. It was hot then, as well. Now, you seem to take every opportunity when you can find cool water.' He knew he was overstepping. 'Would you mind if I took your temperature?'

Tess's face hardened.

'I'm fine.' She said. 'I just enjoy swimming, and it's been hot in the *Meseta*. You know that.'

He put his hands up. 'You're right. I promised I wouldn't be your doctor. Let's go swimming.'

The river water was ice cold as they waded in. Javier and the kids were having a hard time getting acclimated. All three moaned about how cold the water was and eased their way just waist deep. Tess dove in and swam across to the other side before popping out.

'Hey, slowpokes.' Tess called, laughing. 'Don't be chickens!'

Javier turned to Pen for her expertise.

'What is *slowpoke*? I know what a chicken is.'

'*Slowpokes* are people who don't rush into things; they lag behind others. Chickens are fraidy-cats.'

'*Fraidy cats*?' He looked confused,

Pen rolled her eyes.

'People who are scared.' She explained.

'Ah. Well, we can't have that.' He dove into the water and swam to the other side, popping out right in front of Tess, ready to scare her. She smiled at him when he noticed the blood dripping from her nose.

'You have a nosebleed.' He told her. 'Press your fingers to the side of your nose. I don't think the kids have seen because they're still on the other side.'

He led her to the bank, and they sat on a rock. Her frustration at his earlier concern was gone, replaced by fear.

'It's a side effect of the meds I'm taking. I promised John that if I started to notice any, I would get a blood draw and check my levels.'

Javier looked concerned.

'I'll call a friend of mine in León. We went to medical school together, and Amelia is a leading oncologist in Spain. You can have a blood test tomorrow.'

Tess pressed her nose harder and looked around him to see the kids splashing each other with water.

'Is it going to be hard to get in to see her? She may be booked up.'

'She will see you whether she has a space in her agenda or not.' He sounded very sure. 'I treated her grandmother in Madrid before she passed away. We are old friends from childhood.'

Tess agreed, looking at her hands. 'I think the bleeding has stopped. I can swim to the other side now.'

Javier helped her off the rock.

'Let's go back. I'll get some ice. It will help slow down any residual bleeding until it starts to clot.'

They swam back and told the kids Tess had a headache, and they were going to get something for it. There was another topic Javier had hoped to discuss with her.

'When are you planning on talking to Pen about your illness?'

At the question, Tess started to cry.

'I don't know.' Swallowing hard to keep the tears at bay.

'I think you should tell her sooner than later. She needs to understand what you're up against and her part in helping you.'

Tess shook her head vigorously, willing it away. The movement started her nose bleeding again, and Javier gave her his towel.

'I'm going to find hotel rooms in León for tomorrow, and I think you should call John and keep him apprised of the situation.'

'I don't want him to worry.' She whispered.

Javier stopped, failing to keep the frustration from his voice.

'He has the right to know, Tess. Do you want me to call and speak with him?'

Tess closed her eyes. She didn't want her two worlds to touch. John had expressed jealousy of Javier. And Javier mostly avoided acknowledging she was married. She couldn't imagine anything good coming from a conversation between them.

'No. I need to shower and get myself together. Then I'll call John after you've called your friend and gotten me an appointment.'

Javier knew she was stalling, but he also knew how hard this was for her.

'OK,' he said quietly. 'I'll make the call and get you some ice.' He turned to leave the albergue with his phone to his ear and a trail of Spanish in his wake.

Tess stood under the water for a long time. She knew she was supposed to limit the length of her shower, but today she didn't care. As soon as that door opened, everything would change. Crying as the water poured over her face, she struggled to understand how she was dealing with this in the middle of Spain, wondering how to explain it to Pen.

She and Pen had just begun the process of understanding each other. She didn't relish pulling the rug out from under her daughter's world.

Tess turned off the water and dried off as best she could. On the Camino, she had gotten used to never being fully dry after a shower. Putting on underwear in the stall while still wet and balancing on one foot was challenging. She struggled more today than usual, a little dizzy from the blood loss. She found Javier sitting on her bed.

'You have an appointment at 3 pm tomorrow. I sent you the address in WhatsApp.' He told her quietly.

'Ok.' She whispered. 'Thank you for setting that up.'

'Of course.'

He handed her a plastic bag of ice he'd gotten from somewhere.

'Are you going to call John now?' He asked her.

'I want to lay down for a bit. This nosebleed has worn me out.'

Javier helped her to her bunk and laid out her sleep sack. She pressed the ice pack to her nose, but she fell asleep almost immediately, and it dropped to the floor.

Javier felt her forehead, wondering what he should do. She was ill, that was certain. But something more was going on, and he was concerned that her judgment was impaired since she wasn't communicating with John and had yet to tell Pen. He took a deep breath and made a decision. Grabbing her phone from her pack, he input the number into his own. Then he left the albergue, waiting to dial until he was down the street. An American voice answered, and it took him a moment to find the words.

'John?' asked Javier.

'Yes?' said the cautious voice on the other end.

'You don't know me, but my name is Javier Silva. I'm a friend of your wife and daughter on the Camino.'

There was silence on the other end of the phone. Then a steely, 'I know who you are.'

Javier took a deep breath.

'I'm overstepping by calling you. I know that, but I am concerned about Tess, and I want to ensure you know what is going on.'

A beat and then 'OK.'

Javier filled John in on the previous few days and what had happened at the river. He also let him know about her appointment in León.

'Does she know you're calling me?' John asked.

Javier said she did not.

'Her health is the most important thing. And I know you and your son are probably very concerned being on the other side of the world. '

John didn't reply right away. 'I am very concerned.' He admitted. 'But our son, Charlie, is not concerned because he is dead.' John struggled for control. 'Tess didn't tell you?'

Javier held his breath. Tess always spoke of her son as though he were alive—just another college student. He didn't know what to say. What else had she not told him?

'Our son died the night of his high school graduation in a car full of his friends. That was four years ago next week.' John whispered.

They both let that sink in.

'You're taking a big chance, calling me. You know that?' John told him. 'Tess is the loneliest person I have ever known. She doesn't let people in easily. I don't know how you have managed it, but if she finds out, I know her. She will never trust you again.'

'It's a risk I am willing to take.' Javier said quietly.

John held Javier's fate in his hands. All he had to do was to tell Tess about this phone call. Their relationship would be over in an instant.

'Do you think she should continue with this trek?' John pleaded, already knowing the answer he was hoping to hear. 'In your professional opinion, should she come home immediately and start treatment?'

'If it were up to me, she would have left weeks ago and started treatment.' Javier assured him. 'No delay. She will not do that, so I don't think that is an option. But she needs to see the doctor tomorrow, and I did arrange an appointment for her. Afterward, I will make sure she calls you and discusses the results. But I wanted you to have my number, just in case.'

This phone call was the strangest of their lives. Both loved the same woman and were worried sick about her. Neither of them was comfortable with the situation in which they found themselves.

'First,' said John. 'Let me just say, if you were standing in front of me right now, I would punch you in the face.' John took a deep breath. 'But I also want to say thank you for calling me. I'm sitting over here worried to death about my wife and daughter.' he choked up. 'I barely sleep. I need to know what's going on over there, and if you're the one who will keep me informed, then I'll take it.'

Javier closed his eyes. He felt for this man.

'I put myself in your shoes, and if I were you, I would want to know. I am aware that I am betraying Tess's trust by calling you. But if it means she is well when this is all over, then so be it. Then you can punch me in the face.'

John chuckled despite himself. 'I'll take you up on that.'

The call disconnected, and Javier took a couple of deep breaths before walking back to the albergue to check on Tess.

John looked at the screen. Then he made Javier a contact. This guy was now his back door if he needed to stay informed on how Tess was doing. Over the last few weeks, John had spent a decent amount of time imagining a confrontation. But John was no fool. He wouldn't throw away this opportunity.

ELEVEN

LEÓN

G etting up early, they started in the dark with their headlamps switched on. Javier didn't try to engage Tess in conversation. For that, she was grateful.

León came into view by 11 am, and they checked into the Parador. Javier was taking Mateo and Pen for lunch at the home of Mateo's relatives. Pen wanted to know why Tess wasn't joining them, but she said she was tired and needed the rest. Her daughter seemed concerned, but reluctantly, Pen agreed to go without her.

Tess ordered a taxi and gave the driver the address Javier had sent her. Standing at the entrance to the office, she looked up for a full minute before entering. Tess didn't want to go inside; didn't want to hear what this friend of Javier was going to tell her because she knew, whatever it was, it would not be good news. Surrounded by the thick carpets and the soft-hued sofas, Tess calmed down as she approached the desk. The receptionist, who spoke English, took her through to the Doctor's private office and offered a coffee.

Certificates and photos plastered the walls. It appeared Doctor Amelia Garcia Gómez was an active woman with many interests. Tess assumed the woman was similar in age to Javier, so the pictures of a group of young people must have been taken 20-30 years before. Tess rose and studied them more closely.

In one shot, the group was on a boat in the blue Mediterranean Sea. She could momentarily pick out the woman she would speak to based on her prominence in other pictures. Then she spotted a very familiar face. A much younger Javier was smiling at the camera, shirtless and tanned, with his arm draped over the shoulder of a beautiful blond girl. She was looking up at him and laughing.

'College days.'

Startled, Tess turned to see the doctor standing in the doorway, offering her hand. 'Buenas tardes. Amelia.' Said the doctor. 'And you are Tess Sullivan. Mucho gusto.' They shook.

'That photo was taken in the dark ages when we were all students.' Gesturing to the image on the wall. 'You can see Javier before he went grey.' she said, pulling on her own curly salt and pepper locks. 'Back when he won Alejandra's heart, to the envy of us all.'

Amelia looked at the photo wistfully.

'She was stunning, on the inside and out. We were all in love with her, but she only had eyes for Javier.' she said thoughtfully. 'Her death impacted each of us profoundly.'

After a moment, Amelia shook her head.

'I'm sorry.' She smiled. 'Javier gave me some details, but I'd like to hear from you what is going on and get a list of the current medications you're taking. If you don't mind, I'd also like to contact your doctor back in the US and consult. I know you're on the Camino and determined to finish. I want to ensure we are all working together to help make that possible.'

'That sounds fine.' Tess nodded. 'I'll give you her contact details. I also wrote down all the medications and dosages before I came today. I brought them with me, as well.' Tess rummaged in her daypack, lining them up on her desk. The doctor examined the bottles and nodded.

'So. You are experiencing some side effects from some of the targeted treatments. Let's take some blood, and we'll see what we find. It's good you're here now so I can call your doctor with the results when she arrives at the office in the US. We can work together on any adjustments needed for your treatment plan.' Amelia turned from the bottles on her desk. 'Javier also mentioned concern for an elevated temp, so we'll check that too. And look for any secondary infections. Is there anything else you want to tell me?'

Tess went through some of her symptoms, and then began to cry. As an oncologist, the doctor seemed to take this in her stride. Tess told her that she still needed to tell her daughter about her cancer. Amelia listened, then recommended that Tess wait until the results were back before she decided when to speak with Pen. Tess wiped her eyes and nodded. There was no pressure, and she liked that.

The nurse came in and led her to an examination room while the doctor explained what they would do as Tess's blood pressure and temperature were taken. Javier was right. Her temperature was over 100. The doctor checked for signs of dehydration.

'It's been exceptionally hot in Spain this year. I think you are a bit dehydrated. I will put you on an IV and ensure your electrolytes and levels are good before you go. If you lie down, my nurse will get you a blanket, and you can relax while the IV is going.'

It sounded like heaven to Tess. While the nurse hooked her up, she fell into a deep sleep, awakened by the doctor sometime later.

'You are fully rehydrated now, so we'll remove the IV. Your blood work will be back a little later, and I will call you with the results after I speak to your doctor. If we need to adjust medications, I can ensure a pharmacy close to your hotel will have the medications waiting for you. We will take another temp before you go. Javier says you're staying here and will take a rest day tomorrow.'

'Yes. We will sleep in tomorrow and see some parts of old León and the cathedral.' Tess told her.

'Very good. It will give me time to do what I need to do and you the time to take a break from walking. Getting plenty of rest is essential in your condition. I know you want to finish your Camino, and from what I see, I think you probably can—barring anything in the blood work that surprises me. When are you going back home?' the doctor asked her.

'Not for a few weeks. I didn't know how long it would take to walk the Camino, so I wanted to give us plenty of time.' Said Tess.

'I understand. Perhaps, in the end, you can find a good place to rest and relax before you travel home.'

Amelia hesitated before continuing.

'Can I ask why you didn't enter aggressive treatment when you got diagnosed more than a month ago? I understand that while your doctor did not tell you that you couldn't walk, she advised you to start treatment immediately. A double mastectomy is what I would have advised. And with lymph glands in the neck and under your arms, they should have been removed immediately. Allowing no delay. You have a chance if you do this immediately and go through the course of chemotherapy and other treatments.'

Tess closed her eyes. 'I can't explain it adequately. I needed to walk this—for myself and my daughter. I knew I wouldn't be strong enough to do it once I started treatment. And if the treatment didn't work, I might never be able to do it. I'm compelled; there is no other explanation.' She stopped and took a deep breath before continuing. 'My relationship with my daughter has been very contentious. She and I are healing on this walk. We needed this time together. It's that important.'

The doctor nodded, considering her words.

'I will call you later to discuss the results. The good news is your fever seems to be down. Just a little elevated, so perhaps it was the dehydration. You will need to watch that closely from now on. I will devise a plan for when and how much to drink daily and which electrolyte replacement therapy you should use. You'll need to follow this strictly. No variations.'

Tess nodded. 'Of course, whatever you say.'

'Do I have your permission to call Javier and discuss your condition since he referred you to me?' The doctor asked her.

Tess thought for a moment.

'Yes, you can call him. But I must ask that you keep what my doctor in Arizona tells you confidential. That is very important to me. I know Javier is concerned and may have questions I can't answer.' Then she added. 'If my husband would like to speak to you, would that be OK too?'

The doctor raised an eyebrow.

'Of course.' she said.

Tess got up and smoothed out her skirt. 'Thank you so much for seeing me and agreeing to treat me on such short notice.'

'When Javier called,' said Amelia, 'I knew he wouldn't have done so if it weren't important. He is a good doctor; he helped my grandmother as she was in the final stages of Alzheimer's and dementia. We have been friends for all our lives.' She turned away, busying herself with something on the counter. 'He cares about you. I can tell. I think it's difficult for him that you are ill. Did he know that when you met?'

Tess sighed. 'Yes. Javier knew right away.' She hesitated. 'Look. I'm not trying to hurt him. I came on the Camino to do exactly what I told you. I wasn't looking for a relationship, but we both got one. He's a wonderful man. I'm just trying to live, truly live. Then I will go home and fight this.'

The doctor looked thoughtful. 'Home to your husband and your family.'

'Yes. My husband knows about Javier. They know about each other.' Tess struggled to explain. 'If you knew me before, you would never see me in this situation. It's unbelievable, even to me. But my husband is grateful to Javier for helping me. It's a complicated situation. But I am not ashamed.' She whispered, not sure if it was true.

The doctor's face softened.

'You seem like a good person. I am just protective of my friend. I know what he and Mateo went through when Alejandra died. Afterward, Javier moved Mateo out of the family home they shared with her and into a small apartment. He couldn't bear to be in that house without her—and he said it would help Mateo too. But he couldn't face it, and they never returned to the house since moving. He just locked the door and walked away.'

Tess held her breath. 'He didn't tell me that.'

'He wouldn't.' she whispered. 'And now he's found you; you're married and very ill. Out of reach, really. No matter the outcome of your illness. You are out of his reach.'

They looked at each other intensely as tears poured down Tess's cheeks. The nurse's arrival broke the moment. Tess thanked the doctor for her help and all the information she had given her. The nurse walked her out to reception.

'What do I owe you for this visit?' Reaching into her backpack for her wallet.

The nurse smiled.

'The doctor said not to worry about payment.' She assured her.

In the taxi to the hotel, Tess called John and updated him on what was going on.

'So, the fever is nothing to worry about?'

'The blood work will come back, so until then, I have to wait and see. It may just be dehydration. The doctor is giving me a plan, and I've agreed to follow it to the letter.'

'Good girl.'

'Listen, John. I know this is hard being so far away.' She began to cry. 'I'm sorry. For everything.'

'No. Don't. I wanted this for you, and you're doing it. The Camino is difficult for healthy people, and you're doing it. I'm so proud of you. And Pen is changing too. It's what we wanted for her.'

Tess sniffed.

'I mean the other stuff. It's hurting you. I know that. What kind of person am I to do something that hurts you?'

'Tess. Honey, I want you to listen to me. Go, take a hot bath when you get back to the hotel. And re-read my letter. I meant every word. I'm torturing myself, but I don't want you to do that.' He tried to remain upbeat. 'If you're happy, I'll be happy too.'

'I feel scared today, John.' She told him. 'I know I'm not making you happy right now.'

The silence hung between them.

'Well, you don't know what I'm doing here.' He joked. 'I'm on Tinder and having the time of my life! You should see these babes. I'm raking them in, swiping right on every one of them. They can't get enough of me.'

Tess laughed through tears.

'You know you'd clean up if you did that, right?' She laughed.

'Yeah, well, I'll save that for another time.' He whispered.

Wiping her eyes. 'Okay.'

John took a deep breath. He loved her so much it hurt.

'Do what I said. Go, take your bath, and send me a picture of your smiling, tanned face from the bubbles. I want to see you happy.' He said.

Her taxi pulled up to the hotel.

'I'm heading up now.'

'I Love you, my girl.' The line went dead.

Tess followed John's suggestion. She soaked for a long time until she heard her cell phone ring but couldn't get out of the bath in time to answer it. Shortly, there was a knock at the door. Her skin had wrinkled, and the water was getting cold anyway. She wrapped herself in a white hotel robe and opened the door to Javier, standing on the other side of the threshold.

'Hi.' She said, feeling awkward.

'Hello.' He looked worried. 'I thought I would hear from you after your appointment, but I became concerned when I didn't.'

Tess sat down on the bed.

'The doctor said she would call you and give you an update. I wasn't sure I could answer all of your questions.'

Javier's radar perked up.

'I haven't heard from her yet. Is everything alright?' He asked, concerned.

She looked up at him with tears in her eyes.

'Yes, so far, yes.' She went on to explain, sitting on the side of the bed. 'I feel a lot better.' The look on her face told a different story. Javier crossed the room and bent down. He wrapped his arms around her and held her as she cried. Finally, she pulled back, looking up at him as he brushed her hair back and wiped her tears.

'What else? What are you not telling me?' he asked.

'Nothing. That's all I know. Amelia and I chatted for a while. I saw some pictures in her office from when you were young—still in medical school. She's known you for a long time. You and Alejandra.' She told him.

Javier nodded. 'Yes. What did she say that upset you?' Frowning.

'She didn't say anything that upset me. She told me how hard it was for you and Mateo after your wife died. How hard it was for your group of old friends. I think she is very protective of you.'

'Ah. I see.' Javier looked thoughtful for a moment. 'Of course, she knows you are ill. And on top of that, you have a husband. She's concerned I will get hurt in some way.'

Tess was quiet.

'Yes, and so am I.,' she whispered. 'She used the term 'out of reach.' No matter what, I am out of your reach. Whether I live or die.' Her tears flowed again.

Javier's face darkened. He got up, pacing the room but said nothing. Tess watched him, waiting for him to speak.

'I know she means well. I know she is concerned, but it's my life. I am happy today. Every day I am with you. I know it will not last, and in four weeks, you will go home, and it will cost me a great deal when you do. But I went into this with my eyes open. You did not deceive me, and I have not deceived myself.' He assured them both.

Tess released the breath she had been holding.

'She was lovely.' She whispered.

Javier looked up. 'Who?' Confused.

'Alejandra. The pictures are in Amelia's office. One of them was of you all on a boat, with your arm around her and looking so happy. It was wonderful. She was stunning.' Tess told him.

Suddenly, his face looked as though it would break in half. Tears poured down his cheeks.

'She was.' He whispered.

'Amelia said everyone was in love with her, including Amelia apparently, but she only had eyes for you. I find I'm a little jealous of her. It's not logical, but there you go.' She admitted.

Standing by the window, Javier covered his face with his hands.

She waited a few moments before continuing.

'She also told me you locked your house in Madrid after she died and moved into a small apartment. That you have never been back since.'

Javier looked back at her with such anguish; her tears began to flow again. Tess got up and went to him, wrapping her arms around his waist. He spoke into her hair.

'I couldn't face living in that house without her. If you saw it, you would know why. It is filled with her, her paintings, and her style. She was looking back at me everywhere I looked, just beyond the tips of my fingers. Sleeping in our bed was torture. I didn't wash the sheets for weeks to preserve her scent and the last indent on her pillow. I knew we needed a start fresh. So, I bought an apartment, and I closed up the house. We took only a few things with us. I bought new furniture. Even pots and pans.' His voice broke again, and he hugged her more tightly. 'Now, it's a museum covered in dust.'

'I understand.' She whispered. 'It had to be hard. Love like that is so rare and precious. It must be preserved.' She tried to reassure him.

'Yes, it does.' Barely a whisper.

'Hearing her talk about it made me homesick for John and my life there. Thinking of all the things we've collected together over a lifetime. Stupid things. A cheap Eiffel Tower from a family trip to Paris. And our sand jar from the beach vacations together. All the things that would mean nothing to anyone else. They have no monetary value, but they mean the most when you hold them in your hands. Memories. Laughter. Salty kisses. I am making memories here, but they will never belong to John and me. It makes me more than a little sad.' She admitted.

Javier knew precisely just how she felt.

'I struggled afterward. Making memories without Alejandra meant that she would slip away from us. But I know now that it's unavoidable. We had to go on. We had to do things that she wouldn't be there to do with us. But we don't love her any less now than we did when she was alive.'

Tess thought of Charlie at that moment, taking a deep breath.

'And I don't love John less because he's not here. I called him and told him so.'

Javier smiled. 'I'm glad you spoke to him. I am sure he is relieved that your health is stabilizing and you can finish your Camino and go home.'

'Yes, he is. And while he's struggling with this thing between you and me, he also said he is happy, which is weird. He knows I'm happy, and you're part of that. He told me to do whatever you say.'

Javier's eyebrows went up.

'I think he meant on the medical front, but he knows everything else. He says you're good for me.' Tess saw his shocked expression. 'I know.' She smiled and wiped her eyes. 'He told me to do what I need to. But does it make me a bad person for going ahead and doing it?'

Javier shook his head, brushing the hair back from her face. 'No. It doesn't make anyone a bad person. Not John, you, nor me. This circumstance isn't what any of us would have expected in a thousand years. But here we are. I refuse to place those kinds of judgments on things. It will do none of us any good.'

Later, Tess checked in with Pen. The kids wanted to order room service and watch movies in their rooms. She and Javier had a picnic in hers.

'Is it strange for you to spend the afternoon with Alejandra's family?' She asked.

Javier considered the question.

'Not anymore. I know they love Mateo and spoil him when he sees them. They're so proud, and visiting makes him feel closer to his Mother. They adored Pen, showing her all their old photos, and they stuffed us full of food.'

Tess was surprised to hear that Pen had the patience for all of that.

'They sound like kind people.'

'Alejandra's mother and I had some time to speak. She will be coming to Madrid later in the year, and she will stay with us. I asked about her husband. He has never budged in his feelings for me. Even though he is a doctor, I think he somehow blames me for her cancer—an attitude that defies science. Mateo will visit them in the Spring of next year in Barcelona before his final exams. No matter how he feels about me, Sebastian must have time with his grandson.'

Javier had a generous heart and put others first. No matter the cost to himself.

'So, Alejandra's mother is from León?' She asked.

'No. Sofía is from Santiago. But her sisters moved here when they married. Both of their husbands passed away, and now they live together. They're very close and still have relatives and a family home in Santiago. They visit there a few times yearly, mostly for religious holidays like Semana Santa.' He told her.

'If you notice, Mateo has lighter hair and light eyes. If you met his Grandmother, you would see why. In Galicia, the people have Celtic ancestry. Their language and their heritage link them to Ireland. You will see it when we go there. Celtic crosses and imagery everywhere. Mateo inherited his coloring from them. And he has remained close to the culture.'

'Is his grandfather from Galicia?' She asked.

'No, Sebastian is from Madrid. But he prefers Barcelona—I think he likes feeling superior to the Gallegos and the Catalans. Indeed, knowing Basque blood runs through his grandson's veins has brought him no joy. But in fairness, he adores Mateo and is very proud of him. So, as far as Mateo is concerned, I don't want to be ungenerous in my portrayal.' Javier told her.

'Sounds like your father-in-law and your Mother are from the same type of background.'

'They are. And both care very much about what others think. I find that for myself, I don't care what anyone thinks anymore.'

'What would your mother think of me?' She asked.

He made a face.

'You shouldn't concern yourself with her opinion. It won't benefit you in any way.'

He closed his eyes and listened to the city.

'We should get a good night's sleep if we are going to be tourists tomorrow.' He encouraged.

A wave of exhaustion had settled over them both, and they were out as their heads hit the pillow.

Tess woke up as dawn was breaking and looked at her phone. Javier had returned to his room in the middle of the night. She saw a message from her Arizona doctor asking her to call her—no matter the time. Taking a deep breath, she dialed the phone.

'Tess?'

'Hi, Marissa. I got your message. What's so urgent?' She asked as her heart pounded.

'I understand you've been ill and saw a Doctor Gómez over there.'

'Yes.' Said Tess. 'I've been feeling tired, and I've had a fever. I met a doctor on the trail who arranged for me to see a specialist here in León.'

'Yes. I spoke to her today. She and I went over the results of your blood tests.' Marissa hesitated. 'They're not good, Tess. I don't think you should continue this quest of yours. And neither does Doctor Gómez.'

Tess was shocked to hear this. Amelia had indicated that it might just be dehydration, and she said so.

'It's more than that. I think you know it. This adventure would always be a stretch for you, but it's taking a toll. You should come home and let us do the surgery.'

Tess teared up. She'd come so far.

'I'm not coming home right now. I still need to talk to Pen about all this, and I feel better after rehydrating. It's only a few more weeks until I'm finished. Then I can rest.'

She heard Marissa's heavy sigh.

'I can't caution enough against that approach. Your body isn't responding well to this physical challenge. I imagine there is a fair bit of emotional stress, too. I want you to have the best chance, Tess. And your best chance is to come home now and start aggressive treatment.'

Tess's head was spinning.

'Isn't there anything you can give me? Something new that might delay things?' she begged. 'I have to keep going, Marissa. I need to finish this. It's too important. For me and my daughter. Please.'

Her doctor sighed.

'Let me call Amelia back and discuss it with her. But she won't like it any more than I do.'

Tess stood under the shower for a long time before getting dressed. She knocked on Pen's door to see what her tour-guide daughter had planned for them. Taking the rare opportunity to sit with Pen over breakfast before the guys showed up.

'I heard you were a big hit with Mateo's family.' Tess gently teased her.

Pen smiled.

'They're super nice people. One of his aunts gave me a family rosary and said something in Spanish that made Mateo blush. They wouldn't tell me what it was. His grandmother, Sofía, is so beautiful. She's like seventy-five or something, but she's got bright blue eyes, just like Mateo. She loves him a lot. You can tell because she sat on the arm of the couch, hugged him a hundred times, and petted him like a cat. He seemed a little embarrassed, but you could tell he liked it too. They spoil him.'

Tess watched Pen's face as she talked about her encounter with Mateo's family, lighting up from the inside as she described the scene and the emotions flying around the room.

'I think Javier had a hard time being there.' She told Tess. 'He and Sofía went to the balcony and talked for a while. The Aunties stuffed Mateo and me full of sweets and pastries. It's probably good we're walking the Camino, or I'd be 500lbs.' She rubbed her stomach.

"Why did you think Javier was having a hard time?' Tess asked, concerned.

'It was just the way he seemed. Distracted, I guess. And he was on the phone a few times.'

'Maybe to his patients.' Offered Tess.

'Yeah, maybe.' Said Pen.

Just then, the guys showed up. They took their seats and ordered coffee. Then they got up to make their selections from the buffet. Tess watched Javier, wondering if he had told her everything about the visit to his wife's family. When the coffees arrived, the kids rose to get more food, and Javier leaned over.

'I have a message from Amelia. I am going to step outside and call her back. Can you run interference for me?' He asked.

'Of course. I haven't heard from her, so whatever she tells you, you must tell me.' Said Tess, nervous. Hoping Amelia wouldn't reveal too much to Javier.

'Of course.' Javier assured her.

He went to the lobby.

Pen came back to the table alone.

'Where did Mateo go?' Tess asked.

'He wanted to talk to his Dad about something. He saw him go to the lobby. He'll be right back.'

The blood drained from Tess's face. She anxiously watched the doorway for Mateo or Javier to return. Time ticked by, and it was 15 minutes before they came back together. Mateo looked stricken, and Tess wondered what had happened in their conversation.

'You gotta eat so we can go!' exclaimed Pen when they returned.

'Yeah. I'm not that hungry this morning.' Mateo pushed his full plate aside. 'I'll just have the coffee.'

Pen wrinkled her brow but said nothing. Tess was anxious to hear what Amelia had told Javier, but there was nowhere with privacy to find out.

'Shall we.' Javier said, breaking the tension after they finished their breakfast.

'Yes, let's see the first thing on Pen's itinerary.' Tess encouraged. 'Pen, lead the way.'

Pen decided they would first go on the Cathedral tour and led them to the square in the old city. Mateo walked ahead with her but looked back toward his father as they made their way up the street. Tess couldn't wait any longer.

'What did she say?' she whispered.

'She's making some adjustments to your medication. And she wants you to limit alcohol. It will help with the dehydration.'

Tess pulled a face.

'It's a small price.' He assured her. 'A glass of wine here and there, but nothing more. Also, she spoke with your doctor in Arizona, and they've agreed on the new course. I called the pharmacy, and they will send them to the hotel, so you don't need to pick them up. You'll start the new meds when we return to the hotel tonight.'

'Thank you.' She waited momentarily before asking, 'Did Amelia say anything else?'

'No, why?' asked Javier.

'No reason. I was just wondering.' She tried to steer the conversation away from her illness. 'What did Mateo want to discuss with you? He looked terrible when he came back to the table.'

Javier took a deep breath.

'I don't know. I talked to the pharmacy about the medications and having them sent to the hotel. When I turned around, Mateo was there. He asked if you were sick. If you had cancer—he heard me say it on the phone. I didn't want to lie to him, so I told him. But I also told him that Pen doesn't know and that you will tell her.

Tess's heart began to beat out of her chest.

'Oh.' She whispered, trying to figure out her next step.

'I apologize. I had no idea Mateo was there, listening.' Javier looked as though he would be ill. He had betrayed her trust in discussing her condition with his son.

'Do you think he'll tell her?'

'No.' he said with certainty. 'He knows this is something you both need to do together. He wouldn't have wanted to hear about his Mother's illness from anyone but his parents.'

This complicated things. And it might change how and when Tess would tell Pen, although if she was honest with herself, she had been putting it off. Up ahead, her daughter skipped up the sidewalk like a child. Tess needed to figure out the right moment. She saw Mateo look back in their direction yet again.

'He's carrying my secret, and I need to talk to him about it.'

'I think that's a good idea.' Said Javier.

'Did you tell him about us?' She asked.

'No. It didn't come up, and I didn't think it was relevant to your illness.' Tess nodded—one less thing.

They toured the Cathedral and museum, and were having lunch when Pen spotted some amusement rides set up for a local fiesta.

'Can we go on some rides, Mom?' Pen asked with enthusiasm that hadn't diminished since morning.

'Sure.'

Soon, they found themselves in front of the roller coaster. Pen vibrated with excitement.

'Come on, Mateo. Let's ride it!'

The look on his face told a different story.

'I'll sit it out.' He told her.

Pen pouted.

'I can't believe you won't ride this with me.' She looked at her mom. 'I know you won't do it 'cause you're a fraidy cat.'

'That's me!' Tess said happily, volunteering to own the title.

Pen turned to Javier with a pleading look.

'OK.,' Putting his hands up in surrender. 'I'll go on this extremely unsafe pile of metal with you.'

He glanced at Tess and shrugged. She laughed. When they walked away to get in line, Tess took the opportunity to talk to Mateo.

'I understand your dad told you about my illness.'

Mateo didn't turn to look at her. He looked down at his shoes, kicking a rock unenthusiastically.

'Yes, he told me. You went to see my cousin, Amelia, yesterday. She is helping you with some issues you are having while walking. Medication for cancer.' The last word he whispered.

Tess took a deep breath.

'Yes, I have been having some issues, and your dad arranged for me to see Amelia. To make sure everything is OK so that I can finish.'

'Don't worry.' He said. 'I won't tell Pen.'

'I appreciate that.' Tess said quietly. 'Listen, I don't like asking you to keep this secret. I want to tell her. It's part of why I wanted us to take this trip together. But I also want to have all of those important talks on the list. If, for some reason, the treatment doesn't work when I get home, I might not have the time.'

Mateo listened, but when he looked up, he had tears in his eyes.

'She will be angry if she knows that I knew and didn't tell her. I would ask that you please talk to her soon, so the time between now and then is short. I can help her. I have received this news about my mother. It's terrible, and it will change her life forever.'

Tess's tears had started too.

'I understand. After our final two talks from my list, I have decided to tell Pen.'

'What are they?' He asked.

'*Money and Finance* is one. The other is *Marriage and Family*. The first one will be short. The second is more involved.'

He nodded thoughtfully.

'My father likes you very much. I haven't seen him with anyone since my mother died.' His expression broke her heart. 'Please don't hurt him.' Mateo whispered.

Tess had to stop herself from crying out; the pain of his words shot through her.

'I would hurt myself before I would hurt him.' She assured him.

Mateo kicked another rock with his toe, like a lost little boy, instead of the grown man he almost was.

Pen's shouts came at them as they saw her and Javier fly by. He looked terrified. Pen was in adrenalin heaven.

'Mateo. I think so highly of you. You've helped to transform my sullen, angry teenage daughter into this bubbly girl. And you handled the situation in Burgos with great maturity. I was very grateful and very proud of you. I told your dad I should buy you a gift for how you navigated it.'

Mateo smiled his lopsided smile.

'I like her very much. She is spontaneous, and she pushes ahead—always looking for adventure. And she is so beautiful. That makes it easier when she's cross. But she apologizes if she says something or does something she shouldn't. Not everyone is like that.'

Tess was thoughtful.

'Yes, she is all those things. She has a bright future ahead of her. And so do you. I understand you want to be a doctor like your father and both of your grandfathers.'

'Yes, I would. I always thought I wanted to be an oncologist. To perform research to help find a cure for cancer. But sometimes, I look at the quiet work my father does. It's not glamorous; he mainly works with families and older people. His specialty was geriatrics. He is patient with elderly people and helps ease their transition at the end of their lives. There is honor in that. I looked at my grandmother and aunties yesterday, and I know he will

be the one who will help care for them as they get older. I like knowing
that.' He sniffed, whipping his nose on his sleeve.

Tess looked at this boy who was becoming a man. It was a
remarkable speech; she could tell he meant every word.

'I'm sure you'll follow your heart, and your patients and their
families will be fortunate in whatever specialty you choose.'

Mateo smiled.

'I'm glad my dad has you on the Camino. He needed a friend.'

Tess smiled. 'I needed him too. I didn't know it, but I did.'

He nodded.

'I'm going to give you some time to have your talks with Pen so that
you can tell her about your sickness sooner. I'll think up a way to walk
with my father.'

Tess smiled.

'Thank you, Mateo. Do you mind if I hug you?' She asked him.

He nodded, and they embraced just as Javier and Pen walked down
the ramp from the roller coaster.

'WOW!! That was awesome! Were you two scared we were gonna
die?!' Pen laughed. 'You were hugging.'

'Oh, I was a little worried something would happen to you. Mateo
offered me a hug to calm my nerves.' Tess told her.

Pen looked at Mateo with skepticism but didn't push. She turned
to Javier laughing.

'Javier, you were so scared! You looked like you were gonna throw
up!'

'It was a distinct possibility, my dear.' He assured her.

Mateo put his arm around Pen, and they walked ahead.

Javier was green.

'I cannot believe you went on that thing.' Tess laughed. 'I hate roller
coasters. You would never catch me on one.'

'That was the first one I have ever been on, and now I know why.'

'Seriously?!' Amazed. 'Why did you do it?'

'You needed to speak with Mateo. More importantly, Mateo needed to speak with you. It was the only way to give you the space to have that conversation.' He told her.

'Oh, my God. You took one for the team going on that nightmare ride with Pen.'

'Yes, I did. And I expect later to be rewarded for my gallantry. *Taking one for the team,* as you say.'

Tess laughed until it hurt.

'You shall be rewarded handsomely, my gallant knight. Now, let's get you something to settle your stomach.'

They landed in a café for some tapas and ginger ale, and just as the drinks arrived, her phone rang. Tess saw John's name flash on the screen. Excusing herself, she left to stand outside the café.

'Hey,' She said.

'Hey, yourself. Have you heard from the doctor yet?' He was anxious about the results.

'Yes, I did, and she's been in touch with Marissa in Phoenix. They're adjusting my medication, and the pharmacy is sending them to the hotel.'

She failed to mention her call with Marissa that morning.

'Wow, good service. Did Javier have something to do with that?' John asked.

'He did. He called the pharmacy and made the arrangements.'

'Good. So, you don't have to navigate the language barrier.'

'No. I'm grateful for that.'

'You sound a lot better.'

'I feel a lot better.' She waited before saying. 'Listen, John, I've decided I'll have my final two talks with Pen, and then I will tell her about the cancer.'

He was silent.

'Did you hear me?' Tess asked.

'Yes, I did. It's the first time that you've used that word with me. Usually, you say 'illness' or something along those lines. You talk around it. This time, you just said the word.'

Tess knew there was truth in what he said.

'I did say it. Today I had a conversation with Mateo. He had no problem saying the word. So, I shouldn't either. I can't run from this.'

'That's wise.' He told her. 'Once you tell Pen, it will be real. And as much as I've encouraged you to tell her, I have dreaded that moment. Please tell me right after you do it so I know if she reaches out.'

'I will.'

Tess heard him exhale.

'It's going to be okay.' She reassured him.

'I know it is. Because we have each other, and that always makes everything okay.'

TWELVE

TO CRUZ DE FERRO

T he following morning, they left León in the dark, cresting a rise on the way out of town in time to see the sunrise. As usual, Pen spotted it first and called them to turn around. It was spectacular.

When Tess turned to continue walking, Pen was still standing there.

'Mateo said he has something he wants to talk to his dad about after spending time with the family. So, you're stuck with me today.' She told her mom.

'Oh.' Tess was a little surprised. 'Okay. It will be my pleasure to walk with my beautiful daughter.'

Pen rolled her eyes.

'You know it's not just me who thinks you are beautiful.' Tess teased.

'What did Mateo say to you yesterday when we were riding the roller coaster?'

'He said he admired your spirit and your spontaneity.' Tess smiled. 'Even when you're grouchy.'

Pen's cheeks turned red.

'I like him. He's kind. He doesn't try to act cool like the boys back home. He just *is* cool.'

'Yeah. Mateo's got a good head on his shoulders.' Tess agreed.

'I think Dad would approve of him as my boyfriend.' Pen smiled.

'Boyfriend? Well, alright.' Tess squeezed her arm. 'Anyway, I know your dad would approve.'

They walked in silence for a while.

'So, his sunt gave you a family rosary.'

'Yeah. I was surprised, and she patted my hair a couple of times and said some stuff I didn't understand in Spanish. Mateo seemed embarrassed.'

'They liked you.'

'They acted like we were going to get married or something. I mean, I like him, but I'm fifteen. I'm a long way from that.' But she still looked pleased.

'Yes. You need to finish college and establish what you want to do with your life. Marriage and family can come later. Please don't leave it too late, though. If you find the right person, don't be indecisive. No matter what anyone else tells you. Trust yourself.'

'Well, I'm not planning on it anytime soon.' Said Pen.

'Take your time.' Tess decided to push a little. 'As far as kids. Do you think you want to have kids?'

'Of course!' Pen looked at her like she had two heads.

'I mean, well, these days, you know you don't have to have kids.' Said Tess. 'You can have a full life if you decide not to.'

Pen scowled. 'Are you sorry you had kids?'

'No. Not a day goes by that I'm not grateful I had you two. You guys are the best thing I've ever done. I regret the times that I wasn't there when you were growing up. I watched a lot of videos on my phone in taxis and on my laptop in hotel rooms. Your dad was a good recorder of your events. But I've never regretted having you and watching you grow up to be who you are. Sometimes, it feels like it went by so fast. I look in the mirror and am not sure who that person is anymore. Whose daughter is taller than she is.'

'Hmm.' Said Pen.

'Well, let's face it—parenting isn't easy. Your kids don't come with a handbook or map to tell you how to do it perfectly. And each child is different. You couldn't be more different than Charlie. That wouldn't have worked if we parented you the same way we did with him. So, you adjust to the personality each child is born with.'

'And then there are the mistakes you make with each one. Being too hard on one of them and too easy on another. Signing them up for stuff they don't like or not signing them up for something they love. Feeling their disappointment and knowing you screwed up not nurturing their passions.'

Pen glanced sideways at her mom but kept walking. Tess had never been so vulnerable about parenting, acknowledging that she didn't have all the answers. Her parents seemed like they were the experts on everything. But they were human.

'Well, I do want to have kids. Marriage sort of scares me, though.' Pen admitted.

'Why?'

'I don't know. Is it realistic that two people get married and stay together, committed to being exclusive for a hundred years?'

Tess laughed.

'I can't imagine that anyone has ever been married for a hundred years, except maybe in the Bible. But I know what you mean. Half of your friend's parents are divorced. But I think it's about what expectations you have going in. So many people think they're going to change the other person. Or save them from something. But we can't only save ourselves. And if you think someone will change their essential nature after you marry them, you're kidding yourself. That's a recipe for divorce.'

'But I think a happy marriage is possible if you're honest with yourself and with each other. And you ask for what you need. Your crazy aligns with their crazy. The other person has similar quirks and foibles. It's not about how gorgeous they are at the beginning. Because that helps with the attraction and lust side of things but looks fade. The model gets middle-aged with wrinkles. All boobs sag eventually.'

Pen grimaced. 'Yuck.'

'Yeah, it's not pretty.' Tess smiled. 'But then you have shared experiences. Common goals of, maybe raising kids, and loving things about the other person that has nothing to do with how they look.' Tess told her.

Pen thought about what she was saying for a moment.

'What do you love about Dad?' she asked her mom.

'I was always attracted to how smart he is—how he solves problems. He understands my work and gives me good advice. But only when I ask for it. He has a great sense of humor and makes me laugh every day. Your dad and I have learned how to fight the right way. To disagree but still respect each other. He's a rock. I lean on him a lot, and I don't know what my life would be like without him.' She stopped and turned to Pen. 'Your father is truly one of the most remarkable, kindest people on this planet. And I am very, very lucky to have found him.'

Pen studied her mom's face, how much she meant what she was saying, and the tears in her eyes. Suddenly, Pen had the urge to hug her, and she let herself. Tess talked into her daughter's hair.

'That's what I wish for you, whether you choose to get married to that person or just live with them for however long. I hope you find someone to walk through life with that supports who you are. You said you aren't sure if it's realistic. Maybe I got struck by lightning, but I don't think so. It's just a matter of knowing yourself and what you want, then meeting the right person at the right time with an open heart.' She pulled back. 'Above all, never do something you don't want to do to please the other person. That won't turn out well in the long run.'

Pen nodded. She figured this might be one of the talks on her mother's list.

They walked the rest of the day together and met up with Javier and Mateo in the village where they stayed that night. Tess had done an excellent job of following doctors orders. Despite what both doctors said, she was feeling better than before León and was hopeful she could finish. But only if she played it smart.

A few days later, they set out for Rabanal, the last village before Cruz de Ferro, one of the icons of the Camino, and its highest point capped by a cross that dates back centuries. Tess looked forward to placing the rock she had brought from home and asking for the list of miracles she had amassed.

She knew she needed every one of them. The biggest being infinite strength to face what was ahead.

The following day, they made the trek up the mountain in the dark. It was foggy, which lent a mystical air, with the swirling clouds around the huge mound of rocks that held the cross rising a hundred feet overhead, each stone left by a pilgrim who'd made the trek before, including pictures, letters, and prayer cards—pleas for help, healing, or peace. Tess knew she needed all three for herself and her family. Climbing the mound and silently saying the words and prayers she'd said in her head along the way, she placed her rock and the paper under it. Tess turned to see Pen watching her with a curious look on her face. But her daughter said nothing, as Tess clasped her hand when she reached Pen's side.

Javier and Mateo laid down rocks they had brought from home, said silent prayers, then hugged each other. The scene brought tears to Tess's eyes, seeing how bound together they were by their grief.

By late afternoon the group had made it to the stone bridge over the *Rio Maruelo* leading to the picturesque town of Molinaseca. The buildings looked like they belonged more in the Alps than Spain, with black slate roofs rather than red tiles.

The following day, they picked up the pace, arriving by late morning at the village of Cacabelos where they would be staying. Walking through the old town over a high stone bridge and then down by the river, they discovered the families of the entire village picnicking and swimming in the ice-cold water on a sunny Sunday. Mateo and Pen hurried to get into their swim suits while Javier and Tess dangled their feet in the river to cool off. Teenagers from the village were jumping off the old bridge into the water, and soon Tess looked up just as Mateo leaped.

'Oh!' It slipped out of her mouth involuntarily. 'I saw no signs warning kids not to jump when we crossed the bridge. In the US, there would be railings and a ranger telling them how dangerous it is.'

Javier chuckled.

'People have probably been jumping off that bridge for a thousand years. Certainly, every parent watching today has done it. So, they probably figure if they survived it, their kids will too.'

Tess looked at him, surprised.

'You seem unconcerned about Mateo jumping into the river from that height.'

'I have learned that boys need some form of danger, or their spirit withers. This is a relatively safe danger.' Javier told her.

'Jumping off a bridge is a 'relatively safe danger'?' Do those words even go together?' She asked, her heart beating faster.

Javier turned to her.

'Yes. Mateo is not diving in the water from that height. All the kids are just jumping. The worst that might happen is they land on each other and perhaps break a bone. A broken bone is part of life. I would never encourage Mateo to avoid something when the worst outcome is a broken bone.' He said.

This perspective was foreign to how people raised their children in the US. But Tess conceded the point.

'You're right. I would never have allowed my kids to jump off a bridge. No hurt was acceptable to me.' She admitted. 'Perhaps, it's why it's so hard for me to talk to Pen about my illness. I'm protecting her from pain when I know it's inevitable.'

Javier saw the emotion near the surface and told her not to be so hard on herself.

'How Americans raise their children is different than we do it here.' He reassured her.

Tess knew he was trying to cut her some slack. She leaned back on her elbows from her spot on the riverbank and looked at the cloudless blue sky—closing her eyes, feeling the sun on her face; a perfect moment until she heard a scream and looked up in time to see Pen plunge into the river from the bridge above. Her instinct had her on her feet in seconds, searching the water. When Pen's head emerged, Tess was knee-deep in water at the river's edge.

'Pen!' She shouted as her daughter swam towards her. 'What do you think you're doing? You could have been killed!'

Pen climbed out.

'I just did what Mateo did. It's no big deal.' She said, angry that her mom was embarrassing her in front of the whole town.

Tess's heart beat out of her chest, and she hugged Pen's wet body like a life preserver.

'Why are you freaking out?' Pen frowned.

Tess gulped for air.

'I can't lose you.' Tess whispered. 'I can't lose another child.'

Pen pulled back and frowned at her face, angry.

'Look at me, mom. Really look at me. I'm. Not. Charlie.'

Then her face softened as Tess broke down, and she hugged her mom with the same ferocity.

'Don't worry so much. It's gonna be OK.'

Tess cried into her daughter's shoulder before gathering herself. Finally, letting go as Pen walked back into deeper the water. Returning to where Javier was sitting, he looked concerned, squeezing her hand. He had heard the exchange on the riverbank.

'Are you alright?' he asked her. 'I heard you say something about Charlie. What did you mean, 'I can't lose another child.?' John had already told him, but he wanted Tess to know she could talk to him if needed.

Tess covered her face with her hands.

'My son is dead.' She sobbed, looking up at him. 'He's not in college. He's not lighting the world on fire like I know he would have. He died in a car accident on the night of his high school graduation. Four years ago, today, my son was alive. We were waking up at this time back home. Pen and I were hung blue and silver decorations for his big day. Celebrating him. Twenty-four hours later, he would be gone and never come back.'

Javier watched her and the anguish inside her spilling out. He wrapped her in his arms as she cried, looking over her shoulder at the river where Mateo and Pen were swimming. Pen looked back at them but didn't return to the shore. She turned and swam further out into deep water, leaving Tess behind.

Thirteen

The Final Ascent

T he following day they made their way to Las Herrerías, the village at the base of O Cebreiro, the last mountain on the Camino. It's a small stone village nestled in the forest by a river, whose residents embraced all the good vibes of the Camino. Signs festooning the path encouraged peace, love, and hope. Various stations invited pilgrims to write prayers or messages, then attach them to tree branches so they could blow in the wind like Tibetan prayer flags.

Their host for the night was a green and blue kaftan-clad Swiss woman called Marie, who had walked the Camino many years before and returned to give back to the Way. She was perhaps one of the calmest people Tess had ever met, coming forward unbidden, silently carrying Tess's pack to a bunk before checking them in. A courtesy not extended to them before. After finishing up with the administrivia, Marie invited Tess to sit on the shaded deck to enjoy a cup of herbal tea.

They sat in silence, listening to the birds sing, and the wind rustle through the leaves of the trees before her host spoke.

'So, you are ill.,' said Marie.

'Excuse me?' asked Tess.

'You are seriously ill.' The woman stated. 'But you know this already.'

Tess wanted to rise and flee.

'How do you know?' Tess asked her incredulously.

'I don't know. I just do. I would like to offer you a healing. If you are uncomfortable, you won't offend me if you don't accept it.'

Tess had never encountered anyone like this woman with a halo of grey curls and wasn't sure how to react. It was odd that this stranger knew she was sick just by looking at her.

'OK.,' Said Tess quietly, 'Yes. I can use all the help I can get. But can you explain to me what you do?'

A smile broke out across Marie's pale, wrinkled face.

'I studied with some people back in Switzerland who are also healers. Somehow, I know when people are ill. They understood my gift and helped me to refine it.'

'So, you can heal someone with cancer?'

'I don't know what you have. I only know you are ill and struggling. I am not a doctor, and I don't diagnose ailments. I try to heal the illnesses I sense—the root cause is obscured from me.'

'How would you go about healing me?' Asked Tess.

'I prefer to do what I do in the forest, amongst nature. Nature is powerful, and I like to use it to help others. I won't have to touch you except your hands and head at certain points.'

Tess had nothing to lose, so she agreed. They got up and walked through the albergue and out the front, continuing up a path through the tall trees, stopping when they came to a clearing.

'You can sit or stand. But it would be best to close your eyes and hold your hands in front of you with your palms up.'

Tess chose to sit on the ground. She had been walking all day and didn't trust herself to stay upright if she closed her eyes.

The woman got behind her, and after a few moments, Tess could feel her back becoming warm. Then the Swiss *hospitaliero* got up, came to the front, and sat down, holding her hands and saying incomprehensible words to Tess. Then she took Tess's hands and put them on her heart, one on top of the other. Marie kept her hands over Tess's and closed her eyes. Again, she felt her heart and chest warm up.

Finally, she briefly placed her hand on Tess's head, then declared that Tess could open her eyes.

'How do you feel?' Marie asked her.

'I don't know. I could feel warmth a few times.'

'Yes, it often generates heat. For the rest of the day, you should be gentle with yourself. And drink a lot of water. I'll make you more tea.' Marie appeared tired as she smoothed her flowing printed dress, then offered her hand to help Tess to her feet.

'Is that it?' Tess asked. 'Does it work with only one treatment?'

'I only know the results once a person reports back. I have worked with people that live nearby. But, for you? I don't know. I hope I have helped you, if only to give you some temporary peace. I think you felt some of what I do and the energy that comes through me. But I am not the keeper of that energy, just a facilitator to someone who needs it.'

Marie hesitated before continuing.

'When I come in contact with illness, it's as if it speaks to me. It seems to know what I'm there for and naturally, it resists what I'm trying to do. What you have is very dark and very strong. It fights to the death, like an angry bear thrashing and slashing. It swiped at me and roared, but it did not yield. I fear it is growing stronger. Feeding off something I could not see.'

Marie studied Tess.

'But you knew this already. About how strong this is.' She stated, tilting her head to one side. 'Curious.'

Tess choked on her words before she was able to find her voice.

'Yes. The type of cancer I have is severe. Even my husband doesn't know how serious. I asked my doctor to keep that to herself when giving us the treatment options. It's very aggressive.' She admitted. 'Much like the bear you saw.'

Marie reached out and squeezed Tess's arm.

'And yet you are here, nonetheless. On pilgrimage with your daughter. Are you hoping for a miracle?'

Tess wiped her tears. 'Not for myself. But for her. I just need to outrun the bear for a little bit longer.' She whispered as Marie reached out and hugged her.

The two women walked back to the albergue arm in arm. As instructed, Tess went out to the deck to wait for more tea. Javier sat at a table, drinking a beer he had purchased from the nearby bar.

'There you are. I was wondering where you went off to.' He said, smiling.

Marie joined them and offered Javier tea, as well. He raised his beer but thanked her.

'Drink the tea, and you'll sleep like a baby tonight.' She told Tess. 'It's a long climb up to O Cebreiro. You'll need a good rest to make it to the top.'

'I've heard. I'm a little nervous about it.' Tess told her.

'There is another option, you know.' Marie smiled. 'A local man, he makes the trip up the mountain a few times a day with pilgrims on horseback. I could reach out to him and ask if he has horses available. He will take good care of you.'

Tess smiled. 'My daughter would love that. She loves horses.' Said Tess.

'I can see she is a spirited girl. Teenagers can be challenging but possess more understanding, for which their parents often do not give them credit. She can be a help to you if you trust her. Much like you are doing for her.' She said.

Shivers ran up Tess's spine. She saw the shadow cross Javier's face and quickly looked away, yawning and stretching.

'I think we should get something to eat before this tea does its job and I'm asleep.' Turning to Marie. 'Thank you for your help today. And your advice.'

Marie held up her cup and bowed her head humbly.

'I will call Hugo and arrange the horses. Remember to drink a lot of water.'

When they got out to the front of the albergue, Javier stopped her, 'What was that all about?'

Tess filled him in on what had transpired—most of it.

'You think she can help you?'

Tess shook her head.

'I don't know, but I felt something when she did it. It wasn't just a feeling brought on by suggestion. I felt it—heat in my back and my chest.' She told him.

'Hmmm. Did she charge you for this healing?' He asked, concerned.

'No. Marie just wanted to do it and then made me tea after. You heard what she said about Pen. It's like she knows things. Marie is mystified by how she knows, but she knows.'

He was skeptical.

'I'm not going to say there aren't things outside modern medicine that sometimes work. Miracles, most people call them. It sounds like gypsy stuff. But she didn't ask for money or anything else?'

'No.'

'Interesting.' He said.

'You seem skeptical.'

'Of course I am, being a doctor, the bit about Pen was curious. Did you tell her you hadn't told Pen?'

'No.' said Tess. 'We didn't talk about Pen at all.'

The following morning, they had to be at the stable by 8:30, so they lingered over coffee. Tess had more cups than usual, and it made her jittery. She had heard that horses could sense nerves or fear in their riders. Tess wasn't exactly afraid, but the coffee heightened her lack of confidence on horseback. It turned out her worries were unfounded. The guide was experienced, and the horses were too.

Tess watched Pen nuzzle her horse's muzzle and wrap her arms around its neck. She loved animals, and Tess was sure that if she were allowed to ride this horse the rest of the way to Santiago, Pen would gladly do it.

They were given some brief instructions, mounted up, and were off. Javier seemed to know his way around a horse, and it was clear Mateo had been on horseback more than once in his life. Perhaps they learned to ride on the family farm.

The climb through the mountains was daunting, and several pilgrims had to jump out of the way of the horses as they ascended on foot. The villages along the way were small, but the people were friendly, and they waved as the group passed. Further up, they broke out of the trees to a spectacular view down through the valley. But the horses just kept going, and the ride was smooth. As they crossed into the region of Galicia, looking more like Ireland than her previous experience of Spain, the sun came out to greet them.

The horses reached the top, and they dismounted, leaving their four-legged friends to head back down to pick up more pilgrims for the afternoon session. They were just days from Sarria, marking the final week until they reached Santiago.

Javier explained.

'Two more days and the path will become crowded. Many people start their Camino in Sarria. To receive the Compostela, a pilgrim is required to walk 100km. Sarria is nearly that distance from Santiago, so it makes sense that they would start there. We will begin to see buses full of students and many more groups on the way. The albergues will become crowded, so we must get to where we plan to stay early in the day to ensure we have a bed.'

Seeing so many new people starting after so long would be strange. Thus far, they had seen the familiar faces of those who had started simultaneously in St. Jean or Pamplona. And while they were in good shape from walking, the new pilgrims would be on fresh legs.

Fourteen

Sarria to Santiago

When they reached Sarria, they saw student groups piling into hotels out of vans and buses. The mood on the Camino had changed. More subdued. Peregrinos on the road for weeks knew the journey was rapidly coming to an end. Their friendships would also change as they arrived in Santiago, and they eventually made their way back to their home countries. Tess was feeling melancholy about this prospect herself when Javier's phone buzzed. She watched him step aside to take the call.

'That was one of the aunties from back in León. Her son lives in Portomarín. One of his children fell out of a tree, and they would like me to look at him. I will grab a taxi and go there to check on the boy. I advised them to take him directly to a local doctor, but they insist on me seeing him first.' Javier turned to Tess. 'Would you like to come with me?' He asked.

Tess looked at the town and back at Pen.

'No, I think I will stay here with the kids. You go ahead. Let me know how it goes.'

'OK.' He said, a little disappointed. 'I have a feeling that it will involve dinner, and if I'm honest with myself, the family will want me to stay the night. So, I will most probably see you in Portomarín tomorrow, as that is where we would be walking to anyway.'

'Ok.' She smiled. 'The three of us will be fine.'

Suddenly, he looked sad.

'I'm sorry about this.' He told her.

'No. Don't be. I am a capable person, and I'll survive without you. Go.'

Javier waved as the taxi pulled away. Tess turned to the kids.

'Shall we find the place to lay our weary heads tonight?' She offered.

Once checked in and cleaned up, they grabbed dinner.

'It's weird without Javier.' Said Pen over a pizza. 'I'm so used to having him around; it's like he's a second dad.'

Mateo looked at Tess.

'Yes. Well, we will see your *first* dad in a couple of weeks. We are just one week from finishing the Camino.' She told her daughter.

Pen looked stricken.

'One week? That's all?'

'Yup. One week. Then we must decide what we're doing for the last stretch before we go home.'

Pen was silent for a moment.

'Have you reconsidered the offer of visiting Mateo and Javier in Madrid?' She asked her mom.

Tess hadn't given it much thought, but maybe she should. She saw Pen brighten with hope, turning to Mateo, smiling. Tess held up her hand.

'Let me talk to your dad about it first. I want his input.'

'Okay.' She began furiously typing on her phone. 'I'll text him too.'

Tess smiled and didn't try to stop her.

In the morning, they set out for Portomarín, walking through cornfields outside Sarria and listening to train whistles. Then through rolling hills and forests. As Javier promised, the path was much more crowded as large groups of high school students got off buses and out of vans that ferried their packs. Pen was incensed.

'It's not fair that we walked all the way from France, crossing actual mountains, and they get the same Compostela as we do.' She grumbled. 'It's like they're cheating.'

'In Spain, many high schools bring kids from across the country to walk the final stages of the Camino.' Mateo patiently explained. 'It's a rite of passage. But it's not cheating. It's just different.' He looked over at Tess for help.

She jumped in. 'Do you remember that first night in Saint Jean? The French guy who ran the albergue gave us his Pilgrim speech? He said, 'Everyone walks their own Way.' We've walked our way, and for these kids, this may be the only opportunity they will ever have. You know you've walked the entire thing. No one else has to know it. These kids will get a Compostela, and they know they didn't walk from France. But it doesn't matter. It's their Camino.'

Pen was still furious. 'Well, see if they beat me to the next town.' And she plowed ahead.

Mateo looked sheepish.

'Go after her.' Tess told him. 'So she doesn't get herself into trouble. I'm fine walking on my own.' Looking over at the pack of kids next to her. 'Or should I say, with this crowd.'

Tess found the relative solitude a nice change. Pen and Mateo marched ahead, and the high school kids were much faster than she was. It was the first time she had walked alone since the early days of the Camino from Saint Jean.

She was going at her own pace when, suddenly, she felt one of her boot laces hook the grommet of the other boot, and she couldn't catch herself with her poles—landing on her left knee, palms down on the gravel path, pain shot through her. She lay on her side, clutching her knee, trying to catch her breath.

After a few moments, Tess was able to sit up. Unbuckling her pack, the lack of pressure made things a bit better. She examined her knee and hands. They were full of gravel and bleeding steadily. She picked out as many rocks as she could before struggling to a large rock on the side of the path and pulling herself up to sit. The change in position made her knee bleed more, and it was harder to pick out the remaining gravel embedded in the flesh. She was doing the best she could when she heard a voice.

'Are you OK?' in very American English.

Tess's head whipped around at the sound of home, tearing up from frustration.

'I fell. I tripped on my shoelaces.' She said, feeling ridiculous. 'And now I'm sitting here picking gravel out of my knee.'

'Here. Let me help you.'

The strapping young man had his pack off in record time, his first aid kit was out, and he was cleaning her wounds, then dressing them. Tess just sat there, as he seemed like an ex-boy scout and knew what he was doing.

'Such a stupid thing.' She was so frustrated with herself.

'Are you walking the Camino alone?' he asked.

'No. My daughter is with me, and we met some new friends. She's up ahead.'

'Hmm, I see.' He didn't say any more.

Tess tried to explain.

'She's fifteen and very impatient with the pace I walk. So, I told her to go on ahead with a friend.'

The young man stood and surveyed his work.

'I think I got all the gravel out. And the bleeding is slowed down. Can you stand on it?'

Tess got off the rock with his help and put weight on her leg. The area where she fell stung slightly, but it didn't feel like her knee was damaged internally. Thank God. She couldn't imagine getting this far and quitting because she forgot to tuck in her laces. It seemed both she and Pen needed to remember the advice they had received on the first day.

'I think I'm alright, actually.' Said Tess, a little surprised. 'The knee itself doesn't hurt. Just the cut. I think I can still walk today if I put my poles in my pack since my palms are pretty cut up.'

The boy nodded. 'I'm Jake, by the way. I'd shake your hand, but I think it would hurt.'

'Tess,' she offered, smiling. 'I can't thank you enough for your help.'

'No Prob. Happy to do it.' Jake folded her poles and attached them to her pack. Then he helped her put it on.

'Could I walk with you for a while to make sure my knee holds out?' She asked him.

'Of course. Happy to have the company. I've been alone, mostly, for the last couple of days.'

'Where are you from?' She asked.

'I just graduated from the University of Iowa. Walking the Camino is the last thing I'll do before I take a job in New York. I'll work for a charity in the Bronx. Eventually, I'd like to get my master's in public policy.'

Tess was impressed.

'Wow! That is ambitious. If only I were as together at your age. Goodness. You've got it all figured out.'

Jake laughed.

'I don't think so. I know I want to help people. I figure the rest will sort itself out.'

'Well, that's half the battle. Knowing what you want. The rest is easy if you have a clear vision.' She smiled.

'I do have that.' He laughed.

'Then you're unstoppable.' Tess assured him.

Jake blushed.

'So, you came out to do a post-bachelors-degree Camino.' She said, impressed.

'Yeah. I don't know. I saw that movie, and I just had to do it. My family isn't pleased about it.' He admitted.

'They're probably worried something will happen to you.'

'Yeah—my mom is.' He said.

'Well, you're almost done.' Realizing it was true for them both.

Jake nodded thoughtfully. 'Then, real-life starts.'

'Oh, someone forgot to tell you. Real life started a long time ago. It's just a different stage, but it's all real life.'

'Yeah. But no more summer breaks. No more Christmas breaks. No more taking two months off to walk around Europe.' He admitted.

'Well, you can bake that stuff in if it's important. You can have the life you want, no matter what anyone tells you.' She said quietly. 'Just have the courage to have it.'

Jake looked over at her. 'You don't sound like my mom.'

Tess laughed. 'I don't sound like *my* mom, either.'

They walked in silence for a bit.

'So, what's been on your playlist for the Camino?' he asked.

'I haven't had much alone time, so I don't have a Camino playlist.' Tess told him. 'What about you?'

'Oh. I've listened to tons of music out here.' He hesitated. 'OK. I'll ask you what I've asked everyone else I've met. What three songs would you want them to play at your funeral?'

Tess's heart dropped into her stomach. 'What?'

'If you had to pick three songs they would play at your funeral, what would they be?'

Tess gulped. 'I don't like funerals.' She whispered.

Jake missed the tension in her voice.

'OK, I'll go first. At mine, I'd want Eminem *I'm Not Afraid*. Bruno Mars *Locked out of Heaven*. And the last one would be Kanye West *Stronger*. '

Jake asked her why she looked so surprised.

'It's just that I didn't expect a lot of rap from a kid from Iowa. Nothing wrong with it, but I guess I figured Katy Perry or Taylor Swift would be in the mix.'

Jake laughed.

'I just went to school in Iowa. I'm originally from Queens, Long Island. So that's where my music appreciation comes from.'

With the ice broken, she decided to play along.

'Well. My musical choices are a little different. I would have them play *Hotel California* by the Eagles. Paolo Conte *Via Con Me*. It's the song I listen to at take-off whenever I fly. I find it comforting. And finally, *I Believe* by Andre Bocelli.'

'Hmm. Interesting list. Not something I'd expect from a mom from America.' He teased.

Tess laughed. 'Touché'

He smiled.

'Can I have one more?' she asked, suddenly enthusiastic about the game they were playing.

'Of course—it's your funeral.'

Tess took a deep breath. 'Alright. I would want Pink *Let's Get This Party Started.*'

'That's a good one.' He agreed. 'Good for an Irish wake if that's what you're into.'

She laughed. 'I hear you there. Oh! I'd also want Diamond Rio's *One More Day With You.*'

'Listen to you.' Jake laughed. 'It would be the longest funeral in history. I've created a monster.'

They walked for the rest of the day, discussing the universe and the best flavors of ice cream. Then the best live concerts they'd seen and the best concert venues.

Less than a kilometer before the hillside village of Portomarín, the conversation turned back to his family and how happy his mother would be to see him safely home.

'I bet.' Tess said. 'Mothers worry. But she must be so proud of you.'

Jake smiled shyly at the compliment.

'She visited me once at school. I'd lost a bunch of weight, and she was so worried. She wanted me to quit and come home so she could take care of me.'

'But you didn't.' Tess applauded his commitment. 'You stuck it out and finished.'

'Yeah, I did. I guess my mom has every right to be worried all the time. I had leukemia when I was little. I almost died, but a bone marrow transplant saved me. She still struggles sometimes, letting me go.'

Tess stopped in her tracks and looked up at the big healthy young man who stood before her. Full of optimism and a bright future. But with Jake, she saw something more. They'd spent the day in a non-stop conversation, free-associating on every topic, like hitting a ping pong ball between them. Yet it was only the last bit when he chose to share that he was a cancer survivor. He had so many other amazing things going on in his life: opportunities that would take him from the Camino to new exciting experiences. He didn't limit himself by the experience of having leukemia as a small child. Jake defined himself in the present. Tess was amazed at this young man.

They walked into Portomarín, where Tess saw Mateo, Pen, and Javier waiting at the steps on the other side of the long bridge.

'Are you staying here?' she asked him, hoping to continue the conversation and introduce him to the group.

'No.' he said. 'I'm looking to get in 10k more today. If I can get to Santiago sooner, I'll have more time to explore before I go home.'

'Ah.' They walked across the bridge. 'Then I don't think we'll see each other again.' Tess whispered sadly.

'No, I don't think we will.'

They stopped on the other side of the bridge. Jake was heading left down the hill as she would cross the street and meet up with the others.

As Tess hugged Jake goodbye, her son's face flashed into her mind. 'Goodbye, Charlie.' She whispered without thinking before she pulled away and smiled up at him. 'Thank you for being my guardian angel.'

'No Prob. That's what I'm here for.' Blushing, he turned and walked down the hill toward the river. 'Buen Camino, Tess.' Jake shouted before rounding the corner out of sight.

Tess waved with a lump in her throat before crossing the street to the shouts of the kids.

'Who was that?' Pen asked.

'I'm not exactly sure.' said Tess.

'Huh?' Her daughter frowned.

'When you guys went ahead, I had a fall. Jake bandaged me up and walked with me here.'

Javier looked down at her hands and bandaged knee.

'I knew I should have taken a taxi back to Sarria last night.' He said, concerned.

'No. It ended up being a great day!' She told them cheerfully. 'One of the best. He's a nice American boy from Long Island. We had a lot to talk about it.'

The three people standing before her looked amazed.

'Come on.' Tess said. 'Let's get checked into the albergue. I'm starving.' And she ran up the stairs leaving them to follow.

Portomarín is a town perched on the steep banks of the *Rio Mino*. Tess was surprised at how big the river was—more like something you would see in the American West or British Columbia, Canada. Tess got cleaned up, and they took a walk in town after dinner.

Mateo asked about his little cousin.

'He will be fine. We had to take him to the hospital in Lugo. He broke his arm and needed a cast. It was only a small fracture, so nothing to worry about.' Javier looked at Tess's knee. 'I still wish I had returned to Sarria and walked with you today. Is it painful or stiff?'

'Not really. Honestly, I'm fine.' She assured him.

'I would like to inspect it and ensure it's completely cleaned. Some small stones might be in there, and it would not be good if an infection set in. You should ice it tonight.' He advised.

Tess smiled. 'OK, doctor I will let you treat my battle wounds and bandage me up again.'

On the street, they encountered a full marching band playing a rendition of rock anthems from Queen's *We Will Rock You,* and *We Are the Champions*—even *Tequila* by the Tijuana Brass. People danced in the streets, and groups of pilgrims gathered in the main town square before the church to line dance.

Pen appeared surprised when Tess joined them, linking arms with strangers and kicking her feet to the beat of the music. Javier laughed and took videos with his phone as Mateo grabbed Pen's hand and pulled her into the fray. Tess was happy to see her daughter finally letting loose, jumping around with the rest of the teenagers, as Tess linked arms with a guy in dreadlocks, with feathers in his hair, wearing sultan pants and sandals.

She eventually tired and returned to Javier to watch. Pen and Mateo staggered towards them, out of breath.

'I saw you dancing with that guy in the funny pants.' She said to her Mom.

'Yeah. I love those pants.' Tess laughed. 'I think I need a pair.'

Mateo offered up an immediate solution. 'I saw them in the grocery store on the way up the hill, hanging from the ceiling.'

'Well, what are we doing standing here?' Tess told them, and with that, she led the march back across the square. They arrived at the store and discovered Mateo was right. Many versions of the sultan pants in bright colors and patterns hung from the ceiling. Tess had a hard time making up her mind. She asked the owner to bring down a striped one and a blue pair.

'Thoughts from the peanut gallery?' She asked the assembly, holding them up.

Javier leaned over to Pen. 'Peanut gallery?'

'I think it references a crowd of monkeys at a circus. But essentially, my mom wants to know our opinion.' Then Pen turned to Tess. 'Neither.'

'Ah. Well, this monkey likes the blue one.' Javier chimed in.

'Yeah,' said Mateo. 'It will go with more stuff.'

Pen rolled her eyes.

'Sold!' proclaimed Tess, holding up the blue pair and handing over the twenty euros. 'I think I'll wear these tomorrow. Breezy and comfortable.'

'Then you'll be walking alone.' Said her daughter scornfully. 'Are you going to start wearing Patchouli oil instead of Chanel?'

Tess frowned.

'Tsk Tsk, so extreme. No, I'm not going that far. I just liked that guy's pants, and now I'm the proud owner of my own pair.' Pleased with herself.

Javier chuckled at her childlike enthusiasm.

'I will proudly walk with you in your grocery store pants.' He reassured her.

Tess turned to Pen. 'See. I won't be walking alone, and *he* likes my pants.'

Pen left the store with Mateo trailing. Tess thanked the owner, and they made their way down the hill. She could feel Javier's eyes on her.

'Something is different about you today. I go away for one day, and it seems you are changed.'

'They say, 'What a difference a day makes.' She teased him.

'I don't know this saying, but you seem more mercurial.' He smiled. Tess considered it.

'Maybe you're right. Today, I had to walk alone, and then I fell. When I thought I might be seriously injured, I found I wasn't. I would be alright. Even if Jake hadn't come along, I would have been fine. But he did come along, and we spent the day walking and talking about everything. He didn't talk to me like I was an old person or sick. We just talked. He even asked me what three songs I would want them to play at my funeral.'

A shadow crossed Javier's face.

'Yeah, I know.' Tess agreed. 'I was a little freaked out. But apparently, it's something Jake asked everyone he's met on the Camino. He told me he'd been surprised at the breadth of music people like.'

Javier seemed to relax at that, but he didn't ask her the songs, as if it would tempt fate.

'We talked about the cosmos. Jake was so in the present. So optimistic. It was refreshing. In the end, when we walked across the bridge into town, he told me he had leukemia as a child. It's why his mom worried about him walking the Camino alone.'

Javier was silent. He'd been cursed by cancer himself. He knew how it changed the bravest person into the most fearful.

'Jake wasn't defined by cancer. It was the last thing he told me, not the first. I connected with him because I don't want to be defined by it either. I refuse to allow my life to be bookended by this.' Tears began to run down her cheeks. 'I am me, not that!'

Javier cupped her face with his hands.

'No, you are you. Not that.' Smiling into her eyes for a moment before chuckling. 'Just you, with your grocery store pants.'

Tess laughed and wiped her face.

'Ah-ha! I knew it. You are jealous of my pants.' She told him, 'You know you want a pair.'.

'Uh, no, thank you. This unique fashion experience is all yours.'

Tess hugged the bag to her chest as they made their way down the hill and to the albergue. Even with her earlier injuries, she began to skip.

They walked to Palas de Rei the following morning—only four days from Santiago. The trail was a host of ups and downs, and by the time they reached the albergue, they were tired. Each place they had stayed on the Camino was different. Some were ancient, with black timbers supporting the ceiling, converted from their original purpose. Others were new, shiny, and clean. The albergue in Palas de Rei was a new one, and they were pleasantly surprised that they each had their own pod-like bed with a curtain for privacy. It wasn't as luxurious as a private room, but it was the next best thing on the Camino. After dinner, they took a walk around the town. More students were on the streets, and when they returned to their albergue, they found it full of a busload of them. It would be a noisy night. Before heading inside to chaos, Tess called John.

'Hey, you!' He sounded happy to hear her voice. 'I've received reports from Pen. She said you bought some weird pants in a grocery store and insisted on wearing them publicly. She's embarrassed beyond belief.'

Tess laughed. 'Guilty as charged.'

'Picture?'

Tess took a selfie and sent it to John.

'Wow. Those are interesting. Pen was right. They certainly are outside of your normal fashion choices.'

'Maybe I'm changing.' Said Tess. 'More open. Or I just don't care about what anyone thinks of me anymore.'

'I would say it's true after everything that's happened.' He agreed. 'You are more open. I hope you don't change so much that you don't come home. Back to your old life. Back to me.'

Suddenly, the joking was over.

'Of course, I'm coming home. We have a couple of weeks until we land.' Tess reminded him.

'That's all I wanted to hear.' Said John.

Tess closed her eyes, silent.

'Pen also said you are considering visiting Madrid with Javier and Mateo.' He said.

'Well, they asked us, but I told her I would consider it. I wanted to talk to you first. Get your thoughts.'

'If you want to go, go. I don't see a difference between walking the Camino and going to hang out with them in Madrid.' He sounded resigned.

'Hmm.' She said. 'I sort of did make a distinction. But I think you're right. We are coming home not long after we finish. Where we go until then isn't that relevant. Pen likes Mateo, and he wants to show her his hometown. Do you remember how she talked about doing a year abroad? Javier said they would happily host her if she decided that Spain was where she wanted to do it.'

'Interesting.' John said thoughtfully. 'I'm not sure if that would be weird for me, but we have more than a year to decide.'

'Yes, we do.' She said quietly.

'I'm so glad that you're almost at the end. Are you feeling alright?' He asked, concerned.

Tess didn't say anything about falling, but she did tell him about walking with Jake. About their conversation, favorite funeral music, and his leukemia. Like Javier, John didn't ask her to list the music for him, either.

'I think it is great you had an opportunity to walk with someone new. Have a fresh experience. Have you gotten through your list of conversations with Pen?' He asked to remind her of her ultimate goal.

'Almost. Then I'll find the right moment to talk to Pen about everything else.' Said Tess.

'OK. Well, you sound good. Keep me posted, and keep wearing those pants. They're crazy.'

Tess laughed.

'Maybe when we get on hotel Wi-Fi in Santiago, we can FaceTime, and I can see you.'

'I'd like that.' He said quietly. 'I miss you. I miss seeing you.'

The following day, Tess got up early and was downstairs in the lobby area, tying her boots when Pen came down with Mateo.

'Where's your dad.' She asked him.

'He's still sleeping, I think.' Said Mateo.

'Let's let him sleep.' She offered. 'We can walk up and get breakfast. I'll text him and tell him where to join us.'

The kids seemed to like that idea, and they walked up the hill together to find the first yellow arrow of the day. And a nearby café in the process.

Tess would indulge in a rare two café con leches, and Javier could take his time waking up and getting ready.

'I hope we don't have a bunch of stupid high school kids at the next albergue.' Complained Pen, yawning. 'They're so noisy and annoying.'

Tess nearly choked on her coffee. 'You do know you're in high school too, right?' she reminded Pen, who rolled her eyes in response.

'All those boys were staring at me.' She pouted.

'Believe me, I know.' Said Mateo gravely. 'And making comments about you every time you went past them. I think they thought I was American, too, and didn't understand Spanish. I wanted to say something, but my father said to let it go.'

'Really?!' Pen was both surprised and pleased that Mateo would defend her honor. She leaned over and hugged him as his face turned a few shades of scarlet.

Mateo ordered another coffee and some pastries at the bar before returning with their second round. Just then, Javier arrived to the café, looking a little dazed.

'Come sit down, sleepyhead. We have coffee ready for you.'

Javier made a beeline for the chair.

'I don't know what is wrong with me. I'm usually the first up and ready to go. I'm exhausted this morning.'

'Well, we can take it slow today.' Tess said. 'We're in no hurry.'

They finished their breakfasts and were on the trail for more than an hour when Tess noticed Pen itching her neck, and she couldn't stop. Javier stopped to examine her face and then had her remove her pack. He lifted her shirt, and Tess gasped as she saw the raised welts on her daughter's stomach. Javier looked inside her mouth and at her face and scalp.

'I don't like how this is progressing. Pen's having an allergic reaction to something. I will get us a taxi to meet us on the road up ahead. It's only a hundred yards up. It's a Sunday, and we won't find a doctor with an open office anywhere near here. We're going to urgencia in Melide.'

How had this happened? 'I don't understand. She was fine this morning.' Tess said, confused.

'Sometimes, there is something hidden, or allergies develop over time. What is Pen allergic to?' asked Javier. 'Food or medication?'

'She has a couple of sensitivities but nothing major. When she was little, soy could trigger issues. Like a rash. She can't eat garbanzo beans.' Said Tess.

Javier looked confused.

'Like hummus—she can't eat that, or she will get a rash.' She explained.

Pen's face was getting redder. Javier dialed the phone and spoke to the taxi company. Then he said something to Mateo in Spanish, and he uncorked his water bottle and gave it to Pen.

'Do you have any antihistamines?' He asked her. 'In a first aid kit?'

Tess remembered that she had brought some Benadryl. She dug it out and gave it to Javier. He got a pocket knife and crushed some on a bandana from his pack. Then he opened Pen's mouth and rubbed it with his finger under her tongue. She made a face at the bitter taste but said nothing. Then Javier told Tess to take Pen and start walking. He sent Mateo running ahead to meet the driver. He would carry Pen's pack.

Tess watched Javier's quick response and how he reacted to the rash on Pen's torso. She knew something serious was happening, and she didn't know what to do except follow instructions. As promised, the taxi was waiting for them, and at Javier's insistence, the driver stepped on the accelerator, and they took off toward Melide. The trip should have taken nearly 15 minutes, but the driver did it in less than 10. Tess was grateful.

Javier monitored Pen throughout the trip. He called ahead, and the doctor on duty was there to meet them when the taxi pulled up. They rushed Pen into a room with her Mom.

Javier sat in the waiting room with Mateo.

'How is she?' Mateo jumped out of his seat when Tess emerged from the back.

'They gave her a couple of shots, and she's already responding well. She's going to be fine. She slept after the adrenalin hit her system. I think we caught it just in time.' Tess was still in shock. 'It came on so suddenly. I didn't see her eat anything she hadn't eaten before on this trip.'

Mateo spoke up.

'Last night, we went to the store on the corner and got some things to eat before dinner. I saw her open the box this morning. I don't know what they were, but maybe she is allergic to them.'

Tess rummaged through Pen's pack and came up with the box. She couldn't read the ingredients, but Mateo translated. Sure enough, chickpea flour was in the crackers. So much for being safe with gluten-free foods. Tess turned to Javier.

'Thank God you were there. I can not imagine what would have happened if you didn't catch what was happening.' She teared up thinking about it, and Javier put his arms around her.

'I was happy to help.' He assured her.

Mateo watched them but said nothing, turning his attention towards the door where they had taken Pen. Javier tried to cheer Tess up.

'I do have some good news.' He told her.

She wiped her eyes, confused.

'The head of the emergency department offered me a job. She says they're shorthanded, and since I'm drumming up business for them, I should sign on.' He smiled.

'Shameless.' She scolded him. 'Using the injured to climb the ladder of success.'

'But alas, I turned her down.' He teased. 'I couldn't leave you to walk the rest of the way to Santiago while I start my new life as a country emergency doctor. We are only a few days from the end. We need to finish this.'

'Amen to that.' She said.

Just then, they wheeled Pen out, looking drowsy. Mateo jumped up and went to her, wrapping his arms around her. She smiled tearfully.

'Thank you for saving me, Javier. I could have died if you didn't do what you did.' She told him weakly.

'My pleasure, my dear. You have a long life ahead of you, lighting the world on fire.' He squeezed Pen's hand.

'She does.' Smiled Tess, walking over and hugging her tightly.

'I can call a taxi to take us back to the trail. Pen. If we get you something to eat at a cafe, could you walk a few kilometers back to Melide? Mateo and I can share carrying your pack.'

Pen nodded.

'Great. Let's get food, and then we'll get transportation back to where we left off.'

The ride back was much less tense than the one earlier. Tess reminded herself to call John later. She had awoken him when they got to the hospital to tell him what was happening.

The taxi dropped them right where they left off, and they were in Melide before they knew it. A long uphill led into the bustling town, and albergues were plentiful.

'Any preference where we stay tonight?' asked Javier.

'None.' Tess told him. 'I'll sleep in a stable after this morning and be grateful for it.'

'Please don't choose an albergue with shower restrictions.' Pen pleaded. 'I want a long shower. And I want to sleep.'

'A stable with unlimited hot water. Let me look and see what we can do.' He made a couple of phone calls, then they followed him to a lovely albergue with private double rooms available and ensuite bathrooms. Pen was in heaven. Tess was glad she could check on Pen throughout the night without disturbing other pilgrims.

She showered first, telling Pen she could take as much time as she liked under the water. Tess stepped outside and called John.

'Is she OK?' was his nervous greeting.

'Yes, she's OK.' She filled him in, letting out a heavy sigh. 'I'm not being overly dramatic. She could have died if Javier didn't act quickly, getting us all to the ER. Her lips were swollen and blue when we got there.'

'Oh, my God.' John blew out a breath. 'Thank God he was there to help you guys.'

'Yeah. It's weird. Somehow Javier's taken care of us at every turn on this trip.'

John knew it was true.

'Please thank him for me. Tell him how much I'm in his debt for all he's done. Does that sound weird?' he asked. 'I should hate this fucking guy. I do, in the middle of the night when I can't sleep. But then I feel guilty.'

'I get it.' Said Tess. 'And you're entitled. But, it's as if he was sent here to save us from ourselves.'

'Where are you now?' Her husband asked.

'Melide. We didn't get as far as we wanted today, but we'll still get to Santiago in two days. Then get the Compostela. I haven't talked to Javier about going to Madrid if the offer is still open. We've been quite the handful.'

'He's a fool if he says no. And he's no fool. Enjoy the last few days and then be tourists. And please try to stay healthy—both of you. I don't want my girls ill at the same time. You can wait until you get home to do that. It will be my turn to take care of you.'

Tess didn't respond. She knew going home meant fighting cancer. She would be very ill, and John would have his hands full, too.

'I should check on Pen.' She whispered.

'Please tell Pen I'm sending her good thoughts.'

'I will. We love you.' Tess hung up as Javier descended the stairs reading something on his phone.

'I was just speaking to John.' She said.

He nodded. 'I imagine he's been concerned.'

'Yes. But John told me to thank you and to tell you he's in your debt.'

Javier seemed surprised.

'It's been an emotional day. I think perhaps ice cream dinner is in order.' She declared.

'*Ice cream dinner*?' He asked, confused.

'Yes. When the kids were growing up, and something shook us, we always had ice cream dinner. They loved it.' She explained. 'No one can be stressed out eating ice cream. Tonight, it's non-negotiable.'

Javier laughed. 'That is a great prescription for what ails us. I wish I had thought of it.'

When the kids came down later, Pen looking a little worse for wear, they explained the plan. Mateo was confused.

Pen smiled. 'Ice cream dinner cures anything. It's the best!'

Most small restaurants and even grocery stores on the Camino have a board out front advertising all the different packaged ice cream they serve.

But there are also ice cream shops in the larger towns, and Melide didn't disappoint. Javier surprised her by ordering a giant sundae.

'What?' he asked Tess when he saw the look on her face. 'I'm embracing this famous American tradition.'

Tess shook her head and laughed.

'Reaching across the cultural divide suits you.'

He stuck out his tongue at her and resumed his dessert.

Pen hung back with her mom, linking arms as they made their way back to the albergue.

'This was perfect. Thanks, Mom.'

'I knew it would help.' She said quietly. 'You had a tough day.'

'Yeah, I was scared in the taxi when my tongue swelled, and I couldn't talk. I wanted to cry but was afraid I couldn't breathe.' Pen sniffed, remembering the fear.

Tess smiled. 'It's over now. You're going to be alright. And while we're here, Mateo or Javier will read the labels on everything before you eat it.'

They walked in silence for a bit.

'I Love You, Mom.' Pen whispered, resting her head on her shoulder.

'I Love you, Pina. Oh, and Dad said to tell you he's thinking of you and sending you good thoughts.'

'You called him?'

'From the hospital, and I spoke to him after. He says he's in Javier's debt for saving his lovely daughter's life.'

Pen smiled. 'He said that?'

'He did.'

'I miss him.' She said.

'I miss him too.' Tess agreed.

Javier was walking alone, reading a text he'd gotten earlier.

John: 'Thank you for saving Pen. I owe you.'

The following day was their last full day on the Camino, and it was quite literally a walk in the woods. Galicia was already much cooler than the other regions they'd traversed. And while it was hot, the shaded path made for a crisp morning and a pleasant afternoon. They were more subdued than usual, each thinking about the end of their journey and what that would mean when they finished. They had chosen a small Albergue in a little village one day's walk from Santiago. Pen pulled her mother aside.

'It's Mateo's birthday. His grandma, Sofía, texted him earlier, and I saw it. Can we go into the little shop and get him something small? And maybe we could get a small cake or something in the bakery.'

Tess smiled. Pen had fallen hard for this boy, and her selfless enthusiam about doing something for him touched Tess.

'Of course.' She said to Pen.

They brought their surprises back to the café where Javier and Mateo waited, kicking off a small makeshift birthday celebration American style. Tess took the opportunity to solidify their post-Camino plans with Javier.

'Well, hopefully, that offer to come and stay with you guys in Madrid is still open. I think continuing this party for a little longer would be fun.'

Mateo threw his fist above his head. 'Yes!' As Pen smiled ear to ear.

PART IV

THE TALK

Fifteen

Turn Around to See the Sunrise

They awoke in the dark and got their packs and boots on. It would be the final time they would perform this ritual. As they walked out, Pen yelled, 'Turn around to see the sunrise!' And they did for one final time.

It was stunning. The light beams were broken by the clouds, shooting off in a fan-like, now-familiar scallop shell—their last Camino sunrise. Silently, they turned and began walking towards Santiago through eucalyptus forests alongside fellow pilgrims. No one spoke. All the loud conversations and joking they heard on other days were gone. Some pilgrims had their rosaries out and were silently praying. Each of them understood this final day was sacred.

They had to cover 30 kilometers and collect two passport stamps before entering Santiago de Compostela. Trucks stopped for them to cross highways, and they wandered through the last villages and up over a set of steep hills.

Finally, they reached Monte de Gozo, the final place pilgrims can stay before entering the central part of the city. The view showed Santiago spread out at their feet, a moment that seemed unreal to Tess after walking all the way from France. She wasn't sure how they had done it, one step at a time, to be sure. She couldn't articulate the feeling of happiness and grief twisting around her heart. Javier saw the emotion written on her face.

'Shall we walk down into the city?' he asked quietly. 'It's only a few kilometers more.'

Tess nodded as the kids ran ahead down the hill. It was hard for her to contain the tears falling down her cheeks. She knew Javier saw them but said nothing.

The bustle of Santiago was an assault on the senses. They crossed a bridge over a freeway, then walked up the hill through a busy business district with narrow sidewalks. Then down again into the old part of the city. Along the way, they saw other pilgrims they knew who arrived before them. Some hugged them in celebration. Others pointed towards the Cathedral and shouted, 'You're almost there!' then clapped in celebration.

Near the cathedral, Tess heard a lone piper playing the bagpipes. It was then that she could no longer contain her tears. She cried openly as they walked under the church portico and into Obradoiro Square. Pen and Mateo were already there, hugging other pilgrims while waiting for them. Javier stopped and turned to Tess.

'We made it.' He told her.

Tears streamed down her cheeks. There were no words as he pushed her hair from her face, and they embraced. She pulled back, smiling, then they went to join Mateo and Pen, who were waiting on the other side of the square, congratulating them on completing the entire Camino.

'What now?' Tess asked the group, wiping her eyes. 'Should we get our Compostela or check into the hotel and get cleaned up first?'

'Compostelas Now!' They said in unison.

The line was long, with others finishing that day, so they waited to record their entry and obtain their Compostela. The cancer hadn't kept Tess from doing it. She had beaten the bear today.

Finally, it was her turn at the counter. When the administrator asked where Tess had started the Camino, she choked up. 'Saint-Jean-Pied-de-Port in France.' The woman smiled. 'I'm sorry.' Tess apologized. 'I didn't know it would be so emotional.'

'It's alright. Many people cry at this moment.'

'Have you walked the Camino?' Tess asked her.

'Yes. Many times.' Said the woman.

The foursome met in the courtyard near the fountain and proudly showed each other their Compostelas. Pen had opted for the additional paper certifying the mileage she had walked.

'Those high school kids from Sarria don't have one of these.' She was as proud of that as her Compostela.

Tess read the certificate Javier held out. Their names inscribed in Latin listed both his and Alejandra's names, as Javier had fulfilled his promise to walk it in honor of his wife. She looked over at Mateo's, and he had done the same. Tess smiled. Alejandra was a lucky woman to be loved by these extraordinary men.

Sixteen

Santiago and Beyond

Tess stood before the bathroom mirror in her hotel room, wiping the fog from the glass. No more smelly albergues. No more of the same pilgrim dinners. No more walking for hours every day. And yet, she would miss it. The feeling of community. The common sense of purpose of all pilgrims on the Way. The realization that they were slowly reaching their goal and the confidence that comes with doing something that, at the start, seemed so impossible. All of that was behind her now. She decided to call John.

'Hey! Did you make it?' He asked.

'We did!' She said.

'Wonderful! I'm so proud of you.' Tess could hear the tears in his voice.

'Thanks. I'm pretty proud of myself too. They say you can't unring a bell. Well, you can't un-crack an egg, either. And I feel cracked open.' She said through her tears. 'Like all the emotions I've ever had are flowing out of me, and they'll never go back in. I don't know how to explain it any better.'

'You don't have to.' He told her, 'I understand. It was hard for you. Harder than most people. And with everything going on, you still did it. I've been worried every day, and yet you made it. My strong wife.'

Tess sniffed.

'How is Pen?' he asked.

'She's very proud of herself, too. But I think she's looking forward to wearing regular clothes and doing normal things again.'

'She's a teenager. When she's 40, she'll look back on this and understand it more clearly. What the two of you did together at such a critical time.' He whispered. 'For you both.'

'Yes.' She hoped. 'Probably.'

'So, when are you heading to Madrid?'

'I am not sure. I told Javier yesterday that we were taking them up on their offer. Pen and Mateo are ecstatic. I didn't speak to him much today. The last day was more about individual reflection. Most people were quiet, so we didn't have a chance to talk about details.'

'How are you feeling?' He asked.

'I'm feeling okay. Exhausted. I've just walked across Spain, so I get to have that for free.' She smiled.

'True.' John chuckled. 'Well, keep me posted and send me pictures. I miss you. Less than ten days until you're home.'

'Yup.' She said quietly. 'Then, everything begins.'

Tess blow-dried her hair and sent her trail clothes out to the laundry. She looked in the mirror one last time and liked what she saw. She left everything on the trail at 20lbs lighter in body and spirit, and tanner than she'd been since high school. All the baggage. All the sadness. It was gone. She had only love in her heart for everyone. She texted Javier and Pen and told them she would be in the square before the Cathedral.

Walking out of the Parador, no longer a Peregrino, felt strange as she looked up towards the entrance, watching others enter the cathedral square. They all had the same look—relief, exhaustion, confusion. And tears. She spotted the Brazilian couple she met that first night in Orrison and ran over to them. They embraced, and each of them had tears in their eyes.

'How long have you been here?' asked the woman.

'We arrived today.' Said Tess. 'I just enjoyed my first post-Camino shower and thought I would come down to see if anyone I knew was coming in.'

The man smiled.

'We made it! The class of May 28th. We started together on the same day in Saint Jean and finished on the same day.' Choking up. 'How do you feel?' He asked Tess.

. 'I feel overwhelmed by it.' Tess wiped her tears. 'What we've all done is remarkable. It didn't seem that way when we walked, but now it does. I don't think I'll ever be the same.'

The woman smiled.

'I feel the same. Today was like a meditation, walking in. As if we were in church.'

'I understand.' Said Tess.

'What should we do now?' he asked.

'Well, the Compostela office is down the hill and to the right.' Tess told them.

The Brazilian man offered his wife his hand. 'Shall we, my dear?'

The others were still settling, so Tess walked up the stairs to the Cathedral. Inside, people were milling around, but Tess chose a quiet spot to sit down. She looked at the architecture and finally up at the cross. The relics of Saint James were reportedly stored here. People asked for miracles from them every day. Tess didn't bow her head as she prayed. Instead, she felt compelled to look up into the vast expanse of the Romanesque ceiling as she spoke to God.

'Please help me. I don't know what to do. I have cancer—but then we've talked about that several times in the last few weeks. I need to tell Pen, and I need to do it soon. But I don't even know how to begin that conversation. There are no perfect words to keep this from hurting her.'

Just then, Tess felt a hand on her shoulder. She looked up into the round, ruddy face of the Scottish priest she'd met weeks ago in the square of the hill town at the birthday party.

'It's Tess, isn't it?' he asked, concerned.

She wiped her eyes and tried to smile. 'Yes, Father.' She whispered.

'I don't want to intrude on your conversation with God, but you appear upset. Is there anything I can do to help?'

She had just asked God for assistance. Perhaps that's why this man was standing here.

'I don't know, Father.' Tess tried to keep her composure. 'I'm lost. I'm sick with cancer and need to find a way to tell my daughter. I've walked all this way with the one goal of telling her I'm ill. And each time I could have done it or should have done it, I was a coward. I need to find a way without breaking both our hearts, but I am lost.'

The priest sat beside her, reached out, and took her hand.

'Ah, my dear. Most of us are lost in this life. And those who say they are not are fooling themselves. That is the point of the Camino, to empty ourselves out of all the noise and to walk with God. But it's a testament to you that even though you're very ill, you're still more concerned about your child and how it will impact her. I think you're questioning if you're a good mother. It would be best if you let those doubts go. But now is the time, to be honest with her. The hiding is over.'

Tess looked into this kind man's face and nodded. 'You're right, Father.' But she wasn't convinced she knew what to do. 'You know, I'm not even Catholic. Maybe you shouldn't waste your time on me.'

'Ach.' He smiled 'Catholic Schmatholic. God doesn't care about that. Believe me. I know.'

'Mom?'

Surprised, they both turned and saw Pen standing in the aisle.

'How did you know I was here?' Tess asked her, wiping the tears from her eyes.

'When we didn't see you in the square, Javier said I should come to look for you in here. You look upset. What's going on?' She asked, looking from the priest to her mom.

The Father smiled at Tess, squeezing her hand. 'I'll leave you now. If you need anything, I am wandering around looking at some of the relics.

Pen watched him go, then turned back to Tess.

Tess wiped her face and patted the spot the priest had just vacated.

'Please sit down. There's something I need to talk to you about.'

Pen reluctantly slid into the pew, afraid.

'I'm sorry.' Tess took a deep breath. 'I'm struggling to know where to start.' She swallowed before finding her voice again. 'Remember that day when Dad and I told you I was quitting my job?'

Pen nodded.

'Well.' Another deep breath. 'The reason I did that is that I have breast cancer.'

As horror washed across Pen's face, Tess broke down. They both cried as Pen wrapped her arms around her mom's neck and held on for dear life, drowning from the news. Finally, she pulled back.

'Why didn't you tell me?' She asked, clearly hurt. 'All this time.'

'I was going to. We were going to, your dad and me. We'd learned about it the day before, but we hadn't landed on a course of treatment yet. I wanted to wait until we knew exactly what we would do. We had a plan, but then the drug thing happened, and I was more afraid I would lose you to something like that rather than my fear of cancer. I decided that we would take this walk. It would get you away from those people, and I could find a way to tell you while we were on the trail.'

Pen was quiet.

'But you didn't tell me while we were walking.' She whispered.

'No.' Tess tried to calm herself. 'At first, I told myself it was because you were walking with Mateo. And you seemed so happy, so I thought I would let you have more of that. But in the end, if I'm honest, I've been hiding. I knew it would hurt you, and also, it would make it real for me. But I wanted this time with you, without the cancer intruding.' She sniffed. 'We've had a tough relationship these last few years. You know that. I'm not completely sure why. But I wanted us to get to know each other again. For you to know, I'm on your side.'

Tess thought Pen might explode, and she braced herself for it, looking down at her hands. But the only sound she heard was Pen letting out the breath she was holding.

'That's why you made a list of all those talks. Are you afraid you'll die and won't be able to talk to me about that stuff when I'm older?' She asked, searching Tess's face for answers.

Tess closed her eyes. 'I don't know what's going to happen. I wanted this time, in this way, with you.'

They both let that sink in.

'Does Javier know?' Pen asked.

Tess nodded. 'He found a bottle of the medicine I'm taking. It fell out of my pack at one of the albergues. He asked me about it, and I was honest. After that, he's been pushing me every day to tell you, but I didn't know how. Your dad and I talk every evening. Each time he asks me. So, it's not on them; it's on me.'

Tears spilled down Pen's cheeks. 'How have you carried it all this way?' she asked.

'You've needed my support but didn't ask for it. And I didn't offer it because I didn't know. Now I feel terrible. Like I'm the worst daughter in the world.' Pen began to cry in earnest.

'Oh, honey. No.' Tess squeezed her hand. 'You're a teenager. You're doing what teenagers do. I didn't expect you to carry me on this trip. I wanted you to have the Camino you needed, and you did. But now, I need to ask for your help. When we get home, it's going to be difficult. I'm having surgery the following week. Dad will need you, too. All of this has been very hard for him. But he's heard how you've changed on the Camino. We're both hopeful the drugs and the booze are behind you.'

Pen closed her eyes and waited. 'Did you delay treatment because of me?' she whispered.

Tess lifted Pen's chin to look into her daughter's bright blue eyes. She didn't want to lie to her, but she couldn't lay the burden of the outcome of cancer on her young shoulders.

'I made this decision. You can ask your dad. It's something I always wanted to do, even before, and I knew I wouldn't be able to do it once

I started treatment. With the drug thing, it was just further confirmation that this was the right thing to do.'

Tess watched Pen search her face to gauge if what she said was true.

'I want to tell you I'm not angry with you because you're sick. But I am, and you should have told me. But you didn't trust me with that. You always act like you're protecting me, but you're not.'

Tess could hear the pain in Pen's voice and knew she was right.

'You're right.' Tess admitted. 'I've done everything you said. I haven't trusted you. But not because of the reasons you think. I haven't trusted myself. After Charlie died, I struggled so much. I wanted to control the pain swirling around us and to keep it away from you. I was afraid of how it was affecting you. And with my diagnosis, I've been doing the same thing.'

Pen wiped her nose.

'Maybe if you weren't always trying so hard, you'd see that you can lean on us. Me and Dad—we're strong. We can handle things. We've handled you and are tougher than you give us credit for.'

Tess reached out and brushed Pen's hair back. 'I see that now. I know you're strong.'

'And sometimes you get to be weak.' sniffed Pen. 'You don't have to manage everything. We can take care of you. That's what you do when you love people. You let them help when you need it.'

Tears poured down both of their faces.

'Shouldn't we go home now?' asked Pen wiping her face with her sleeve. 'So, you can start treatment? Wouldn't that help?'

Tess sniffed.

'We're already at the end of our adventure. In the grand scheme, a few days won't make any difference. Let's go to Madrid and decompress. Then, we'll go home.'

Tess pulled Pen to her feet and hugged her. She saw the priest over her daughter's shoulder, praying over a lit candle. Somehow, she figured it might just be for her. Pen didn't seem to want to let go when Tess pulled back.

'Listen.' She told Pen calmly. 'One thing I would suggest is that you talk to Mateo. He's been through what we're about to go through. He knows what it feels like to have a mother with cancer. Lean on him. I know he'll be there for you.'

Pen nodded.

They walked out of the church slowly, arm in arm. Each knew that as they entered the bright sunlight of Santiago, nothing would ever be the same. Javier and Mateo spotted them and waved, quickly realizing something had changed. Pen left her mom and fell into Mateo's arms.

He looked at Tess over her shoulder and mouthed, 'Thank You.'

'You've told her then.' Javier whispered.

Tess nodded, and he hugged her while she cried.

'Pen?' She said, pulling away from Javier. 'I think we should call Dad and talk to him about it. What do you think?'

Pen nodded.

Tess put her arm around Pen's shoulder as they walked across the square. Javier and Mateo watched them go. Neither sure what would happen next.

The video call to John lasted for more than two hours. Tess knew John wished he was there to support them both. But by the end of the conversation, Pen appeared to be in a better place.

'Can I sleep in here with you tonight?' asked Pen her mom.

'Of course.' Tess smiled.

'I know you have cancer, but I was already feeling sad. I think because the Camino is over. I know we're going to Madrid with Javier and Mateo, but it won't be the same.'

'Oh, honey. I know. It's alright.' Tess squeezed her hand. 'We have to go back to reality. And, you've had an emotional day, with some big news dropped on you. But the good thing is, we'll ease into it. First, Madrid. Then home.'

'I feel like we live in Spain now.' Said Pen. 'I don't think Dad would like it if I said that, but I do. I'm used to it here. Home feels a long way away. The stuff I used to do seems babyish now.' She hesitated before whispering,

'And I feel like you wouldn't be sick if we stayed here. You don't seem sick. Just tired.'

Tess tucked a stray hair behind Pen's ear.

'Oh, I wish that were true. That a miracle happened on the Camino.' Tess smiled. 'But then I look at you, and I think maybe we did get our miracle. This trip changed you more than a little bit. You seem very different. Maybe my baby isn't such a baby anymore. Growing up right in front of me.'

Pen smiled and hugged Tess. 'But tonight, I need my mom.' Pulling back the covers and burrowing in.

Tess got in beside her, and Pen snuggled in. She listened to her daughter's breathing until it evened out. It was lovely to have her little girl back, even for just one night.

The following day, they slept in before meeting up with Javier and Mateo.

'It feels strange to know we aren't packing up and walking tomorrow.' Pen pointed out as they hunted for coffee. 'We've taken rest days before. But we never took two days off.'

Looking around, other pilgrims also looked lost. They had reached their goal, their sole focus for weeks, with no thought to after. Now, *after* had arrived, they were all a bit unmoored. The prospect of leaving new friends and the routine of the Camino was daunting.

'I thought I would go to the train station to book our tickets to Madrid tomorrow.' Said Javier.

'I'll go with you.' Tess turned to both Pen and Mateo. 'Do you guys want to come with us or do your own thing?'

Pen looked torn. She should stay with her mom now that she knew she was sick. Tess let her off the hook.

'We're just going to the train station. Nothing exciting or dangerous. If you guys want to do something—Go! Enjoy our last day in Santiago.'

'Okay,' whispered Pen.

Tess placed some euros in her daughter's hand and hugged her tightly. Then she watched the two of them head off. Tess and Javier walked in silence toward the station.

'How did the conversation with John go?' He finally asked.

'I think it went OK. Pen needed to hear his voice and what he was thinking and feeling. I needed that, too. Then she spent the night with me. As though she was afraid to leave me, for fear I would disappear.'

Javier understood.

'We haven't had a chance to talk since yesterday. I know you needed time with Pen, but I was up all night thinking of you and wondering what was going through your head. Would you still want to go to Madrid? Or would you rather take Pen and go home? More importantly, how I could help you.'

Tess reached for his hand and squeezed.

'I would never have gotten to Santiago without you.' She told him. 'We are going to Madrid.'

Javier exhaled.

'I am glad to hear it. I think Pen has changed on this trip.' He told her. 'She seems more mature.'

'She does. Last night, I was surprised when she wanted to stay with me, even after telling her about the cancer. She hasn't been that snuggly in years.'

Javier helped purchase the tickets for her and Pen at the station before they walked back through town.

'I'm looking forward to seeing Madrid and your home. I've only known you here, mostly in bunk beds and with all your belongings on your back. It will be strange to see you in your everyday surroundings.'

'An animal in his natural habitat?' He smiled.

'Something like that.' Tess agreed.

'You will not be that impressed. We live a simple life. My world is small and unexciting. Every day looks much like the last and the next one. You will see.' He assured her as they walked back up the hill towards the church where they had promised to meet the kids for the final pilgrim blessing.

Recommendations said to sit on the side of the vast Romanesque cathedral to get the best view of the swinging of the *Botafumeiro*. It is the only place in the world where a group of *Tribaboleiros* hoists the large silver thurible hanging from the ceiling on thick cabled ropes, filled with hot coals and frankincense, swinging it out over the congregation. As it swings, the people can see the hot coals, and the church fills with the smoke of the burning frankincense.

They secured a spot, and the service began. Tess was not religious and had not raised her children to be. Pen had been in more churches on the Camino than her entire life up to that point. But Tess always felt something whenever she walked into these old ones in Europe, and the Cathedral of Saint James in Santiago was no different.

In this building, over 1000 people could fit under the giant Romanesque arches of the church, with standing room only. Perhaps it was the collection of believers that gathered here for centuries. Maybe there was something to a faith she had never understood but could feel somehow.

Soon it was time to swing, and a group of men dressed in scarlet robes with thick cords wrapped tightly around their waists entered and began the centuries-old ritual of first lowering and packing the *Botafumeiro* with hot coals. They began hoisting it violently into the rafters. The motion caused it to swing and smoke as it flew. Higher and higher it went, over the pilgrims, one way, swinging back over the altar, and the pilgrims on the other side. All heads were turned towards the ceiling of the enormous Romanesque Cathedral as it went back and forth.

Eventually, the men in robes brought it down, and the priest gave a final blessing. As they filed out, Tess told Javier she needed a few minutes, and he took Mateo and Pen out to the front. At the candle stations, she put a few euros in the coin box and took out some candles, placing them together on the stand and lighting them individually—for each of those she loved.

'I'm sure Charlie is up there somewhere, so, God, please make sure he's
OK. I don't want him to worry about us.'

Tess bowed her head once more.

'Please take care of John and Pen.' She swallowed. 'And Javier and Mateo.
Help them when I'm gone.'

She rose and left the church. The sun was bright outside, and she
shielded her eyes as she found them in the crowd.

'You look like you've been crying.' said Pen, concerned as she
approached.

'I think it's just going from the darkness to the sunlight.' Tess smiled.
'Shall we get some lunch? I'm starving after all that smoke and singing I
didn't understand.'

'I don't think it would have mattered if you had.' Javier assured her.

SEVENTEEN
THE FINAL TALK

They took the high-speed train to Madrid the following day, and Javier let Tess sleep the entire way. He took the kids to the dining car, and they lingered over lunch before Pen rose.

'I'm going to check on my mom.' she told them.

Something was bothering Pen. Javier wanted to give her space before they got to Madrid.

She found a groggy Tess looking out the window.

'Is everything alright?' Pen asked, sliding into the seat opposite.

'Yes.' she smiled. 'I'm fine. I was just sleepy, I guess. I've been sitting here thinking.'

Tess reached for her daughter's hand across the table.

'We've had a great adventure. Haven't we?'

'Yeah. We did. But it was hard.' Remembered Pen. 'There were days I didn't want to get up in the dark and walk.'

'Oh, I know,' Tess laughed. 'I had to coax you more than once.' She reminded her. 'But I felt the same plenty of times myself.'

Pen seemed surprised. 'You never acted like it. You never said.'

'Oh yeah. On more than one morning. But I tried to focus on propelling us forward. We had to keep going if we wanted to get to Santiago. And to do that, we had to get out of bed. After that, we just needed to put one foot in front of the other.'

'And we did it.' Smiled Pen 'But it wasn't easy.'

'No.' said Tess. 'It wasn't. And we could have stopped so many times. We had some good reasons, too. They would have been sympathetic if we told anyone that we couldn't finish because of my cancer back in León or when you had your allergic reaction at Palas de Rei. 'Of course, you had to quit.' They would have said. But we didn't quit; we kept going. And aren't you glad we did?'

'Yeah. I'm happy we did.'

'Remember this, Pen. The Camino is a metaphor. It's like life. There will always be valid reasons you could stay in bed and pull the covers over your head. Or to give up when difficult things happen. It's inevitable. The world will tell you it's understandable. But at your lowest ebb is when you find out what you're made of, and sometimes, all you have to do is get up and put one foot in front of the other until it all makes sense again. But you don't have to run. You can go as slow as you need to until you find your strength.'

Just then, over the loudspeaker, they heard the announcement of their arrival in the capital. Tess collected her things, and Pen got up to get her bag down from overhead as Javier and Mateo arrived at their seats. He looked from mother to daughter as they gathered their belongings, ready to disembark. Something was different.

Madrid is the largest city in Spain and its capital. Tess and Pen craned their heads as they made their way through town in a taxi.

'Our apartment is in Chamberí.' Javier explained. 'It's more like a village within the city, and everyone knows each other. We like it, and it is my hope you will too.'

Traveling through other cities on the Camino was nothing compared to the vastness of Madrid. The noise and the sheer volume of people were overwhelming. Tess took it in through the window as the taxi stopped in front of an older building. The driver helped them get the bags onto the sidewalk.

'Home sweet home.' Said Javier, spreading his arms wide and leading them toward the lobby, where a uniformed man came out to help them.

'Buenas tardes, Doctor Silva. Bienvenido.'

'Gracias, señor Ruiz. Bueno estar en casa.'

The marble interior was cool on the top floor on a hot summer day. Tess found herself standing in the living room of a large penthouse apartment filled with light. The A/C was on, and a giant orange cat rubbed against her leg. Mateo reached down, lifting it up.

'This is Patas.' He said, smiling and rubbing cheeks with the purring animal. 'She missed me.'

Pen walked over and petted the cat.

A tiny, older woman in an apron came out of the kitchen, wiping her hands on a towel, as Javier introduced her to Tess and Pen. Inés, their housekeeper, inclined her head when he explained how invaluable she was in keeping their lives running. Inés crossed over to Mateo, hugging him and kissing his cheeks. He picked her up, and she laughed, then swatted him with her kitchen towel.

'Bienvenido.' She teased Mateo.

He smiled down at her.

Javier gestured towards the hallway.

'Let me show you to your rooms. Inés has ensured that everything is ready for you.'

He led them down a long hallway, stopping at the first room. It was cozy with a single bed and decorated with white gauzy curtains and a sea-blue duvet. In the corner was a small bench where Javier deposited Pen's backpack.

'Please make yourself at home. You can unpack and use the armoire for your things. We can store your pack in the closet in the hall.'

Pen smiled. 'Works for me.'

The next room was Mateo's, complete with all the markings of a teenage boy, including posters of his favorite futbol stars. Turning to the right, they continued down the corridor and came up short in front of Javier's room. A room much larger than the other two, complete with a canopy bed and an antique armoire. Moroccan carpets covered the parquet floors, with windows hung with curtains so heavy she was sure he could make the room pitch black at midday for a nap. A door to an ensuite bath was barely visible.

'This is my room. I don't spend much time in here.'

He continued down the hall before Tess could get a closer look.

'The last room is yours.' he said, opening the door.

Decorated all in white, Tess felt afraid to set anything down. She was still lugging dirt around from the Camino. The Turkish carpet was the one-color exception. The combination of blues and creams and the reflection from the window made the room seem to be floating in the clouds.

'Wow, Mom! You got the best room.' Said Pen, looking around as she ran her hand across the dresser.

Tess smiled. 'I think I'll be happy here.'

'Good. That is the idea.' said Javier. 'Now, everyone can get unpacked and settled. If you need to rest, please go right ahead. I will be in my office just down the hall and around the corner, returning patient calls. Later, if everyone is up for it, we can go to one of our favorite places and introduce you to the neighborhood.'

Tess felt like a princess in this room of white. Inés had even thought to put fresh flowers on her bedside table. Feeling contented, she kicked off her shoes and lay down on the bed, and before she knew it she was asleep. When she woke up, a kiss on her lips startled her.

'What's going on?' she asked, sitting up.

Looking around the room, Tess remembered where she was.

'Not a thing.' Javier smiled. 'It's time to get something to eat.'

'Where are the kids?' she asked, looking over his shoulder at the closed door.

'They're in Mateo's room playing a game on their phones. I wanted to take the opportunity to see how you were doing. How do you like your room?'

'It's lovely. The perfect temperature. And the light here makes me dreamy.' She laid back down.

'I can't take credit for decorating it. My mother did that when we moved in.' He explained. 'She wanted a room for herself, even though she lives in Madrid and has her own home.'

'Well, thank your mother for me.' Said Tess. 'She has wonderful taste.'

'I'll be sure to do that. Now, as far as the bathroom, you can use mine. I know you like to take a bath, and I have a rather large bathtub, so instead of sharing with the kids, you can take a grown-up bath.'

'Ooh, that sounds tempting.' Tess smiled. 'Perhaps later.'

'I'm counting on it.' He said with a wicked grin. 'If you want to freshen up, I'll give you space. We can leave here in 20 min, hmm?'

She watched as the door closed behind him.

Tess grabbed her makeup bag, then padded down the hall to Javier's room. She was entering when she saw Pen coming out of Mateo's room.

'Why are you going to Javier's room?' Pen asked.

'He said I could use his bathroom instead of sharing it with two messy teenagers. I'm just getting ready to go.'

Tess met them in the living room, as promised. Walking down a street teeming with people, they walked to a small café, greeted like heroes by the owner and his wife, with many shaking hands and hugging Mateo and Javier—then rapid-fire Spanish.

'They are giving us a special menu. We are to sit here and enjoy each course as it comes out.' He explained.

'That sounds very dangerous and very fattening.' Said Tess.

Javier laughed.

The food got progressively richer over the next several hours, and Tess struggled to eat it all. But she certainly gave it her best try. Finally, the coffee appeared. Even Pen looked full.

'That was really good.' Said Pen. 'I don't know what some of it was, but I figured if it tasted alright, I didn't need to ask.'

Javier smiled.

'You are developing a palate. This is great progress from the first meals we ate together.' he teased. 'When the only thing you would eat was pizza.'

'Hey, there's nothing wrong with pizza!' Pen cried. 'It's got a bunch of the food groups.'

Javier put his hands up in mock defense.

'I agree. But not for breakfast, lunch, _and_ dinner.'

Pen and Tess both giggled. It was true; Pen was venturing out on the culinary side. And in most other areas, Tess admitted. The girl sitting before her seemed lighter, without the sharp edges that had cut so deep. Tess closed her eyes and leaned back. When she opened them, she caught Javier watching her.

'You look happy.' He said.

'I am happy. The temperature and company are perfect, and the food is delicious. What else could I ask for?'

Before he could answer, Mateo and Pen laughed, and Javier looked over to see them staring into Mateo's phone, sharing earbuds.

Javier shook his head. Mateo looked up and caught his father's eye.

'Can we go to Emiliano's house? They're having a party and asked if I want to join now that we're back.' He turned to Tess. 'I'd like to take Pen if it's OK with you.'

Tess looked at his puppy dog eyes, but it was Pen to whom she directed her next question.

'Alcohol?'

'No way! Don't worry, Mom, I'm not doing that again. Coke.' She stumbled, 'I mean Coca-Cola. That's it.'

Tess gave her a serious look and to Mateo, 'May I have the address of this party? Is it far from here?'

'It's not far. It's near our old house.' He told her. 'We can take the Metro.'

Javier's face tensed, but he said nothing.

'I don't know where that is, so if you can, please message me the address so I have it, and then you can take Pen if your Father says it's OK for you to go.'

Mateo looked at Javier, who, with a smile, waved his hand toward the kids.

'Go. At least you'll be talking to these people in person rather than watching the party in that thing.' Pointing to the phone.

Pen hopped up and kissed her Mom on the cheek.

'Are you sure it's OK? I can stay here with you if you want me to.'

Tess smiled. 'No. Go and have fun.'

Pen wrapped her arms around Javier's neck.

'Thank you!' she hugged him before they ran off.

Javier laughed. 'I think it would have been nice to have a daughter. It takes so little to make them happy.'

Tess rolled her eyes.

'I don't know.' Javier told her. 'All I must do is say 'Yes' to whatever she asks, and I'm her hero.'

'Oh, my God. If you had a girl, she would have wrapped you around her little finger.' Warned Tess.

'That is most definitely true.' He conceded.

They got up and took their time strolling back to the apartment, walking hand in hand with Tess's head on Javier's shoulder.

'Will you spend the night with me tonight?' He asked her.

'I think it's a bit risky with Pen being there.' She warned.

'Well, at the very least. Lay down with me for a while. This is Madrid. That party won't end until dawn.'

Tess looked stricken.

'Don't look so worried. What will they do at 4 am they can't do at midnight?' He asked.

'True. I guess it's the idea of Pen staying out all night. We have a history with this.' She reminded him.

'Remember the bridge? 'He asked her. 'Here, there are fewer signs. They must learn on their own. And we have to let them do it.'

Tess sighed. She knew he was right.

'Do you mind if I take a bath in your big tub?' She asked.

'Not at all. I will wash your back.' He offered, ushering her into the apartment.

'Mmm. We'll see.'

She filled the tub with bath gel from the cabinet, then piled her hair on top of her head. Soon she slid among the bubbles, so happy to be in the water again. Javier came in with a glass of wine and sat on the side.

'I have my very own mermaid.' He smiled.

Tess blew bubbles like a child and slid even deeper beneath the water with only her head and toes peeking out. She closed her eyes, leaning back.

'Does it feel weird to be home and to have us here with you?' She asked him.

He considered the question.

'It feels strange to be home after being gone so long. But not to have you here. I wish you could stay much longer.' whispering. 'Forever.'

He drank from his glass, trying to regain his composure.

'It's strange.' she said, looking up at him. 'I feel perfectly at home. I know it's only been a few hours, but it's comfortable here. It smells and feels like you.'

Javier sat his glass on the side and rubbed her shoulders where her pack had caused some marks. Then kissing the side of her neck as his fingers worked their magic.

'You're finally relaxing.' He whispered.

'Mmm.' She closed her eyes.

'This is good.'

'This wasn't the bath I had in mind originally for today.' She said as he switched to the other end, rubbing her feet.

'Oh, no? I hope it meets the standard.'

'I thought I'd be in here alone, shaving my legs. I haven't done that for weeks, and it's what I envisioned when I saw the tub. Although, this is much better.'

'Where is your razor?' He asked.

'I'm not going to shave my legs right now.' She told him.

'No, you're not. I'm going to shave your legs right now.' He took the razor from her shower bag on the counter and lathered up the soap.

'Give me your leg.,' he directed. Tess leaned back and reluctantly complied as Javier spread soap on her outstretched calf, then dragged the razor up to her knee.

'Are you sure you know what you're doing?' She asked, a little nervous. No one else had ever shaved her legs before.

Javier pulled a face.

'First of all, I'm a man. We shave on the face; I might add, daily. Granted, weekly these days for me. And secondly, I'm a doctor. I've operated on people. I know how to hold a knife.' He continued making paths up her leg.

Tess was struck by how focused and thorough he was.

'I hadn't noticed how harry your legs so were. If I had, I don't know if I would have made a move back on the farm. You really let yourself go.' He teased her, trying not to smile.

Tess blew bubbles at his face and piled some on the top of his head. She found it hilarious and laughed, shifting in the tub.

'Hey!' Javier scolded her. 'This is serious business. I have a razor in my hand. If you want to survive another day, you better hold still, young lady.'

'I'm so sorry, doctor. I'll be good. But you look like a giant 3-year-old with the bubbles in your hair.' She laughed.

He grabbed the other leg and finished up, rinsing them and rubbing the soap off.

'I'm very glad you are here.' Javier said quietly. 'That you didn't go straight back to Arizona from Santiago.'

Tess closed her eyes. 'I could be nowhere else.'

Soon, the water had cooled, and she got out and dried off. Tess had promised to lay down with him in his bed for a little while, and she snuggled up, wrapped in his robe. Javier lay in the dark with her, holding her tightly and feeling her hair on his cheek, wishing for time to stand still as they drifted off.

Tess woke with a start. Seeing the sun peeking around the curtains, she sat up, suddenly alert. She had not meant to spend the entire night. Where was Pen? Did she go to her room when she got home from the party and notice Tess' bed wasn't slept in? Javier was lying next to her, still asleep. Tess got up and went to the door. Peeking out, she tiptoed down the hall to her room, opening her door, finding her covers were thrown back, as though she had only gotten up a moment before. She was confused because she knew she hadn't slept in the bed.

She dressed and brushed her hair before remembering she had left her toothbrush in Javier's bathroom. She'd have to get it later. Making her way to the kitchen, she began looking through cupboards for what she might need to make coffee when Inés came around the opposite corner from the large dining room.

'Buenos días.' Tess greeted her.

Inés smiled. "Buenos días, *señora*. Can I help you with anything?'

'Oh, you speak English. That's good because my Spanish is terrible.'

Inés smiled and inclined her head.

'Yes, I do. Are you hungry for breakfast? Doctor Silva is usually up by now but is sleeping in today. I am happy to make you something. Eggs, perhaps? Coffee?'

'Coffee would be wonderful. And yes, eggs would be great. Is there yogurt? I usually have yogurt in the morning, but I didn't think about going to the store last night.'

'There isn't any yogurt, but you don't have to go to the store. I will pick up some things later today and get some.'

'Thank you, Inés.'

Tess got herself a glass of water, sat down at the small table in the kitchen, and took the handful of pills she had brought from the bedroom. She didn't see Inés watching her.

'Are you well, *señora*?'

'Yes, of course.' Tess smiled. 'Why do you ask?'

'You are taking a lot of pills. If there is anything I can do for you, please let me know.' The housekeeper offered.

Tess wanted to deny that she was ill, but that seemed disrespectful somehow.

'I have been sick. I saw a doctor in León. A friend of Javier's. She ensured I have everything I need to get better.' She assured Inés. 'And it seems to be working.'

'That is good.' Inés turned back to the omelet she was making.

Tess decided to steer the conversation away from her illness.

'Have you worked for the Silva family long?' she asked.

'Yes. I have. I have been the housekeeper for the Silva family since Javier was a child. And then, I became his housekeeper after he married. We had some other help then, too. But this apartment doesn't require much work, and the doctor and Mateo are easy to care for.'

Inés continued.

'So you are American. You and your daughter.'

'Yes.' explained Tess. 'We came to walk the Camino and met Javier and Mateo on the way.'

'Hmm.' Inés responded.

'And they invited us to stay with them.'

'So, you will stay here in Madrid until you go home?' The housekeeper asked.

'Yes. We had planned to go to Barcelona or even Tarragona, but Pen and Mateo have become friends, and Javier was kind enough to extend the invitation to us. So here we are.'

'It's nice for them to have guests and noise here. Mateo is very quiet at home, and the doctor works a lot. So sometimes being the housekeeper is lonely.' She smiled.

'I know what you mean by a quiet house. Pen likes to go out with her friends, but it's nice to have noise again when she has them over for a pool party or a sleepover. Do you have children?'

'Yes, just one son. He is grown with children of his own. He lives in another city, but I see them often.' Inés explained.

'That's nice. I don't know what I'll do when I'm a grandmother. Probably spoil them rotten.' said Tess, wondering if she would ever see her grandchildren.

Inés laughed.

'Yes, you will. Whatever my grandchildren want, they know to ask me for it.'

They looked up and saw Javier at the door to the kitchen.

'Buenos días.' He said to them, crossing to the small table and squeezing Tess's shoulder. Inés turned away to plate the omelet and to make coffee for them, but she didn't miss the gesture.

'The kids got in very early this morning, I think.' He said.

'Yes, they came in just after I arrived at 5:30. I heard Mateo in his room rustling around.'

'Wow.' Tess grimaced. 'That must have been some party.'

'Emiliano is a good boy.' Said Inés. 'He likes my tortilla when he's here in the morning. I will have to make him one before he leaves for University.'

Javier smiled at the pride Inés took in her cooking. She was a godsend during Alejandra's illness, and after her passing. He crossed the kitchen and picked some eggs off the plate before she gave them to Tess. Inés slapped his hand away playfully.

'No, this is for *señora* Tess. I will make you the next one.'

She pushed him towards the empty chair across from Tess.

'Sit down and have a coffee.' She scolded him.

Javier playfully tried to enlist Tess's help. 'Do you see how she pushes me around all the time?'

'Because you are naughty.' Shaking her finger at him sternly, turning to Tess conspiratorially. 'He has always been like this.' Shaking her head. '*Muy difícil.*'

'You should do what she says, or you won't get a yummy omelet yourself.' Tess chided him.

Inés waved the spatula in the air.

'Exactly!' Then she pointed it at Tess 'I like her.'

Javier raised his hands in mock surrender.

'*Vale*. I will behave and eat the omelet you are making me.'

A 'Humph' was all he got in return.

Tess smiled over her coffee cup and then let out an audible moan. 'Mmm. This is good coffee, Inés.'

Inés turned from the stove.

'I am known for my coffee. I will make you another when I finish with this omelet.'

Tess winked at Javier. Inés hadn't asked if she wanted another coffee. Tess knew better than to mess with the captain of the ship.

'How did you sleep?' he asked Tess.

'Like a rock. I had no idea I slept that late. I woke up, and the sun was up. My body wants to walk a long way today. It's like a compulsion now after walking the Camino.'

'I feel the same way. I want a long walk, myself.' He finished putting sugar in his coffee. 'How about we walk to some of the bigger sights of Madrid. Have a tourist day. It's not the Camino, but it will keep your muscles from cramping up.'

'That sounds good.' She agreed.

Javier ate his omelet and complimented Inés to the point of irritation. She pleaded with Tess.

'Please. Take this rascal out from under my feet immediately.' Then she patted his face and kissed the smiling cheek he offered. 'Go.'

Javier reached around her and grabbed one of the cookies she had made earlier that morning. Inés just waved him away.

Eighteen
Chasing Ghosts

'I'll head to my office. Come get me when you're ready to leave.'

It didn't take her long. She made her way down the hallway and turned the corner the way he had gone. The apartment was a big square. All the rooms had large windows that allowed light to illuminate the hallway. She found him in the office on her left, still on the phone. He waved her to a chair, providing a good view of a space that was all his.

On one wall hung three small paintings side by side, each depicting a different season in a place she recognized, the family winery in La Rioja. They were good. Tess wondered where the fourth one was. Perhaps he hadn't acquired it yet. The artist captured the light of each season perfectly. Summer, autumn and winter. Getting up and walking around the room, she saw photos of Mateo at all stages, from birth to earlier this year. He looked to be the smiling, happy kid she knew.

The bookshelves contained medical volumes neatly organized. In this day of digital access, it seemed quaint and old-fashioned, but Tess enjoyed running her hands over the leather spines, sure that these were Javier's books when he became a fully qualified doctor decades ago.

He held up one finger, begging for a few more moments with whomever he spoke to on the phone.

'It's okay.,' she mouthed back.

Tess enjoyed seeing a new side of this man. His desk was organized chaos with the surface covered in folders and notes. And one picture. Just one, next to the small desk lamp. Alejandra smiled back at her, with a much younger Mateo's arms around her neck from behind. For a moment, Tess felt a pang of jealousy. This beautiful woman frozen in time; she'd held Javier's heart entirely. Her loss created a void in him. But she knew competing with a ghost was futile.

The black and white photo was a close-up; a gentle breeze from her right played with Alejandra's hair. The light hit her blond head so that it seemed to shine through even in the grayscale. Whoever took the photo had captured her. She looked happy. Something about the expression on her face made Tess tear up. Happiness is not guaranteed in this life, but this woman had experienced it, and so had Tess.

Javier hung up the phone.

'Finally. I'm sorry about that.' He said before following her gaze. 'Alejandra.' He whispered. 'I took this shortly before her diagnosis. We were in the nature preserve on a summer afternoon. It seems like a lifetime ago.'

She wiped her eyes. 'Mateo looks so much like her.'

Javier swallowed hard.

'Right after she passed away, I couldn't have that picture out. I couldn't bear the reminders of what I'd lost. Now, I think I am finally healing. I don't often cry anymore, and I can remember her and smile about our years together. Good years.'

He was lost somewhere on a summer's day, taking photos of his wife and son before it all came tumbling down.

'Are you ready? Time to be a tourist in my hometown. I haven't been to many of these places for decades, so it should be fun.'

Tess grabbed her hat, and they set off. Javier wasn't kidding about the walking. They started at the Prado museum. The collection was awe-inspiring and reminded Tess of the Louvre in Paris. It would take more than one day to see it all, but they spent the entire morning there, then found some lunch. Like most European capitals, it was a city built to impress the population and showcase its power to any potential invaders. Madrid did both, with architectural masterpieces that spanned the centuries. Some copied from other, equally grand cities. Some, uniquely their own.

'We have done a lot today.' Said Javier. 'I think we will walk through the park before we return home for a nap.'

'Are you tired?' she asked.

'A bit. Getting back into the routine of everyday living. Of course, not the tourist part. Just the cadence of life.'

'A walk back through a shady park sounds wonderful.' She said, linking her arm through his.

They strolled through Parque del Retiro with its famous Crystal Palace and Rose Garden, out the other side, past the archaeological museum.

'We can go there another day if you like. It's interesting. Many civilizations occupied Spain, and the evidence is there. It tells a compelling story.'

'I'd like to see it.' She smiled. 'We have a few more days, so there's time.'

They crossed a wide boulevard.

'This is Salamanca. The area where we used to live.' He said. 'Not far from here. I don't come here much, but the kids were here for the party last night.'

It felt odd to Tess that Pen had been here in the middle of the night without her.

'Can we walk past your old house?' she asked. 'I'd like to see it.'

Javier hesitated for just a moment.

'Of course.'

After several turns, he led her down a tree-lined street.

'This is it.' He said, standing in front of a large yellow stone building surrounded by a black iron fence, with an imposing set of marble steps leading to a formidable front door with heavy hardware. There was an entrance further down the block with a set of large wooden doors reminiscent of a barn. Tess assumed it must have been how carriages came and went in the old days.

'Your house is in here?' she asked, 'It's beautiful.' Scanning the carved stone façade.

'This is my house.' He told her. 'The whole thing.'

Tess was dumbfounded.

'You used to live *here*?'

'Yes.' He said. 'I inherited this house from my grandparents when they died. I was a starving medical resident living in a mansion. It was odd for Alejandra and me. The house still had all the old furniture, filled to the brim, like living in a museum. I couldn't sell it, so we lived in a portion of it while Alejandra renovated some rooms and painted. Sometimes, we had other medical residents from the hospital living with us. It was very Bohemian. When Mateo was born, we stayed. He had most of a floor to play and run his toy cars on the old parquet floor. He would have friends over and play fútbol upstairs, in a small ballroom.'

'Would you like to see it?' Javier offered.

'Yes.' she said, 'I would love to.'

He took the keys from his pocket and unlocked the black iron gate that creaked loudly in protest. Climbing the steps to the front door, Javier let them into the spacious foyer. An imposing carved staircase rose towards a dark second floor, and higher still.

'Wow.' Tess was impressed. 'This is amazing. Imagine coming down those stairs in a ball gown. Quite a sight.'

'There are five staircases in the house, but this is, of course, the most impressive.'

The place felt deserted. But it wasn't as dusty as Tess had imagined.

'I didn't ask her to, but I think Inés comes here sometimes and runs a mop around.' He said, running his hand across the frame of the mirror in the foyer. 'I walked by once, and the windows on the upper floors were open, so I think she was airing it out.'

Tess didn't know where to look first.

'Do you come here at all? Inside?' she asked. 'Not just walking by.'

'Not really. I came here a few times after we moved. It was easy to feel Alejandra in this house, and I didn't want to break down in front of Mateo or the staff at the office. So, I came here. But after a while,' he whispered. 'I didn't come anymore.'

Javier led her into a vast grande salon to the left. A space filled with sofas and multiple seating areas, all covered in sheets. A large hand-carved desk dominated the room. But what caught Tess's eye were the large paintings. They were stunning works of art and infused with light, even in the darkened room, as though generated internally by the picture itself. Large windows, draped with heavy curtains and floor-to-ceiling shutters, blocked glass doors that led out to an interior courtyard. Tess pulled one back and peered out. The garden was well-tended, and the fountain was running. Like the secret garden in the book she loved so much.

'I think Inés has been doing more than running a mop.' She pulled back the curtain and shutter for Javier to see. His surprise told her he had no idea.

'I didn't know she was doing this.' He frowned. 'Honestly, I didn't even think about it.' Concerned. 'I will speak to her. If she has been putting in all this extra work, perhaps she needs more help.'

He pulled back another set of curtains and opened a glass door, unlatching the shutters that led to the courtyard. They stepped out into the sunshine, the trees and ferns providing shade. Walking to the sizeable bubbling fountain, Tess saw fish swimming in the pool.

'How is it possible I didn't know this?' He asked no one in particular.

'Inés cares for you and Mateo like you're her family. Perhaps she didn't want to see something so beautiful die.' As the words came out of her mouth, she regretted them instantly. But he didn't seem to notice.

'For five years, she has maintained our garden. It's the last living thing in this house, and she didn't let it die.' He whispered.

'I wonder what else you didn't know has gone on here. Shall we explore?' Tess asked.

'Yes, I think we should.' He said.

They returned inside and removed the sheets from a group of overstuffed couches.

'They look just like they did before.' He said.

Then he went to a door on the other side of the room and opened it. It led to a boot room where cloaks and rain gear were left when disembarking from carriages more than a hundred years before. It was shiny and clean.

'Let's go upstairs.' He said. 'I want to see if anything is different up there.'

Anxiously climbing the grand staircase two steps at a time, Javier led them through some of the rooms as they made their way down the hall. Many were frozen in a time warp circa 1930. Finally, they reached the main bedroom. Javier stopped with his hand on the door handle, admitting he hadn't entered in several years. He opened the door, discovering a room filled with light. The curtains were pulled back, and the bed was made up with a new duvet.

Entering slowly, he seemed afraid the past would jump out at him. The furniture was polished to a high shine, and no dust was visible, as though he had walked out of it this morning.

Something caught Tess's eye. *Spring* was here—the missing painting from his office in the apartment. Rebirth and renewal; it's what had been missing from his life.

'My God.' he said to himself, 'All this time. I had no idea. No clue that this was going on.'

Tess saw his hurt, but there was something else. Relief, she thought. Perhaps, it was a relief that it hadn't all turned to dust. That this life he had before was still here, just waiting for him to hit *Play* again. He walked through and looked at the bathroom. It was clean, and fresh towels were on the bar.

'I don't understand why.' He whispered.

'Maybe she wanted to be ready.' Offered Tess. 'Just in case.'

He shook his head, running his hand through his hair.

'Maybe.'

Then, he seemed to realize that Tess was there and that he hadn't been talking to himself.

'It's a beautiful room, Javier. It glows from the light bouncing off the yellow stone walls outside the windows.'

He looked around, a hint of a smile at the corners of his mouth. 'It does, doesn't it?'

'You look like you've missed it.' Tess said quietly.

'Maybe I have.' He said thoughtfully. 'I hated this house when I inherited it. It seemed pretentious and old-fashioned. But we had nothing and no one except each other, and we needed a place to live. It was too big for just two people. Back then, we had ideas of filling it with children someday. But that didn't happen.' He stopped himself. 'I don't know. Maybe I associate this house with an unfulfilled promise.'

He looked around. When he turned back to Tess, he was smiling.

'I don't know what to think. But I'm glad we are here.'

He crossed the room and wrapped his arms around her. She tilted her head to look at his face, and he kissed her.

'I'm so glad you are here with me. In this house. In this room. Today.' He leaned down and kissed her again. She wrapped her arms around his neck. The kiss deepened, then he pulled back, brushing her hair from her face.

'You are so beautiful. I look at you sometimes when you're sleeping, and you look like an angel. My angel.'

He laid his right hand in the space between her breasts.

'I like this spot.' He whispered. 'Where your heart is.'

'You have my heart.' She told him, smiling.

'What—The—Fuck?!'

Tess spun around as Pen shook her head in disbelief.

Tess took two steps towards Pen before she felt her daughter's hand strike her hard across the face. By the time she recovered her senses, Pen had turned and run from the room. Mateo looked momentarily stunned, then ran after her. They heard him calling her name down the long hall, then feet loudly descending the staircase.

Javier and Tess were like deer caught in the headlights.

'Shit!' She cried, massaging her face with her ear still ringing from where her daughter had slapped her.

'Are you OK?' Javier asked her.

Tess nodded, but she wasn't OK. She wasn't sure she would ever be OK again. 'This is not good. We need to go after them!'

They hurried out of the house, choosing a direction when they got to the street.

'There is a park nearby.' Javier offered. 'Maybe they went there.'

They ran the few blocks to the park. Nothing. Tess paced, out of breath. She looked at her phone, not sure what she hoped to see. Pen's number went straight to voicemail. Tess texted her asking where she was but knew she wouldn't have much success in getting a response. Next, she called John to tell him what had happened before he heard it from Pen.

'Hey!' He said, still sleepy when he picked up the call.

'Hey. We have a situation.' And she went on to explain what had happened while massaging her jaw. She didn't try to paint herself in a good light. She just told him the truth. John was silent. She knew it was one thing to imagine what was going on here. It was quite another to lay it out for him explicitly and to have their daughter see it.

'I don't really know what to say, Tess. Hearing the details has left me speechless. I figured you'd tell me it all when you got home, but now that Pen is involved, it seems more sordid than before. I want to tell you I'm not angry, but I'd be lying.'

She could tell he was trying to keep from losing it altogether.

'I'll call her and talk to her.' He promised. 'But there is nothing I'm going to say that will make her feel better. I know that because I can't imagine feeling better myself. But I can listen.'

Tess was stung by his words, but she knew she deserved them. 'I think that would be best. But I need to talk to her, too. And I can't do that if I can't find her.'

'I'll text you when I reach her.' She heard him sigh. 'She's in shock, and she doesn't understand the situation.

'John?'

'Yes.'

'I love you.'

'I know you do. And God damn it—I love you too.' The line went dead.

Tess sat on the bench with her head in her hands and sobbed. Javier put his arms around her. There was nothing he could say to eliminate the pain of this situation, and he couldn't imagine how John was feeling. Then he thought of Mateo. His son must have been equally surprised. But he knew Mateo was aware something was going on between them.

Tess fought to pull it together.

'They could be anywhere in Madrid. What should we do?' she asked him, wiping her eyes.

Javier considered the question.

'I think we will stay at the house. If they don't return by the time it gets dark, we can always go home and wait. I will message Mateo, too. Perhaps he will tell me where they are.'

He did, but his text remained unread. They returned to the house and sat in the great room. Tess busied herself with taking the sheets off the furniture and opening the drapes and shutters. Javier didn't try to stop her. Neither knew what to say. They sat in near silence for several hours, each of them pacing the room in turn.

Around 8 pm, there was a knock at the door. Tess jumped up, and Javier went to answer it. Inés stood on the step with a basket that dwarfed her.

'Mateo let me know that something had happened at the house. He told me you came here with *señora* Tess, and there was some kind of fight.' She held up the basket. 'So, I brought you something to eat.'

Javier stood back so she could enter. She walked past him and into the great room where Tess was pacing. Inés put the basket on the desk and started to unpack it.

'You can decide when you are hungry.' She made to leave, but Javier stopped her.

'Thank you for all this, Inés. We appreciate it. If you hear from Mateo again, and he tells you where he is, I would appreciate you letting me know.'

She smiled, reaching up to pat his cheek.

'You know,' he said, 'I haven't been here in a long time. But today, I wanted to show Tess the house. I thought we would only step inside for a moment, but we didn't. We looked around. I noticed you've been keeping the house clean. The only room that appears like it has been untouched is this one.'

Inés took a deep breath.

'Yes, that's true.' She admitted. 'I left this room as it was when you left. I did dust and vacuum, but I didn't take the dust cloths away.'

'Why?' he asked, confused. 'If you were cleaning and keeping up the rest of the house, why did you leave this one?'

Inés closed her eyes, searching for just what to say.

'Because Mateo asked me to leave it.'

'Why?' Javier looked confused, 'I don't understand.'

She chose her next words carefully.

'He thought if you ever came here, you would get angry if the house was not shut tight. So he asked me to leave this room as it was. He believed this would be as far as you might venture. When you saw that it was as you left it, you would be okay.'

'Mateo?' Javier shook his head. 'Why?'

Inés remained silent.

'You've been taking care of the garden.' He said, looking out the windows at the small paradise she had been maintaining.

'I have not been taking care of the garden.'

'What? Then who?'

Inés took a deep breath.

'Mateo has been caring for it. Ever since you left, he would accompany me sometimes when I would come to dust and clean. At first, it was as you left it—every room covered in sheets, like a house filled with ghosts. He went out into the garden that first time and fed the fish in the fountain. He was a child, and he was worried about them. Then, one time he got into the carriage house for tools and began tending the garden. He said his mother wouldn't want him to let it die because she loved it so much.'

She stopped. Thinking she had gone too far.

Javier was stunned. He stared out the window at what his son had done.

'Eventually, Mateo began taking the sheets off the furniture in other rooms. He said he didn't like the feeling of it being hidden. I think he came here on his own because I would find candy wrappers sometimes. I found him once, asleep on your bed. It had no sheets or a blanket, so I brought some and made it up. He seemed to like being in there, so I kept it ready.'

'He used to spend time in his old room, too. I would catch him playing with some of his toy cars. Running them down the hallway. Do you remember when he would do that?' She shook her head, smiling at the memory. 'Always so busy when he was little. He brought a friend here once. But that was unusual. I think he liked to keep it all for himself.'

Javier's eyes filled with tears. 'Why did he never tell me? Why did *you* never tell me?'

'Because it wasn't my secret to tell.' She waited. 'I believe he did not want to hurt you. You moved to the apartment because you couldn't bear to be here without her. He asked me to leave the sheets on the furniture in this room so that you wouldn't know. He didn't want you to think he didn't like being with you at the apartment. But he misses home, and he misses his mother.' Inés looked around. 'She is everywhere in this place. Her studio in the attic is as she left it. Mateo wouldn't allow me to touch it. He feels close to her when he comes here.' Seeing the tears sliding down Javier's cheeks, she went to him and hugged him. Her tiny frame dwarfed as he hugged her back.

'You have been so good to us, Inés. I have not deserved you these last five years.'

She pulled away, wiping her tears.

'Tut tut. Of course, you have. I have been needed. That's all anyone wants in this life.'

She turned to Tess.

'Do not be so hard on yourself, *señora*. Whatever has happened, you will get through it. Families have problems all the time. But in the end, they forgive and move on together.'

She retrieved her purse from the couch.

'I will leave you to eat something.' She patted Javier's shoulder and quietly let herself out.

Tess went to him. While she was worried about her situation with Pen, this was a big moment for Javier and Mateo, facing ghosts in this house.

'She's right, you know.' Said Tess. 'We should eat something.'

Inés had brought them a feast. Tess looked through the basket and spotted something else. Inés had bagged up her medication from Javier's bathroom and put it in the bottom. Somehow, she knew.

They waited until it was past dark. And again, Tess texted John. He'd attempted to call and message Pen but was getting nowhere. She asked him if he wanted to talk, and shame washed over her when he declined. She shouldn't have allowed herself to get into this situation and drag Pen with her. And John too. She had no idea that the kids would come to a deserted house. But she should have been more careful. She had hurt John deeply—a crushing blow.

Just before dawn, Tess woke to the sound of rain. It was pouring outside—a summer shower with thunder rumbling in the distance. She got up from the sofa and went to the glass doors leading out to the garden. Sheets of water poured off the palm trees and the roof above.

Turning the handle, she stepped outside barefoot in her cotton dress, walking to the courtyard's center and looking up at the dark grey sky. Somewhere over the horizon, the sun was coming up. Lightning flashed, and the booms of thunder were rolling overhead with their vibrations coming up through her feet. She raised her arms and invited the water to wash over her. Standing motionless, Tess lifted her face to a sky that was raining its fury down upon her. Tess knew there wasn't enough water in the world to wash away her sins. For her, there would be no absolution.

'We had a deal, you and I. Remember?' Tess said to the sky. 'I'm ready. Do you worst to me.'

Javier had awakened, and he stood at the window, watching her. But he didn't attempt to bring her inside. Whatever was going on with Tess, she needed to do it alone. Then he heard the front door open.

Pen and Mateo walked into the great room. They looked tired and wet and seemed surprised to see Javier standing by the window. Not sure how to start, he waited for one of them to speak. Pen walked over, looking out the glass.

'Why is she standing in the rain getting soaked?' She asked him.

'I don't know. We've barely slept worrying about you both. When I woke up on the sofa, I found her outside, as you see her now.'

'Has she gone crazy?' asked Pen. 'Aren't you going to get her?'

'I was just giving her a moment.' He walked out and quickly became soaked himself. Whispering into Tess's ear, she turned to look towards the windows where Pen was standing.

Mateo grabbed a sheet from the pile, wrapping it around Tess as she entered.

There was so much water pouring down her mom's face, Pen couldn't tell if it was rain or tears. Tess sat down on the sofa, shivering. But she smiled up at Pen.

'I'm so glad you're alright.' She said through chattering teeth. 'I've been so worried about you.'

Pen could tell her Mother was crying now.

'I'm as okay as I can be seeing my mom making out with a guy who isn't my dad.'

Javier put his hand on Tess's shoulders. Pen saw it.

'That's right. You guys can keep fucking. Don't let me stop you.' She turned to go upstairs, but Tess reached out and grabbed her hand.

'Please, can we talk about this?' She pleaded.

'What's there to talk about?' Pen said, shaking her head. 'You've been fucking Javier since you met him, and now, I finally know it.'

Tess hung her head. The words stung.

'I have not been having sex with Javier since I met him. It happened along the way but not the whole time.'

'Oh, that makes me feel so much better.' Pen replied sarcastically, 'You've only been lying to me for a few weeks instead of months.' She shook her head. 'And Dad. He's going to hate you. Do you get that? He will hate you for coming to Spain and betraying him when I tell him. Betraying our family. And you don't get a free pass because you have cancer!'

Pen looked down at her mom with disgust. Tess took some deep breaths.

'Please Pen. Sit down and hear me out, just this one time. After that, you can go on and hate me forever. You can call your dad and tell him everything. Just sit down, and please let me talk to you.'

Tess cried through her words. She lowered her head into her hands, unsure of what to do.

'Fine. You get two minutes.' Mateo moved to sit next to Pen, but Javier stopped him and led him from the room. When her mother sat next to her, Pen moved to another sofa. Tess struggled to keep her emotions under control.

'There is something I want to show you.' whispered Tess.

She retrieved the letter out of her bag and handed it to Pen.

'What's this?' asked Pen.

'It's the letter your dad wrote to me. It's the one I opened in Barcelona that first night. He'd put it in my pack. You saw me, remember? You asked me if it was a sappy letter from Dad. Just like the one you got. But it wasn't like that at all. Please read it.'

Pen saw her father's writing on the envelope. She unfolded the paper and began reading. At one point, she stopped and looked up at her mother.

When she finished, she sat holding the sheet of paper—stunned. It was then Tess realized she was crying. She wanted to go to her but was afraid to scare her off.

'How could you sleep with Javier?' She asked through her tears. 'How could you betray Dad like that?'

'I'm not betraying your father. He knows.'

'What?!' She looked up at her mother in surprise.

Tess pointed to the letter.

'You've read what he wrote. He wanted me to have this time. To experience everything that life has to offer. Everything. I couldn't have imagined doing anything like this when I read it in Barcelona. It's not me. Or it wasn't. I knew he was giving me a 'free pass,' but it didn't matter. I would never use it.'

'But you did.' She whispered

'Yes, I did. Your dad and I even talked about it beforehand. I told him about Javier and how we walked with him and Mateo and spent so much time together. He told me he meant what he said.'

Pen seemed shocked by that.

'Your father is an extraordinary man, Pen. He understands me like no other person on this planet. Sometimes he understands me better than I do. And he always puts others before himself. I've never met anyone quite like him.'

Pen sat still, confused.

'When did it start? On the Camino? When did you start having sex with him?'

Tess took a deep breath.

'On the sheep farm.' She said, ashamed. 'When we went to deliver the lambs.'

'You had sex with him while you were delivering lambs?' Pen asked, incredulous.

Tess laughed.

'Of course not.' She wiped her nose. 'It was after. We were exhausted, and one thing led to another. I won't go into detail, but that's when it started. We'd already been walking with them for over a week. I didn't plan it out. But when we got to the vineyard and were having lunch, I stepped outside to call your dad. I told him where we were, what we were doing. He reiterated what he had said in the letter. He wanted me to be free on this walk.'

Pen looked stunned. It was not how things were supposed to be in fairy tales.

'We were exhausted after a night of lambing. I think my inhibitions were a little down, and because of what your dad had said, I didn't stop myself.' She explained.

Pen looked up at her. Still angry.

'Do you regret it? Do you wish you didn't do it?' Searching her mother's face for any dishonesty.

'I regret that it hurt you.' Tess said honestly. 'But I don't regret the time Javier and I have spent together. He has been very good to us. I was extremely ill that day in the river before León. He found me a doctor in the city, and while you were visiting Mateo's grandmother and aunts, I went and had some tests done. They changed my medication, and I've followed doctor's orders to the letter ever since.'

'You were sick that day?' Pen looked upset by this news. 'I didn't know. But I knew you were tired.'

'I didn't want to worry anyone. Javier helped me and got me back on track. Your dad is very grateful we've been with him all this time. He says, weirdly, he's indebted to him.'

Pen shook her head. She could see her dad saying that. Javier had saved her life, too, when she had that allergic reaction.

They sat on the sofa, silent.

'Don't do that anymore.' Whispered Pen. 'Don't pretend you're fine when you're not.'

'I don't want you to worry about me.' Said Tess, smiling reassuringly.

Pen sighed.

'Don't you get it? You don't have to hide from me. You don't have to pretend all the time.' Shaking her head with tears in her eyes.

'I'm not sure what you mean.' Tess said quietly.

'That's the problem right there. You have no clue what you're doing to us. And that's what's killing me. I feel like you hide everything from me—every emotion. Even now, with cancer. And after Charlie died, it was like you didn't want anyone to feel sadness. You kept it all bottled up for yourself. We moved away, from where he's buried, for *your* job. I can't even visit my brother. It was like you wanted us to erase him because it's too hard for you.'

Tess cried out. If she had eaten something, she would have vomited. But, at long last, her daughter told her how she felt.

'I'm only supposed to be happy, or you can't handle it. But life's not like that. I can't keep acting like everything is OK when it's not. And you having cancer isn't OK. It's terrible. You're ill—you can admit it. You're tired—you can take a rest. You're sad but you smile—like it's a badge of honor. You're always upset with me because I never smile. But I'm angry because that's all you ever do. You leave no room for anyone else's sadness because you're always pretending everything is OK when it's not. You're lying. To yourself and me.'

Tess sat there, stunned.

'You're so desperate for me to be happy you can't see that all I've been is sad since Charlie died—for years. You even admitted it in the church in Santiago. You can't handle my emotions. But with this, I won't pretend that you're not sick. I can see it, Mom. I'm not a baby anymore.'

Pen took a breath.

'You ask me why I do the things I do. You want me to talk to you, but you don't talk to me. I've had a lot of time to think on this trip. All the stuff about your mom and the pain you went through as a kid. You never told us. You never shared yourself with your own children. It's like we have no idea who you really are.' Pen gulped to take a breath. 'I'm sorry, but you don't get to go through cancer alone. It's not fair to Dad and me. It's happening to us too.'

Everything Pen said was true. And it hadn't started with the death of her son. Protecting her children meant they'd been robbed of knowing their mother. She thought she was protecting them from pain—when she was protecting them from her.

Pen wiped her nose.

'Do you think, wherever Charlie is, he's happy seeing what we've become?' She asked Tess.

Tess was crying too hard to answer. Pen waited for her to gather herself.

'Be honest with me.' whispered Pen. 'No more holding back. Are you going to die?'

Tess closed her eyes, wiping her tears. 'I don't know. But I won't lie. It isn't good, Pen. I'm going to fight it, though. I already am, with some of the meds I'm on. And we'll go home, and I'll have the surgery and the treatment.'

'Does Dad know about yesterday?' Pen asked.

'Yes. I called him right afterward.'

'I bet that was an awkward conversation.' She said sarcastically.

'Not my favorite. But your Dad has known all along. He's angry with me for putting you in this position. But mostly, we're both just worried about you.'

Tess sniffed.

'Listen. I know I have cancer, and it's difficult for everyone around me. And my choices on this trip have been hard for you. But please know that your Dad and I are strong. Our marriage is strong.' She choked up. 'No marriage is perfect. If you're looking for a prince on a white horse, he's on vacation for the duration. But what we need, Dad and me, we have that. It works for us. And that's not going away.'

Pen looked at her shoes. 'Do you love Javier?' She asked quietly.

'Yes, I do. But you can love people and not have it take away from the people in your life that matter most. Love is an infinite resource.'

'Did you have affairs on all your business trips?' Her voice hardened.

Tess supposed she deserved the suspicion.

'No. I've never been with anyone but your dad throughout our whole marriage. Until now.'

She sat next to her daughter, brushing the hair back from Pen's face.

Pen wiped her nose on her t-shirt.

'Are you going to keep having sex with Javier while we're here?'

Tess thought for a moment.

'I haven't given it a thought. That's not my focus. Mostly, I've been worried about you.'

Pen looked at her.

'Well, I guess you don't have to pretend anymore. But don't expect me to forgive you any time soon.'

Tess squeezed Pen's hand.

'I don't expect anything. But I will tell you what Inés told me last night. Families forgive the worst transgressions, and they move on together. I will need your help, Pen. For what's coming. You'll need to hold my hair back when I'm throwing up from cancer treatment.' She looked into her daughter's eyes before whispering, 'As I've done for you more than once.'

Pen looked at her Mother and silently nodded. She allowed Tess to hug her.

'Where did you go when you left here?' Tess asked her. 'I've been frantic.'

'I didn't know where to go.' Pen told her. 'I was hyperventilating when Mateo caught up to me. I've never cried that hard.'

It was difficult for Tess to hear.

'I'm so sorry, honey. For all of it.'

'Mateo was worried about me, so he took me back to the apartment. He knew you weren't there and thought it would be the best place for me to get it together. Inés was in the kitchen.'

'She made me some tea and cookies, and then I told her what happened. At first, she seemed a little surprised, but then it was like she sort of took it in stride. I told her I hated you and all the lies you told me.'

Tess wondered what Inés thought.

'What did she say?' whispered Tess.

'She just listened. She told me not to be too hard on you. That there's enough pain and suffering in this world without adding more. I told her you were the one adding pain and suffering. She said, 'No. Your mother is adding love.' But I didn't believe her.'

'Did she explain?'

Pen took a deep breath.

'She asked me if I thought she was a good person. I told her. 'Yes. Unlike my mom.'

Tess winced.

'I was mad. You've let me down.'

Tears slid unchecked down Tess's cheeks.

'Anyway. Inés said I shouldn't speak about my mother in that way. Then she said, 'Let me tell you a story.' Pen sniffed. 'A long time ago, she'd been young and beautiful. She could have had the pick of boys in her village, but only one caught her eye. He was a prominent man and a doctor from Madrid. He came to the village from time to time. His family owned a big house and land. She fell in love immediately.'

'They started seeing each other, even though she knew he was married to someone from a rich and powerful family in the capital. She didn't care, convincing herself that his wife was horrible and didn't truly love him, so what they did wasn't wrong. After a while, she got pregnant. She considered trying to have an abortion but decided against it. She told the man, worried he would be angry.'

'But he didn't get angry. Instead, he offered to move Inés to an apartment in the city, where he could still see her and his child. He loved her and tried to save her from the shame she would face in the village if anyone discovered she was pregnant.'

'In Madrid, people assumed her husband had passed away, and a young, pregnant widow got sympathy. But after her son was born, she was lonely. The man was very busy, and she didn't see him much. Sometimes, she would read his name in the newspapers. His wife liked to throw parties covered in the gossip columns. One day, she saw an ad in the newspaper for a housekeeper and got the job.'

'Not long after she started working in his house, she bumped into the man while dusting his office. He was furious at first. But then he got used to having her in his home. His wife told him the story of the young widow with a small child, and she was allowed to bring her son with her to work when he wasn't in school. The man and his wife already had a son of their own, and while there was an age gap, the older son treated the younger one like the brothers they were.'

'Years went by. Inés said, but the relationship became more of a friendship. When her son was 20, the man became ill. He suddenly passed away. Inés was happy she had worked and saved because there were no provisions for her or his son in his will. But she continued to work for his wife before she came to work for Javier and his wife.'

Tess's jaw dropped. She thought back to what Javier had told her. Inés had worked for his family since he was a boy.

'Where was Mateo when Inés told you this story?' she asked Pen.

'He left us alone in the kitchen. To give us some privacy.'

Tess nodded. 'So, how did you feel after your talk with her?'

Pen wiped her nose on her sleeve.

'Well. As Inés says, good people do things they shouldn't sometimes. Like me. It's kind of like what you and I talked about that day on the Camino.'

Her daughter had been listening.

'Inés told me life is messy. She said part of growing up is seeing your parents for who they truly are and loving them anyway. And that no matter what, a mother's love for her child is the one thing that endures.'

Tess wrapped her arms around her daughter, and after a few moments, she felt Pen's arms encircle her too.

She made up the sofa for Pen and sat watching her sleep. Tess could see how everything had unraveled over the previous two months. Even she was confused about who she was anymore. It wasn't any wonder that her husband and her daughter were struggling to keep up.

Javier and Mateo appeared in the afternoon, and Pen finally woke up. She was sullen and silent but seemed less angry than she was before.

The four of them returned to the apartment, where Inés was waiting. Pen and Mateo went to get cleaned up while Javier decided to connect with his office. Inés and Tess were alone in the kitchen.

'Thank you again, Inés. The hamper was just what we needed yesterday.'

'It was my pleasure.' She took a drink of her coffee. 'It appears you were able to talk to your daughter.'

'Yes. Pen and Mateo came back to the house early this morning. I think it will be OK.'

'That's good. I am glad it was able to be worked out. Discord in a family is a terrible thing. It eats from the inside out.'

'I agree.' Tess took a deep breath. 'When Pen ran out of the house, I was so scared. I wondered how I would find her to explain. Somehow, she came back.'

'Children have a way of surprising us.' Inés smiled. 'They are difficult one moment, but then they turn around and need us more than ever. Pen needs you. It's clear to me. Especially right now.'

'What do you mean?' Asked Tess.

Inés cocked her head but said nothing.

'I know.' whispered Tess.

Inés patted her hand.

'I think you and your daughter have been good for Mateo and his father.' She offered. 'When they left here, they were on a quest. I don't know any other way to describe it. It was plain to see. They have always been close, but still, they needed to find their way back to each other. They each hurt themselves rather than the other with their grief. Now it is finished. I saw it when they came home this morning. I think this is down to both you and Pen.'

Tess considered her words.

'I didn't feel like we were doing anything for them. Javier was so helpful with the medical stuff that came up when we were walking. Pen adores Mateo.' Tess said.

Inés squeezed her hand.

'It's more than that. When a heart is so broken, it believes love is no longer possible. Food has no taste. The sun has no warmth. But now, they both know that love is possible and the future awaits them. You've helped them see that life can go on and take them with it.' Inés said thoughtfully.

'Javier says it's time to move back to the house.' Tess told her. 'Mateo told him this morning he doesn't want to live in the apartment anymore. He wants to move home.'

Inés smiled knowingly.

Tess stopped at Pen's room and knocked on the door.

She waited as her daughter opened and let her in.

'Did you talk to Dad?' Pen asked.

'Yes, I did. He's anxious for us to get home.'

'Yeah. I talked to him, too.' said Pen. 'He is worried about me.'

'He is.' Tess agreed. 'He knows this is a lot. Even without Javier, it's a lot.'

Pen frowned.

'I don't hate you, you know?'

'Well, thank you for that.' smiled Tess, reaching out and squeezing her daughter's hand. 'I appreciate it.'

'I guess, when I was little, I thought you were perfect. Somewhere in the last few years, I found out you weren't. It's made me mad—like you'd lied to me. And yesterday, when I found out you are even less perfect than I thought, I got mad.' Pen sniffed.

'I know.' whispered Tess.

'But then I think, what would I do if they told me I had cancer and I might die? I'd probably go a little crazy. Maybe I'd go bungee jumping or skydiving or something. Maybe I'd get super drunk and run down the street naked.'

Tess chuckled at that.

'I can't see that happening.' She told her daughter.

'Maybe not, even for me.' Pen smiled. 'But I might do something no one would expect me to do. Completely out of character.'

'Yeah, maybe you would.' Tess agreed. 'It is a shock when they tell you the diagnosis, like an out-of-body experience. As though it's happening to someone else, and you're just observing it all. When my doctor told me, I could hardly understand what she was saying. She had to repeat it. Your dad said he felt the same way when he came with me the next day.

'I wasn't very nice to you guys that day.' Pen said through her tears.

'No. But you didn't know what was going on.' Tess reminded her, letting her off the hook.

'You must have still been in shock. And then seeing me like I was.' She left it hanging.

'We were.' Said Tess. 'But we knew we had to do whatever it took to save you.'

'Does it hurt? Is that how you found out? You were in pain, so you went to the doctor?'

'No. I just felt lumps under my armpit and then at my throat. I scheduled an appointment with my doctor but had to change it a couple of times because of work. Finally, they did an ultrasound and a scan, and I had a biopsy. When the doctor called me and suggested I come in for a discussion, I knew it wouldn't be pleasant. We talked through options and treatment plans. I told them I needed to think about it.' Taking a deep breath. 'But the Camino flashed into my mind then, and I couldn't shake it.'

'I understand.' Pen wasn't perfect herself. She had made significant errors in judgment that had impacted her family, too.

'So, you think Dad will ever forgive you for being with Javier?' She asked.

Tess closed her eyes.

'He told me to embrace romance, Pen. I didn't make him write that or say it. So, he's hurt and angry, but I didn't sneak around. And while it kills me that he's hurting, I am not a bad person. No matter what it looks like to you.'

Tess knew Pen was struggling with the events of the last 24 hours. At fifteen, seeing the world in black and white was easy. Experience had taught her that shades of grey would only come over time. Tess decided to go a different way.

'I don't want this final week to be about my cancer or Javier and me. I want it to be about gathering our strength because we will need it.' Tess smiled through tears. 'And for you to have fun, too. Let's forget the mistakes we've made, you and me. Just for a little while. Then we'll go home.' Reaching out and squeezing Pen's hand.

Pen wiped her tears and nodded. 'Ice cream dinners?' offered Pen.

'Oh yeah.' Tess smiled. 'I need a whole lot more ice cream dinners in my life!'

Pen sniffed, then hugged her mom. 'You're insane.'

Tess closed her eyes and hugged her back. 'Totally.'

Pen seemed to orbit Tess as they wound down their time in Spain. She stayed close to her mother. And she still struggled with the after-effects of her mom's diagnosis and the discovery of her affair. Mateo asked what they wanted to do for the rest of their vacation.

Tess and Pen had already talked about it.

'We would like to help you move back into the house. Knowing you're there and settled when we go home would make us both very happy. How does that sound?' Tess asked.

Javier made a face.

'We don't want to put you to work while you're our guests. No, I will have a moving company come and take everything.'

'Sure, the big stuff. But the little stuff, and getting the house opened and ready to occupy? We can help with that. Inés is only one person, after all.' She reminded him.

They informed Inés of their plans to get the house ready.

'This sounds wonderful.' She said. 'I am happy to have extra hands.'

Tess had spied boxes stacked outside the far end of the dining room in the apartment. Inés had already gotten a head start, noticing Tess's eyes flitted in that direction, smiling.

The next day the group loaded boxes into Javier's car, and he drove them to the house. They helped Inés get the kitchen cleaned in the big house and ready to use. It didn't take long, and it was no time before Javier and Mateo arrived with another load from Mateo's room.

Afterward, Javier plopped down on a couch. He was tired but happy. The house was starting to feel lived in again. One of the neighbors had stopped by to welcome them home. Unaware that they had been across town for the past five years.

'Later, we can tackle getting clothes over here.' Said Tess. 'That's easy to take in the car. I'll also bring Pen's and my things so that we all stay in the same place.'

Javier agreed and gratefully accepted a cold drink from Inés.

'I called a moving service for the larger pieces.'

They headed up the stairs to check on Mateo's room. Tess looked around. The toys from when he was little were now on a shelf above his desk. They'd put the fútbol posters on the walls and new sheets on the bed. Pen looked pleased with herself.

'What do you think?' she asked them when they entered the door.

'How does Mateo like it?' Tess asked.

He surveyed his old domain.

'I like it. It's still got stuff from when I was little. It's a good blend.' Javier agreed.

He and Tess walked down to his bedroom when he stopped and looked around.

'The painting. Spring. I think it's time we unite her with her other seasons. Let's go back after lunch and get the paintings. I want to hang them today.' He said boldly.

Tess was impressed. He hadn't hesitated for a moment since Mateo insisted they move back to the house. Instead, he'd jumped in with both feet. Ready to conquer the grief that had plagued him for so long.

After lunch, Javier laid out the plan for the group.

'We will return to the apartment to get some of the artwork. Would you both like to help us?'

Mateo was the first to respond. 'Yes. I want to bring Mama's paintings back to the house. I know where they go.'

'What do you mean?' asked Pen

'She painted them for specific spaces where she hung them. For the light in that space, she told me. I remember where they were before we moved.'

Javier marveled at his son's enthusiasm. He had underestimated the impact of moving all those years ago.

The four of them headed back to retrieve the art; to ensure it spent the night in its rightful place. By the time they returned, they had noticed a few things that appeared out of nowhere.

On the entry table, a tray caught Javier's eye. It was small and blue, made of lapis with a gold edge. Alejandra bought it for him as a gift on holiday to Morocco. It had held his keys and wallet, but he hadn't seen it in years. Yet here it was, looking the same, under the mirror in the foyer. He ran his hands over its smooth surface, then set his keys and wallet inside as if time had never passed.

Tess followed a delicious smell into the large kitchen. It sparkled down to the colored tiles on the walls and the stone on the floor. Inés was cutting through a haunch of meat on an ancient woodblock attached to a long, well-worn wooden table in the middle of the room.

She looked up and smiled. 'Ah, you're back, I see.'

'Yes. We gathered the paintings from the apartment. We're going to start hanging them now.' Said Tess.

'Wonderful. Mateo must be pleased.'

'I think he is. He says he knows where they go.' Tess told her.

'I am sure he does.' Said Inés knowingly. 'I will go back later and pack some more things. Since the kitchen is here now, this is where we will eat. We can have most everything moved from there, in a few days, except the large pieces.'

'Where will all the extra furniture go?' Tess asked her. 'This house already has furniture.'

'I think Mateo has thought about that. I will wait for him to unveil his plan.' Then she returned to the giant meat cleaver in her hand.

Tess heard hammering and followed the sound upstairs to an area she had never been to. They were hanging pictures on existing hooks, and *voila!* The art was back where it belonged. Each painting came to life, suspended in the place for which Alejandra had painted it. Tess offered to help, but Javier declined.

'Why don't you lay down? Have a nap.'

'Yeah, Mom.' Pen said, looking over her shoulder. That's a great idea. Go rest and make sure you take your medicine.'

Tess frowned. She was being dismissed like a child by both Javier and Pen. But she knew they were right; a nap would do her some good. She lay down in Javier's room and went into a deep sleep, with dreams filled with pictures—flashes of her life and people who meant so much to her. Tess awoke with a sense of peace.

Rolling over, she tasted copper and felt a wet spot. The pillow was soaked in blood. Holding her nose, she ran into the bathroom to get some cold water and stem the bleeding. It took a bit before she was successful at getting it to clot. Then she cleaned up her face and grabbed the pillow from the bed.

Creeping slowly down the stairs in bare feet, hearing muted laughter from the garden, she found a garbage can in the boot room and hid the pillow beneath some of the plastic bags. Then she straightened her skirt before heading out through the glass doors.

'The princess has awakened.' Javier rose and pulled out a chair.

Unlit candles dotted the table already set for dinner.

'We weren't sure if you would get up in time for dinner.' he said. Pleased that she had.

'My stomach woke me up. What is that divine smell?' Tess asked them.

'Inés is in charge.' declared Pen. 'I think she likes being back here with the big kitchen. She even made homemade bread!'

'Well, I completely approve of that.' said Tess, touching her nose to ensure the bleeding had stopped.

'It's a homecoming dinner. Inés says it's bad luck not to bless the house with a good meal when moving in. In our case, it's moving back in, but I don't think that matters.' Mateo patted his belly. 'All my favorite dishes.'

Javier poured Tess a glass of garnet red wine and topped up his own. She looked around the garden, listening to the water burbling in the fountain, sure she could fall asleep on a sunny afternoon in the hammock they had set up during her nap.

'What are we talking about?' she asked. 'I heard laughter.'

'These two were just listening to an old man tell stories about his college days.' Javier informed her. The wine had made his accent very thick and his cheeks red.

'Javier was kind of wild, Mom.' Pen told her.

'Shocking!' Tess said in mock surprise. 'What's the craziest thing you did in college?' She asked him.

'Oh. That is a difficult question.' He said. 'Because I was unfettered in competition with my friends to do the most terrible things.'

'Terrible? Like what?'

Javier took a deep breath.

'One time, Amelia and I stole a goat from a farm outside the city. It was just a small goat. And we took it back with us on the train to the Universidad de Barcelona, leaving it in our professor's office. It was so small. We thought it a harmless joke, but the goat ate nearly all the papers on his desk. Who knew that goats could climb?'

'Who knew?' Tess laughed until her face was purple. 'Everyone. Haven't you heard of mountain goats?'

He scowled. 'Of course, I have. But this was a small farm goat from a flat farm. I didn't know flat farm goats could climb. It seems those papers were quite important. They wanted to kick us out, but in a twist of fate, Alejandra's father stepped in and saved us. That was during the time he still thought I had great potential.'

At that moment, Tess realized he was a little drunk. Javier pointed to Mateo.

'Be sure to ask your grandfather about it next time you visit him in Barcelona. He loves that story.'

'I bet.' said Tess sarcastically.

'Anyway, the train ride was the worst part. Goats don't like trains, and they make a lot of noise. *Y se caga en todas partes.*'

He took another sip of his wine.

'I can see your tender heart in your eyes, mi amor.' he told Tess. 'Do not be sad. We took the goat back to the farm. But I will warn you. Do you know what eating paper does to a goat? Goat bloat. It's not something you want to experience.'

Javier pointed at Mateo.

'I borrowed your grandfather's car to return the little goat.' Laughing at his old stunt. 'When I brought the car back to him, it smelled like a farm. I think he was finding goat shit in there for years.'

'Okay,' Tess stood up. 'This concludes *Drunk History-Spain edition.* I'll take the rest of this bottle.' And to Mateo, 'How many has he had?'

'This is the second one.' he laughed.

'Ah.' She grabbed it and went back into the house through a door that led into the kitchen. Inés was reading the newspaper, waiting for something to come out of the oven.

'Good news, Inés! The rest of this amazing wine is all yours. To drink or cook, it's your choice.' She looked around. 'I thought I smelled bread, and I need some before our doctor falls asleep in a drunken stupor.'

Inés laughed.

'I baked many loaves. You can have that one over there.' She pointed to a large baguette on the wooden table, cooling on a rack. She got up, producing a small dish, and filled it with olive oil before handing it to Tess. 'This will help too.'

'*Muchas gracias.*'

'*Nada.*' She sat down and picked up her paper.

Back in the garden, Tess set the bread and oil on the table.

'Time for a little something to eat, my friend.'

Javier stuck his tongue out but broke off a piece, dipped it in the oil, and plopped it in his mouth.

'Mmm. That is good. You must try it.' He encouraged.

Tess did and discovered the best bread she'd ever had. They ate the entire loaf in minutes.

Soon steaming dishes began to emerge from the kitchen. Pen found matches and lit the candles. It was like eating dinner in the secret garden, not in the wet English countryside, but in the warm half-light of the Spanish capital. The temperature was perfect. And the food, divine.

Inés had baked a *Tarta de Santiago* for dessert, which they didn't eat until midnight. Finally, stuffed with food and wine, Javier suggested they stroll through the city to aid in digestion.

'It's nearly one am.,' Said Tess. 'I'm not sure that's such a good idea this late.'

'Madrid only starts getting warmed up at midnight.' He told her.

Tess looked over at Pen, and her daughter nodded in agreement.

'Everyone was on the street when we were out the other night. It was busier than daytime.'

It seemed Pen didn't exaggerate. The streets were teeming with people in the middle of the night.

'Don't these people have jobs to go to in the morning?' She asked.

'Yes.' Javier assured her. 'They'll get to their offices by 9 or 10 am.'

They stopped and chatted with people Javier knew. Mateo texted his friend, Emiliano, and the boy met up with them, huddling as teenagers do.

'Mom. Can we go with Emiliano?' Pen pleaded.

'Yes. But you'll be home by dawn, right?' Tess surprised herself. 'We have more moving to do tomorrow. We can't sleep all day.'

The kids ran off.

Javier put his arm around Tess, and they walked for a while. The meal seemed to have sobered him up.

'How does it feel to have arrived in Madrid only a few days ago, and you're already moving back into the big house?' she asked.

'It feels good. Like we've been there the whole time.' He mused. 'Maybe not physically. But emotionally, in many ways, neither of us ever left.'

Tess was happy the move wasn't causing him pain. They walked for a while longer before rounding the corner to the front door.

'Why does Inés live in an apartment on her own? You have more than enough room. She's getting older, and she could live here with you.' Tess suggested. 'That way, she wouldn't have to commute, and another person would be in the house.'

'You are always so full of good ideas.' he smiled. 'You are right, of course. I will speak with her about it tomorrow.'

They climbed the giant staircase and went to bed, never hearing the kids come in, just as the sun rose.

Tess awoke feeling something on her nose and swatted it away. She rolled over, but it came back again. Opening her eyes, she saw Javier leaning over her with a feather.

'You are mischievous.' She laughed.

'Yes. Sadly, this is one of my best qualities.'

He leaned over and kissed her. It deepened, and they made love quietly and slowly. Afterward, Javier asked her what she wanted to do for the day.

'Please, no tourist stuff.' She pleaded.

'As you wish.'

It set the tone for the rest of their stay. In the mornings, they woke late. Tess enjoyed helping Inés in the kitchen in the afternoons. And their final week in Spain flew by.

'You will be gone 48 hours from now.' Javier quietly observed while enjoying a glass of wine after dinner.

'Yes. I will.' Whispered Tess.

'I am having a hard time with that, suddenly. My butterfly, flying away.'

She didn't know what to say. There was no way around it. She had to start treatment, but it didn't make it any easier.

'I will miss you more than I can say.' She said. 'You have gotten me through the last two months. Every day, you've been there. Every day, I knew you would be. And in a moment, you won't be there anymore.'

Javier reached for her hand.

'I will still be here, wishing you only good things. I want your treatment to succeed and hear that you are cancer-free. That it's all a bad memory.' He told her.

Tess blew out a long breath.

'I did something today. I hope you don't mind.' She told him.

'What did you do?' he asked.

'I emailed my doctor back in Phoenix. I asked her to keep you informed of my treatment. I gave her permission to tell you everything if you wanted to know.'

He looked into her eyes, full of pain.

'Of course, I want to know.' He whispered, 'Do I need to get in touch with her myself, or will your doctor give me regular updates?'

'We didn't get into those details, but I'm sure you could reach out if you didn't hear from her. I will send you her details.' She promised.

Javier struggled to control his emotions.

'You don't have to do this, you know. For me. I won't be able to do anything about it.'

'I know. But if I were you, I would want to know.' She told him.

Leaning forward, he kissed her hands and looked up.

'Thank you,'

They headed to bed through the kitchen, telling Inés they were too tired for coffee and climbing the stairs, thinking about their last full day together. They lay down, and Javier held her.

'It was so easy on the Camino. We didn't have to think about real life. Every day, I just thought about that single day.' Said Tess. 'How far we needed to walk, where the food and water would be along the path. Nothing else.' She smiled. 'Some days, when someone asked me where we had stayed the previous night, I couldn't remember the name of the town or the albergue. It was already in the past. The future was one day away, and this day was the only thing. Just walking.'

He sighed. 'And every day, I was so happy to awaken. I had to sleep away from you, and waking up before dawn meant we would be together again for the whole day. I could touch you, hold your hand, and care for you.' Tears spilled from his eyes. 'Soon, I will no longer have that privilege.'

Tess rolled over and hugged him tightly.

'I will think of you so often, you'll feel it. You'll just know. And I'll know you are thinking of me. At key moments, I'll know.' She promised.

Javier kissed the top of her head as she clung to him. They lay in the dark until the sun came up.

PART V

HOME

Nineteen
The Grief of Goodbye

Tess rolled over as the late-morning sun streamed into the room. Javier lay beside her, but his breathing told her he was still asleep. Slowly, she crept out of bed, retrieving his robe from the bathroom and opening the door as quietly as possible. Tess padded down the stairs and made her way to the kitchen. She found a note on the table from Inés. She and the kids had gone to continue packing up. They would be back for lunch. Inés left some fresh pastries on a plate, and Tess gathered them on a tray with juice, making her way back upstairs.

The door to the bedroom was tricky, and she made so much noise balancing the tray and opening it that Javier was fully awake when she finally crossed the threshold.

'Good morning, sleepyhead.' She smiled.

He yawned and stretched. 'I thought I would find you in bed when I awoke. But instead, a herd of elephants was beating down the door, and my love was nowhere to be found.'

'Well, this elephant was downstairs foraging for food.' She set the tray on the bed and handed him a glass of juice. 'Inés was here very early this morning, baking. The kids are with her now.'

'Ah.'

'So,' she said mischievously, 'we have this giant house all to ourselves for the next few hours. What shall we do? Dance in the ballroom? Bowl in the hallways? Run naked in the garden?'

He laughed. 'All excellent ideas. But I think you should come back to bed.'

'I do wish we could lay in bed all day.' She told him. 'Just us, here. Doing nothing.'

'Really? Nothing?'

'OK, not nothing. But I know we can't. Inés said they would be back for lunch.'

'But we can still laze about today. I don't want you out of my sight for a moment.' He said, wrapping his arms around her.

'Mmm. Whatever you say.' She snuggled in.

Later, they went down to the kitchen. Javier was cooking them breakfast when he turned from the stove and saw the blood dripping from her nose. He grabbed a towel to try to stop the bleeding.

'You're going home tomorrow, or I'd have you see someone here in Madrid.' He said as he tilted her head back.

Tess smiled and squeezed his hand.

'It's not the first time since León, is it?' He asked.

She shook her head.

He reached up and felt her forehead. 'Why didn't you tell me? I could have done something.'

Tess took the towel from him.

'Because I don't think there is anything you could do.' She whispered. 'I'm going home, and I'll do what they say, but what I have is very aggressive. It's getting worse. I know that. I haven't given up, but I think this thing will get the best of me.' She smiled through her tears, trying to reassure him she was OK.

Javier looked panicked.

'Don't say that. There are all kinds of new treatments. Please don't say it. Don't even think of it.'

Tess closed her eyes and tried to calm herself.

'It's alright.' Tess reassured him. 'I came here for Pen. I got my daughter back. And I got you in the bargain. Gift with purchase. No matter what happens, it's all good.'

Javier bent down and kissed her, the coppery taste of her blood on his tongue.

They were washing their dishes when they heard a violent pounding on the front door. Javier and Tess ran to the hall, assuming the kids carried heavy boxes and required swift entry. On the other side of the door was a reed-thin, raven-haired woman in her seventies with a face that could slice through stone. She looked beyond Javier to Tess, then back again. Rapid-fire Spanish ensued before he put a stop to it.

'Please speak English, Mother. I have a guest, and she doesn't understand Spanish.'

The woman turned on Tess with a withering look. But she complied.

'I haven't heard from you or Mateo in weeks! Imagine my surprise when I went to your apartment today, and the doorman told me you were moving out.'

'Yes, well. We have decided to move back here.' He explained with more patience than Tess could have mustered. 'Mateo wanted to come home.'

'Hmm. And then, *el señor Ruiz* tells me you have been home for some time. And brought some backpacking Americans with you.' She snarled, looking Tess up and down with open disdain.

Her reference to Tess and Pen woke up Javier's manners.

'I'm sorry. Tess Sullivan, this is my mother, María Francisco Gómez. Would you like to come in, Mother, or shall we have this conversation in front of the neighborhood?'

The woman pushed past Javier and moved on to Tess, carefully examining her from head to toe.

'Hmph!' was all she got.

Tess didn't take that as a good sign, but she had no time to react. María had already marched past her and into the great room.

'So, you have finally come to your senses and decided to live like a man of decent social standing.'

'Actually, Mother. Social standing had nothing to do with it. Tess,' Javier gestured in her direction, 'helped me face some things. Things I hadn't wanted to face in a long time. I see now that moving back here is part of the healing process.'

'Healing from what? She's been dead five years, Javier.'

His sharp intake of breath warned Tess he was fighting hard to stay composed.

'Her name is Alejandra. And have *you* ever recovered from Papa's death?' He asked his mother boldly.

'That's different. Your father was the most famous doctor in Madrid.' She hissed, with her chin in the air.

Javier stopped himself from saying something he would later regret. María looked past him.

'Where is Mateo? I would at least like to see my only grandchild.'

'He's with Inés. Tess's daughter, Pen, went with them. Inés is moving in with us.'

'Finally. You will have some live-in help. There are servant's quarters in the attic.' María waved toward the roof. 'I'm sure she will be comfortable there.'

'No. The attic was Alejandra's studio. It will remain as it is at Mateo's request. Inés will take a room down the hall from him.'

Maria registered this with horror.

'That is unacceptable. Mateo sleeping on the same floor as the housekeeper?' Her shocked expression made Tess snigger. María wasn't amused.

'Inés is family, as you well know.' He said quietly.

They heard a commotion in the hall. The others were back. Mateo led the way carrying a heavy box, followed closely by Pen. The look on his face when he saw his grandmother told the story. María saw the box he was carrying and turned back to Javier.

'Can't you hire men to do the moving? Making your son carry boxes like a bin man.' She said, shaking her head.

Javier ran his fingers through his hair as Mateo set the box down and hesitantly kissed his grandmother's boney cheek. She smoothed his hair and swatted dust from his shirt.

'Really. Tut tut.' María looked past Mateo to Pen, whose ponytail was askew from packing. The woman's lips pressed into a hard spidery line. Javier saw where it was going and jumped in.

'Listen, Mother. Would you like to come and have a coffee? We can sit down and talk about it.'

María's eyes narrowed, and she lifted her chin defiantly.

'No. I have an appointment. But it would be nice to be invited for lunch sometime,' looking Tess and Pen up and down for the fourth time, 'when you are settled. Imagine, I must hear from your doorman that you're back in Madrid! And you don't even think to call your mother.'

She turned her fury on Inés.

'I would have expected more from you.' Her ruby red lips cut a severe gash across her thin face while looking down her patrician nose.

Inés met her gaze. Unafraid.

María grabbed Mateo's face and squeezed it. Then she turned in a fury, leaving a trail of Spanish and a signature scent in her wake. Reminded of the Wicked Witch of the West in the *Wizard of Oz*; if Maria had pointed a bony finger at Tess and said, 'I'll get you my pretty!' it wouldn't have been a surprise.

Javier sat down on the sofa, closing his eyes. Tess joined him, speechless.

'I'm so sorry about that. I should have phoned my mother when we got back. But you were here, and I was distracted by everything with the house.'

Inés stepped in.

'You have been very busy getting your house in order. She will calm down, and I'll make a special lunch with all her favorites for her next visit.'

Javier smiled gratefully at Inés.

'That lady is scary!' said Pen, finding her voice. 'I thought she was going to hit me.' She reached up to touch Mateo's cheek. 'Your face is red where she squeezed it.'

Mateo massaged his jaw.

'Come.' Inés said, trying to change the conversation. 'We've had enough excitement for the morning. If you can help us get the boxes from the taxi, I'll start on lunch.'

'I need to pop out for a little bit.' Javier told Tess. 'Will you be fine here on your own for a half-hour?'

Tess wondered if it had to do with his mother.

'Sure. These two can entertain me.' She smiled up at Mateo and Pen.

Later, Tess enjoyed the quiet and took the hammock in the garden for a final ride.

Inés brought out some coffee.

'You've had a busy morning. Sit down and keep me company.' Tess encouraged her.

'Okay, just one. I have some unpacking I would like to do.'

'Inés, I just wanted to say, *Thank you*. You've taken care of us while we've been here. And I don't think we have been easy guests. Pen seems to have adopted you like her new Spanish grandmother, and I would take you home with us if I could.'

Inés just smiled.

'I will miss both of you very much. Doctor Silva said that Pen has the invitation to return here to go to high school for one year to help her improve her Spanish. I hope she can.'

'Yes, I think it would be good for her. For her studies, but also to come here and spend time with all of you.' Tess reached over and squeezed Inès' hand.

'*Señora*. I don't want to speak outside my place. But I hope everything goes well with your health. I don't know precisely what is happening, but I know it is serious. Pen was crying the other day.'

Inés held up her hand when she saw Tess's expression change.

'I have watched a child in anguish, and I think hiding it is unhealthy. She was in the garden and didn't believe anyone could hear her. I saw her from the kitchen window. And I let her cry for a bit before I went out to see if there was anything I could do. She told me about your cancer. Not the same one as Alejandra's, I think. But serious. Please make sure she does not cry alone. She doesn't need protection from your feelings. You can cry together. Anything else will break both your hearts.'

Tess's eyes welled with tears. She knew Inés was right, and hearing Pen was having a hard time, and keeping it from her, was difficult to hear.

'I will speak to her.'

'Exactly this.' Said Inés.

She squeezed Tess's hand and patted her shoulder before returning to the kitchen. Tess sat back, stunned. How had they ever lived before the Camino? Before Madrid? They were sleepwalking, and now she and Pen were awake. She hoped it wouldn't end when they got home.

Later, after a dinner where Inés outdid herself, they sat back, enjoying the evening in candlelight.

'We didn't talk about what happened with my mother today.' He said, examining the last of the wine in his glass. 'She can be difficult.'

'It seems so.,' agreed Tess.

'She loves Mateo. Fiercely.' He assured her. 'But she believes the world revolves around her. My father fed that myth, and it did her no good. He always let her have her way. But there were times I knew he couldn't take it. Then he would take me up to the farm to check on things. To take a deep breath.'

Tess smiled. 'I think perhaps I would have liked your father.'

'He died when Mateo was a toddler. You would think my mother was frozen in grief, but she just likes to play the martyr. Alejandra tried to help her, but my mother rejected her sympathy out of hand. When my wife died, María took the opportunity to make it about her, and she relived my father's death all over again.'

'So, you didn't have her support as you went through the grieving process.' She said quietly.

He looked as though what she was suggesting was such a foreign concept that he could not comprehend it.

'Support? From María? No, these words do not go together.'

Tess was silent. She couldn't believe that his mother was so heartless.

'Her life revolves around her friends and a social calendar that nobody cares about anymore. She is living in another century, entirely.' He told her.

'How does Mateo feel about it?' Tess asked.

'He never says a bad word about her.' Then he thought for a moment. 'Actually, he never talks about her at all. He loves seeing Sofía, and they speak on the phone. She sends him small treats to let him know she's thinking of him. He set up a Facebook account for her, and she comments on everything he posts. He only does it for her, so she can see what he's doing and feel a part of his life. I can't imagine my mother ever doing anything like that. It would require her to recognize that she is not the sun around which we all orbit.'

'What was she like when you were growing up?'

He thought for a few moments and answered honestly.

'My mother was perfume and cold kisses on the cheek before bedtime. I can still smell her scent.' He said, transported to a time so many years ago. 'She looked like the princesses in the books my *niñera* would read me. Untouchable. Just out of reach. I don't remember her hugging me, except on my birthdays when she would throw elaborate parties and invite the children of all her friends. She said it was so I could establish good connections from the start. But I don't see most of those people now.'

'That's so sad.' Said Tess.

'Hmm. Perhaps. But I didn't know any better. My father was very affectionate with me. And the staff in our house could see how she was, especially Inés, and they spoiled me with treats. So, I knew I was loved.'

'How did Alejandra deal with her?' She asked.

'Oh, that was a fiery relationship. Alejandra was a passionate person. Painters often are.' He smiled, remembering. 'She would get so angry at how my mother treated me. But that was nothing compared to how she treated Alejandra. It wasn't until after Mateo was born that María would acknowledge her daughter-in-law when she walked into a room. My father could do nothing about it. The episode today was just one of a thousand before it. There is no winning. Just a cool détente that breaks down without warning.'

'So, it's just you and Mateo.' Tess sighed. 'You're on your own.'

'We have Inés, and we have other friends. You met Amelia. She and I have been friends all our lives. She's also my cousin, so she knows how María is.'

Tess squeezed his hand reassuringly, and Javier smiled, squeezing back.

'I wish I could hold on to you,' he said, 'but you must go. Back to your real life.'

His smile turned sad.

'And I wish you weren't about to enter such a dark time. But I will be with you in spirit. I'll even go to church and light candles for you. I'm sure Inés will go with me.'

'A bold step for a lapsed Catholic.' She said, surprised.

'You have to be a believer to lapse. But I do feel something. Those times on the Camino when I would go with you. There is something there, and if it can help you, I'll do whatever I need to.'

Tess hated to see the pain on his face.

'It will be strange to be back in the US. I've gotten used to hearing Spanish in the background of everything.'

'You will be busy with other things.' He whispered—an understatement.

'Yes. I will.'

That night, Tess fell asleep in Javier's arms. He lay awake, remembering another such night long ago when he had to let go of the woman he loved. It didn't get any easier.

The final morning, Tess woke as the sun rose. She rolled over and saw Javier lying beside her, staring at the ceiling.

'You're awake.' She put her arm over his chest. He hugged her back but said nothing.

They heard the sounds of Inés leaving her room down the hall. And birds chirping in the trees outside the window—everyday sounds.

'I am sitting here listening.' He said. 'I haven't slept.'

'I'm sorry.' She said.

'I've heard car doors slam and the world waking up. While this is a tough day for you and me, the rest of the world hasn't stopped. The earth has turned, and the sun came up like a river that continues to flow to the sea. The diversion of a couple of drops doesn't alter its course. And we are the drops. Life continues when hearts break; when loved ones go away. It just does, like an unstoppable force. Even when you don't want it to.'

Tess was silent as he gathered her in his arms.

'We have lived a lifetime in only a few weeks. It's the only life we will ever get together. I have loved every moment. Every breath. Every word. Every look. I have taken them all in, and like water across rock, they have worn a groove that will never go away. You are the water flowing away from me, but I will never be the same after knowing you.'

Tears welled in her eyes. She sat up to face him.

'I want to pretend I'm not leaving today until we walk out the door.' Her sad eye pleaded with him. 'Please, let's have our last few hours be some of our best. I don't want to spend it being sad.'

He reached up, brushed the hair from her face, and stroked her cheek. 'Of course.'

Inés had already begun making a big breakfast when they entered the kitchen. She saw how hard this was for them and shooed them outside.

'Go. I will bring you coffee and then finish breakfast. Those children are still sleeping. Late night.'

They padded across the garden, and Tess sat down in the hammock.

'This thing has been a torture device the few times I've tried to nap out here. But I will miss it. The view of the deepest blue sky from this spot is magic. I was willing to deal with the pain just to see the sky.'

She got up and came over to him as he wrapped his arms around her waist. Just as he'd done that first moment in the kitchen at the farm, Javier nuzzled her belly.

'I know why Mateo took so long to be born. Inside a woman is the best place to be.'

Tess clutched his head tightly, running her fingers through his hair. Inés made a racket to announce her arrival, and Tess went around and sat at the table.

'Your *café con leches* are heaven, Inés. I will need to drink 10 of these today. So, I can ensure my body is fully caffeinated for travel.'

She smiled. 'You can have as many as you like, *señora*.'

They sat back, drinking their coffee.

'You know.' Tess mused. 'If there is reincarnation, in my next life, I want to be born in Spain. To grow up in a house like this, full of love and light. With a garden like this one, where I could think grand thoughts, write poetry, and plot my future.'

Javier chuckled. 'You want to be reborn in 1850's Spain? Wearing gowns and dancing at balls? You'd have a lot of suitors.'

She stuck her tongue out at him.

'No. I want to be thoroughly modern with unlimited choices, stunted only by my imagination.'

'Isn't that pretty much the life you have now?' He teased.

'Yes,' she said quietly, 'Except *Spain and this garden* part.'

She looked at him thoughtfully.

'And you. I would want you there.'

He reached over and squeezed her hand.

'Drink your coffee.'

Inés brought out a buffet for them, filled with her famous tortilla, freshly sliced, perfectly ripe tomatoes, red onions, and capers. She'd made some croissants, and they were still warm. Tess grabbed one and slathered it with the creamy white butter and some of Inés's homemade quince jam. She moaned audibly, and Inés smiled.

'I thought you deserved something special this morning.' Inés told her. 'So, you don't forget us.'

Tess shook her head and spoke with a full mouth. 'I could never forget you, any of you. You'll live in my heart and on my thighs for years to come.'

'You need to keep your strength up, *señora*. When you go home, you need to eat.'

Tess saluted her. 'Aye, aye, Capitan.'

Inés waved her away and marched back into the kitchen.

'She has adopted you and Pen, you know. You may not hear from me, but expect a Christmas card from Inés.'

'I'm counting on it.' Tess told him. It was a thin red thread to this place. She wanted to make sure it would not break.

They lazed about the house, finally getting organized before it was almost time to go.

Tess wandered into the garden one final time and sat down on a chaise lounge. The sky was still blue, her favorite shade. She sat back but didn't open her eyes when Javier came out with a bottle of something. She heard the cork and felt a glass against her cheek.

'What are we celebrating?' She asked him.

'Life. Love. Happiness. Take your pick.' He said.

'OK. I'll choose Love.'

She raised her glass and drank the familiar liquid she instantly recognized. It was the wine reserved just for *la familia*. Javier squeezed in behind her. She lay her head on his chest and smiled.

'The perfect moment.' He said into her hair.

'Mmm.' She agreed, '*All good things must come to an end.*'

'A phrase that seems to haunt my life.' Javier said wistfully.

Tess sighed.

'I guess I was right.' Tess told him.

'About what?'

'What I told the Scottish priest back in that hill town. The one at the birthday party you skipped. Didn't I ever tell you?'

'Remind me.'

'He asked me what I would be when I walked into Santiago. I said I would be a butterfly and fly away. Today I fly away.'

'I've always liked butterflies.' He said quietly.

Javier asked her to sit up. Then he reached into his pocket and pulled out a box.

'I was looking for the right time to give this to you. I didn't want you to leave without having something to remember me.'

He opened the box, and inside lay a blue lapis butterfly edged with gold on a matching chain. He took it out and asked Tess to lift her hair.

'This was my grandmother's. She left it to me when she died. I had forgotten about it, but it flashed into my mind when you told me the butterfly story on the Camino. I knew then that I wanted to give it to you. It matches your eyes.'

She felt the edges with her finger and laid back against his chest. Her tears fell, wetting his shirt, but he didn't care. Soon the sun pushed them back into the cool depths of the great room. It was time to go. Standing by the front door with their bags, checking they had everything, Tess frowned.

'Let me make sure I didn't leave anything. I'll check one more time.'

'I can go.' offered Javier.

'No! I'll do it.' She ran up the stairs and was gone for only a few minutes. Running back down, she gleefully announced. 'Nope. I didn't forget anything.'

They drove to the airport in silence. At security, all four of them were crying.

'We should go.' Tess told him.

She turned, grabbing Pen's hand to peel her away from Mateo.

'Pen, it's time.'

Pen kissed Mateo and entered the line with her mom. Tess looked back when she got to the guard, checking tickets and passports. Javier stood there, waiting for one final look before she disappeared.

She raised her hand in goodbye. Javier smiled, turned to his son, then they walked away. It was all Tess could do not to shout his name as the guard prompted her to move along. When she looked up, the crowd swallowed Javier and Mateo. They were gone.

Twenty

Making for Home

Looking out the plane window at their final glimpses of Spanish sunlight, they'd barely spoken since leaving Javier and Mateo at security. Now Pen laid her head on Tess's shoulder, squeezing her mother's arm for comfort.

'Do you think Charlie was watching over us on this trip?' Pen asked Tess out of the blue.

'I think Charlie watches over us all the time.' She said.

'What would he say if he saw us over the last few months? Me, with the drugs, and you and Javier?'

Tess thought about it. 'Well. I think he would say you were a teenager, and he'd have faith that you'd turn it around. As to me? I don't know. I'm his mom, so maybe he'd be disappointed.'

'Maybe.' Said Pen. 'You don't have to worry so much about me. He always put you up on a pedestal. But I never did. With me, you don't have as far to fall.'

Tess laid her cheek on Pen's head. She had brought a troubled teenager to Spain and gotten back her daughter. And just maybe some pieces of herself. She hoped it would last.

'I'll miss Mateo. And Javier.' Pen said, tearful. 'And Inés too. She's easy to talk to.'

Tess understood.

'Will you promise me something?' asked Pen.

'Of course.' said Tess. 'Name it.'

'I don't want us to pretend anymore.' Tears ran down her cheeks. 'Promise me you'll open up. You'll stop hiding yourself from us. I'd like to know who my mother is—even the dark parts. No matter what. About everything.'

Tess took a deep breath. She was ready.

'I promise.' she told Pen. 'Right now, I can't think of anything I'd rather do with you.'

Tess kissed her daughter's head. The Camino had worked its magic on both of them. In the end, that's all she needed.

A day later, as John opened the front door for his wife and daughter in Phoenix, across a continent and an ocean, Javier locked up the apartment for the final time. The movers had come, and Inés had cleaned after they had gone. This chapter in his life was over. It was time to move on.

He felt in his pocket for his keys and fingered the curved metal pieces. Her boot charms. After dropping them off at the airport the day before, he returned to the house and found them on his bedside table. Tess had worn them laced to her boots, the whole Camino. Engraved with the words:

She believed she could

So, she did

There was also a letter. Javier hadn't allowed himself to read it yet. He would, someday.

Javier wiped his eyes, then looked at his watch. Tess would have landed and seen John by now. Gone just 24 hours, she had given him back his life, this woman who, it seemed, would lose hers. She had opened up a space inside him, and he could breathe again.

Javier decided to walk home instead of taking a taxi or the Metro. Strolling through Madrid after dark, he saw people heading out to dinner. Lovers held hands, and older people sat on benches, smoking and gossiping. He smiled. This was his city; this was his life. He was finally ready to live it again. And he picked up his pace towards home.

Epilogue

The weather was warm for a Spring day in Madrid. John kissed and hugged his daughter before she went upstairs in the large house near Alfonso Martínez Square to get ready for her big day, trailed by her gaggle of fussing bride's maids. It was uncomfortable being here. He couldn't deny that while sitting in Javier's home, preparing for Pen's wedding to Mateo. But he wouldn't have missed it for the world.

Pen was happier than he had ever seen her. Mateo was a good man and a fully qualified doctor now. The two had been through a lot together in the past ten years, and their similar life experiences would mean they could weather the storms that would inevitably come. He was sure this was a marriage that would last.

John rubbed his hands together and rose to look out the window into a courtyard filled with potted palm trees and a beautiful fountain; a cool, shady place to spend a sunny afternoon. He knew he would need to get upstairs soon to put on his tuxedo. This event was a very formal affair. They told him Spanish weddings could have five hundred people at the reception; all dressed the nines. The drinking, eating, fireworks, and dancing would last until the wee hours.

They had taken care of the civil ceremony the day before and would have another reception at a winery somewhere in Northern Spain in a few weeks, thrown by relatives of Javier. John would miss it. By then, he would be safely back in the US, away from the discomfort of this whole situation.

A door opened, and he turned to see a linen-clad Javier enter the room; the great room, lined with books and stunning art, was large enough for several collections of seating areas. Dominating the space was an oversized hand-carved desk, and this is where Javier headed. He was looking for something, rifling through the papers stacked on the top; it was a moment before he noticed John was there.

'Ah.' he said. 'I was just looking for a patient's record. I've misplaced it somewhere on this desk. I need to get back to them, and my nurse is occupied with fussing about the wedding.' Stopping. He knew John didn't care what he was doing.

John looked at this man who had loved his wife, body, and soul. He had to admit the guy was handsome. After all these years, Javier still reminded John of that guy on the 1970s tv show *Fantasy Island*. Very suave. Very sophisticated. Very Spanish.

'Would you like a drink?' Javier offered. 'I imagine being the *Father of the Bride* is stressful.'

'Not half as stressful as being the groom.' John chuckled. 'I saw Mateo a little bit ago. He looked terrified. You guys do know how to throw a wedding.'

'In Spain, it's one of our superpowers.' Javier smiled.

Mateo's grandmother had handled most of the arrangements, grudgingly accommodating Pen's American touches into the ceremony and reception. The woman scared him a little.

Javier came over to where John was sitting. He opened a bottle of something, poured two glasses, and handed one to John.

'Sláinte.' Said John, raising his glass.

'Salud.' said Javier, and they both drank.

'This is quite a room. The art is incredible. It looks to have been painted by the same artist.' John was restless, getting up to stand in front of the painting closest to him. 'Not what I think of when I think of Spanish painters like Goya or Dali. This is light. It makes me happy to look at it.'

'My wife, Alejandra, painted all of these.' Said Javier. 'She was a very happy person. Full of light.'

John sat back down, feeling like he'd crossed an invisible line; he struggled to find his footing. Javier stepped in to fill the void.

'We have never really spoken much, you and me, since that day before León. We have been to countless parties for this marriage, but we have never really talked about anything of consequence.' observed Javier.

'No.' said John as he looked down into the liquid he held.

'It must be strange for you to sit here with me. *The Other Man.*'

John took a moment. This man was fearless and direct.

'You were, and you weren't. I gave Tess my permission.' He said. 'My blessing, actually. So, you didn't do anything wrong. Either of you.'

'That's very generous.' Javier smiled. 'You are a better man than I.'

'Oh, I'm certain of that.' said John wryly. Smiling, he took another sip.

Javier chuckled. 'She was an amazing woman. Tess would have loved all this. She liked celebrating, and she would be so happy to see Pen so happy. And she loved Mateo.'

John swallowed hard. It was weird to hear this man speak about his wife of more than 25 years when he had only known her briefly.

'She was amazing.' He agreed. He could still see her face in his dreams, even though he could no longer conjure that vision while awake. 'I have loved only one woman in my life. My wife.'

Javier contemplated what he had said.

'I have only loved two women. My wife,' he hesitated, 'and yours.' Drinking deeply from his glass.

They sat in silence for a few moments.

'Did you know I saw you there?' John glanced up at him. A look of anguish hovered in his eyes.

'Where did you see me?' Javier frowned.

'At the hospital. They told me it was going to be a matter of days. I didn't want Tess to be alone, so I got up in the middle of the night and headed there. I saw you in her room, holding her hand and kissing her forehead. I saw how she looked at you.' John gulped more of the drink than he meant to and coughed. 'There was one time when I came early in the morning, and you were still asleep in the chair beside her bed. I went down to the cafeteria to wait for you to leave.'

Javier held his breath. 'Why did you say nothing?' He whispered.

'I didn't want her to be alone. I would be with her all day if you were with her at night. She was surrounded by love.' John finished, struggling to control his emotions.

Javier waited for a beat.

'Tess gave her doctor permission to keep me informed on her condition. After she went back to the US, she never contacted me again. It was how it needed to be. We both knew that. She was going back to you and your family. And she was going back to fight the disease. She needed to focus on all of that. But I wanted to know how she was, and one day before she left, she told me she had emailed her oncologist and asked her to keep me informed at critical points. I am a doctor, after all.'

'Yes.' John conceded.

'I got a call that she was near the end. Mateo was finishing exams, but I canceled all my appointments and got on a plane. I went to be with her. She was still conscious when I arrived, and we had some good conversations before the final day. I didn't know how I would handle it after losing my wife the same way. If I could handle it at all. But I am glad I went, and I got to see her the night before she passed. The doctor called me at my hotel the next afternoon to tell me that she was surrounded by family when she slipped away. I flew home the following day.'

Both men had tears in their eyes—the grief still with them ten years later.

'We were there, Pen and me. We got to be with her at that moment. Pen rubbed her feet with her favorite lotion, and I read *Pride and Prejudice* to her and held her hand. It was a beautiful and terrifying moment, letting her go. I don't think we've ever been the same.'

Javier had no words. He stared into his glass.

'The next year, Pen came to you guys here for her year abroad. My pride told me I should fight it, but it was strangely comforting, knowing she would be with people she knew so well. That Tess knew so well. You would take care of her. As you had on the Camino.'

Javier gathered himself.

'She looks more and more like her Mother. Sometimes I find it hard to look at her if she catches the light just right.' Javier looked down, a little ashamed of this admission. 'Again, I don't know if I could have done it if I was in your position.'

'Oh, I think you would have.' John stopped. 'She talked about you. Did you know that? Towards the end. She told me a lot of things about you.' He shook his head. 'Not the specifics of the other stuff. Just about who you were. How you helped her to live those weeks over here.'

Javier stopped breathing. Then he looked up at John with tears streaming down his face. His reaction took John off guard, and he struggled for control.

'I never asked you where she is buried. If I'm ever in the US, I would like to visit her grave.' whispered Javier.

'She was cremated.' John told him. 'She's in an urn in my house. I couldn't bear to think of her alone in a marble niche somewhere with strangers. She asked to be sprinkled at the places in the world that she loved visiting. I'm afraid I haven't done that yet, either. Still trying to let go, I guess.' He hesitated before whispering. 'A few of them are along the Camino.'

Javier looked up.

'I think I probably know where they are.'

'I'm sure you do.' John conceded.

They both thought about what that meant.

'Listen, John. When Mateo and I walked with Tess and Pen, it was in honor of my wife, Alejandra. She was an extraordinary person and deserved a pilgrimage of her own.'

John nodded. 'Tess told me at the time. I thought it was extraordinary.'

'Yes, but not unusual for those in Europe.' Javier chose his words carefully. 'I feel strange suggesting it, but perhaps you and I could walk it. Together. In Tess's honor. You could fulfill some of her last wishes and visit the places Tess loved along the Way.' He stopped, wondering if he was mad to suggest it.

John thought about it.

'I don't know. That sounds odd; her husband and her lover?'

Javier chuckled. 'On the Camino, you will hear many stranger stories. Believe me.'

John was retired now. This suggestion was so far outside his comfort zone, yet, it felt oddly comforting.

'When would we go?' he asked.

His quick reaction took Javier by surprise, but then he remembered. This was the person Tess had described. The man who had written the selfless letter that had set all their lives in a different direction. A man who didn't let his fears stop him.

'I am winding down my patient list. Mateo is taking over the practice. I could go in the autumn.'

John thought about it for less than a minute.

'I can make that work.'

Just then, the door opened and Inés came into the room.

'You both need to get ready if we're going to stay on schedule and avoid the wrath of Pen.' She'd broken the spell, and both men finished their whiskey in one gulp and stood. John surprised himself by reaching out to shake Javier's hand. 'The Fall.'

Javier nodded and clasped his hand. 'The Fall.'

Then they went off to get ready to see their children marry, sure Tess was smiling wherever she was.

Sign up to be the first to know what happens in Book 2 of the Camino de Santiago Family Trilogy!

linktr.ee/authorkellifield

For Book Club Discussion

1. What do you think are the main themes of the book?

2. What impact does the death of Tess and John's son have on Tess' decision to walk the Camino with terminal cancer?

3. What role does Western society's definition of motherhood play in the story?

4. How do you think the author views motherhood in the book? How does Tess' childhood story impact her mothering of Pen?

5. How did Tess' relationship with Javier impact your feelings about her?

6. How do the old tropes about the whore, Madonna, or crone impact how you see the women in the story?

7. How do Tess' avoidance of the past and insistence upon optimism for the future impact her family?

8. What did you think of John's character, and how did you view him? Weak? Heroic?

9. John's letter to Tess was a selfless act. Do you think he regretted writing it after the reality of Tess and Javier's affair came to light?

10. Did you feel sympathetic towards Javier even though he's sleeping with another man's wife?

11. What impact do you think the death of Javier's wife from cancer has on his relationship with Tess?

12. What emotions does the character of Pen evoke? Typical teenager, or is there something more?

13. Grief is a main character in the book, carried as a burden by each person in their own way. How does grief vary for each of them? Did this knowledge make the character more sympathetic?

14. Did Tess and Pen fully realize the redemption they were seeking?

15. How does religion and the history of the Camino de Santiago play a role in the story?

16. Do you believe Tess struggled after her affair with Javier began?

17. Is Tess selfish or selfless on her journey to Santiago? Especially in light of Javier's vulnerability at the loss of his wife?

18. Should Tess tell Pen about her cancer diagnosis sooner on the journey?

19. The characters are all holding onto their secrets and their grief. How might the story be different if they had been more open with each other?

20. Tess hides the death of her son, Charlie, from the reader until she caresses his tombstone. How did that scene make you feel?

21. Which character were you rooting for the most along the way?

22. How does the experience of walking the Camino de Santiago

impact our four main characters?

23. What role does Inés, the housekeeper, play in this family drama? And how does that intertwine with Javier's mother, María?

24. How do the ghosts of their pasts impact Tess and Javier?

25. At any point, did you feel Tess wanted to stay in Spain and remain with Javier? Would Javier have encouraged her at the expense of her relationship with John?

Acknowledgments

Writing this book began as a lonely pursuit in a new country. The characters quickly became my best friends, and I was sad to finish Tess and Pen's Camino. But it turned out to be just the beginning, as publishing a book takes a village. Or, in my case, A Tribe. My Tribe. Including the regular readers of my blog, www.vivaespanamovingtospain.com – Carol, Karen,, Gina, Maria, Tricia, Andy, Raul, Donna, Wendy, Deanna, and many more in both the virtual and real worlds. If your name isn't listed here, don't believe I haven't felt your encouragement daily. Knowing you were out there as I screamed into the void kept me writing and moving this book toward publication.

I want to thank Brian Skillen and the team at Publishing Hackers for their incredible skill and guidance in bringing this book to market. Your expertise, kindness, compassion, and commitment to the story I needed to tell gave me confidence that Tess and Pen were in good hands.

To my friends who agreed to read the many versions and provide feedback, you shaped the story in invaluable ways.

This book would not have been completed without John Rafferty, the wizard of the Camino. Your steadfast friendship and constant encouragement to keep writing about the Camino and Spain at just the right time mattered more than you know; the ripples of your quiet influence continue.

And a shoutout to Fr. Stephen for your committed editing skills and sage advice.

To *The Santiago Book Club*—you know who you are—a group filled with unconditional love and support. Maybe this book will make the cut one of these days!

To Emilie, who walked the first Camino with me. A million-step journey all those years ago before these words ever hit the page. I could see your shadow in every keystroke.

And, finally, to Jeff. You moved to Spain for me and told me to write. You believed in me without hesitation. You're every man I write. Like John's letter to Tess, this book love letter to you.

To the pilgrims on the Camino from all over the world, you have inspired me with your stories and courage, from the first step on the trail to the bagpiper in Praza de Obrardoiro in Santiago de Compostela.

Siempre, mucha gracias. *Buen Camino.*

About the Author

K.D. Field is an American writer and blogger living on The Camino de Santiago in Galicia, Spain. *The Grief of Goodbye* is her first novel. She maintains the blog vivaespanamovingtospain.com chronicling the adventures of her and her husband, Jeff, from the decision to move to Spain after walking the Camino from Saint-Jean-Pied-de-Port to the present day. She also writes a monthly humor column for Euro Weekly News—Spain's most prominent English Speaking newspaper. You can follow along on all her social channels:

linktr.ee/authorkellifield